Praise for Sarah Mlynowski

Monkey Business

"Another delightful tale about an
unlikely group of friends."
—*Booklist*

"Warning: do not attempt to read *Monkey Business*
while drinking. Sarah Mlynowski's hilarious
writing had me snorting tea all over my
new unvarnished oak dining table."
—International bestselling author Chris Manby

As Seen on TV

"Sarah Mlynowski's *As Seen on TV* is funny…
Tapping into the crazy world of 'reality' television
and those who live it, the book is filled with witty
characters and Steve, a lovable boyfriend
whom you can't help rooting for."
—*Columbus Dispatch*

"Mlynowski has managed to create lively characters
that defy traditional romantic archetypes."
—*Calgary Herald*

"*As Seen on TV* is simply irresistible—one of the best
reasons you could find for reaching for the
TV remote and hitting the off button."
—International bestselling author Nick Earls

Fishbowl

"Mlynowski is out for a rollicking good time right from the start."
—*Arizona Republic*

"Mlynowski wisely focuses the most on the girls' relationships with each other, creating fully dimensional characters and a terrific story."
—*Booklist*

"Undemandingly perfect...wonderfully bitchy."
—*Jewish Chronicle*

"A fresh and witty take on real-life exams in love, lust, trust and friendship."
—Bestselling author Jessica Adams

Milkrun

"Mlynowski is acutely aware of the plight of the 20-something single woman—she offers funny dialogue and several slices of reality."
—*Publishers Weekly*

"Jackie is a likable heroine.... Singles will relate to her frustrating search for love in the big city."
—*Booklist*

"If Bridget Jones ever found herself at a loose end in Boston, she'd find a great friend in Jackie Norris. A sexy, sassy story of singledom from the skilled pen of Sarah Mlynowksi."
—Bestselling author Carole Matthews

ME VS. ME

SARAH MLYNOWSKI

RED
DRESS
INK
TM

First edition August 2006

ME VS. ME

A Red Dress Ink novel

ISBN-13: 978-0-373-89588-5
ISBN-10:   0-373-89588-7

www.RedDressInk.com

Printed in U.S.A.

For Sylvia Harris and Dora Stein,
grandmas extraordinaire

Many, many thanks to:
My fab new editor, Selina McLemore, my fab former
editor, Farrin Jacobs, Tara Kelly, Margaret Marbury,
Sarah Rundle and the rest of the RDI team, my awesome
agent Laura Dail and superb publicist Gail Brussel.

For their brilliant insights and edits: Elissa Ambrose
(thanks *again,* Mom; you're the best), Robert Ambrose,
Lynda Curnyn, Alison Pace, Lisa Callamaro,
Jessica Braun, Melissa Senate, Kristin Harmel,
Dari Alexander and Chad Ruble.

For their never-ending love and support:
Larry Mlynowski, Louisa Weiss, Aviva Mlynowski,
Jen Dalven, Gary Swidler, Darren Swidler, John Swidler,
Bonnie Altro, Robin Afrasiabi, Jess Davidman,
Ronit Avni. Special thanks to Vicki Swidler for being
a dream mother-in-law, and luckily for me, nothing like
Alice. And of course, Todd Swidler, the one for me
no matter which road I would have taken.

ME vs. ME

"Close your eyes, Gabby," Cam said.

"Now? I'm watching." Closing your eyes during a meteor shower was like wearing a bikini when taking a bath. You were definitely going to miss the important parts.

We were lying in the back of his Ford pickup, admiring the desert sky exploding above, drunk on merlot sipped straight from the bottle (with cork remnants to spice it up— I could never open a bottle properly), while the light rained down on us from every direction.

"Come on, just close them," he said.

As usual, I did as I was told. "Happy?"

I heard the metal creak. He squeezed my left hand and then slipped something cold and hard around my fourth finger.

Was that…did he… My eyes shot open. Holy shit.

Cam was no longer lying next to me, but crouched in

an awkward wannabe-knight kneel. "Will you marry me?" he asked. A massive Cheshire-cat smile stretched across his normally serious face, making him look off-kilter.

Sparkle, twinkle, glitter. *Ohhh*. I had my very own meteor shower on my finger. At closer glance I could see it was a pear-shaped diamond (one carat or two?) set on a thin platinum band.

The man I loved had just proposed marriage.

The blood rushed to my head and my face felt hot. I wanted to say yes. Yes. Yeeeeeeeeeeeeeeeees! This was the moment I'd been waiting for my entire life. The moment I'd been romanticizing about since I first saw Cinderella when I was six and imagined my own glass carriage ready to roll me toward my happily-ever-after castle. A castle I later decided would be filled with thousand-thread-count bed linen and Italian-marble Jacuzzis. All I had to do was respond. To give some sort of affirmative response. Like *yes*. Or *okay, let's*. And I *was* going to say yes. The word was at my lips, begging to be released. Yes! An orgasmic, hallelujah, couldn't-be-happier yes. Yes!

All I had to do was open my mouth. Unfortunately, my lips were swollen and sticky, like I'd spent the day licking envelopes. They wouldn't let me say yes. They knew I couldn't say yes, because I was moving to New York on Sunday. In thirty-six hours. At least, that had been the plan until the will-you-marry-me curveball. Two weeks ago, when I had told Cam of the offer and my decision to take the job at TRSN in New York (the twenty-four-hour news network owned by the TRS network), he had agreed to try long distance. I had to take the job—it was the chance of a lifetime. It was national. It was cable. It paid a six-figure salary. I'd be producing legendary Ron Grighton's show, which in any lifetime could not compare to my small-fry executive producer's job in Phoenix. I'd invited Cam to come, to make the move with me across the country, but I knew he wouldn't. I loved him, but this was my *career*. I had to go for it. And it wasn't like the move was a surprise; I'd always told him what my dream was—apartment in Manhattan, jogging in the park (not that I jog, but I've always wanted to), snowflakes on my nose. Hadn't I?

"Perfect, huh? This way you don't have to go to New York," he said, nodding. "We both know long-distance relationships never work out."

We did? I wanted to ask since when, but my mouth was still annoyingly uncooperative. I smiled, no easy feat with frozen lips.

"And I don't want to lose you," he continued, oblivious to my condition. "I want to marry you."

So he'd said. I smiled (sort of) again. I never would have pegged Cam as one of those lame-ass romantic-comedy run-to-the-airport-gate-with-flowers-to-catch-the-girl-before-she-flies-out-of-his-life guys, but what did I know? I yanked my eyes away from the sparkling diamond, up to Cam's soft lips, to the slither of a space between his two front teeth that had made me realize way back when that he wasn't perfect, made me realize he was a man—not just a guy with adorable curly blond hair, not just a guy who had the answer for everything, but someone with flaws (like me), someone I could fall in love with.

Except I had to tell him no. I was going to New York.

Nothing came out. Apparently, my lips were too swollen for that word, too.

Yes.

No.

Yes. No. Yes, no, yes, no. Yes no yes no. Yesnoyesno.

Cam was now blinking his eyes furiously. I was going to miss those swirling patches of greens and blues. They'd always reminded me of little globes.

Could I really say goodbye to his globe eyes? Should I? I hated making decisions.

The real problem was that Cam would never in a million years leave Arizona. Career-wise it would be a huge pain in the ass since he's a lawyer, and he'd have to take the bar in a new state. Although the corporate bankruptcy firm he worked for, Banford and Kimmel, did have a branch in New York. Truthfully, the real issue was his close relationship with his parents (particularly his mother), his sister and her two and a half kids (she's pregnant). California, maybe, but clear across the country? A different time zone? He didn't see the point.

I wanted to tell him I was the point.

Now suddenly he'd decided that long distance wouldn't work. Not that I blamed him. It was like after that breakup when you said you'd be friends, but of course you wouldn't be. When you ran into him a year later at a shabby bar downtown, all you talked about was the weather. Which was always the same here. Hot.

So that was my choice: marry Cam or move to New York. I wanted to take a deep breath, but I was afraid to move, since I still had no idea what to say. Time felt stuck, frozen in a frame, paused by TiVo.

If I left, I'd miss the way he always bought me two cards every Valentine's Day, one sexy and one mushy, in each envelope a chocolate heart. The way he'd throw me over his shoulder and spin me around. The way he'd wrap me in a towel when I got out of the shower and then kiss me on the forehead. The way he reminded me to use the bathroom before long car drives.

If I stayed, I'd miss out on a major job opportunity.

If I went, I'd have to sleep alone. I hated sleeping alone.

If I stayed, the Arizona heat, like a vacuum cleaner pressed to my head, would slowly suck the dreams out of my brain. I'd never go on another date. I'd be *engaged*. I'd never have another first kiss. I'd never get to wear cute pink earmuffs.

I needed to breathe. I inhaled sharply, but felt as if my air was turned off. What was wrong with me?

I'd never get to date an Aries, my true love match (I am a Gemini, and Cam is a Libra, which is nowhere near an Aries). Not that I followed such things, but that tidbit had stuck in my mind ever since I'd read it in *Seventeen* when I was twelve. If we got married, I'd never know for sure if I could have found eternal bliss with an Aries.

If I said no, would I ever again meet anyone as patient as Cam? Someone who had spent hours of his free time editing my final college papers, then later my résumés and cover letters, and more recently my story scripts? Someone who would calm me when a virus attacked my hard drive and ate my important files, and then reinstall all my software? Someone who would take off work to be with me when I got my wisdom teeth pulled, and then tell me he loved me even though I looked like a deformed chipmunk? Someone who would build me a bookshelf, not from IKEA, but from planks of wood he bought at the hardware store because he liked making furniture (hence the need for a pickup truck)?

If I said yes, I'd get to marry this wonderful man. Plus, I'd get to wear a diamond ring. A big, pear-shaped diamond ring. If I said no, I'd have years of girls' nights out. Apple martinis till dawn. Sexy first-date outfits. If I said no, I'd break Cam's heart. If I said no, Cam would marry someone else.

If I said yes, I'd be part of a real family. An annoying family, yes, but still. If I said yes, I'd spend the rest of my life with a man I loved. But was he *the* man?

His globe eyes were looking at me with expectancy, and I wanted—oh, I so wanted!—to say yes, and I tried, honestly I did. But my mouth still felt gummy and anesthetized, and nothing came out.

Did I still have a mouth? I wasn't sure. I tried to shake it into working. Which Cam must have mistaken for an implicit yes, because the next thing I knew he was kissing my neck, my chin, my lips.

Interesting. Apparently, I was getting married. Getting married? Getting married! It sounded so mature. Married. A married woman. But Monsieur, I'm a married woman!

I ogled the ring while embracing him. It fit perfectly. How did he know my ring size? *I* didn't even know my ring size. Though, why would I? I'd never been one of those wife-wannabes who went to jewelry stores and tried on engagement rings just in case.

Cam's soft hands began to roam under my sweatshirt. I gently pushed him off. "What are you doing?" I asked, relieved that my mouth was back in working order. Well, not totally, because I think I meant to say, "What am *I* doing?" As in, was I really going to give in? Get married? Give up the dream of New York? "We can't do this."

"Why not?"

"Because—" because I wanted to move! "—someone might see."

He tugged at the green wool blanket and held it to his shoulders like a cape. "We have a cover." Cam the Man. Cam the Superman. Cam the Husband. Why didn't men wear engagement rings? Maybe he should tattoo his finger to mark him as mine. Then I'd feel safe moving to New York.

I didn't know what to say, so I said, "But still." Actually, I didn't know what to feel. My two longings were head butting against each other and I hadn't yet decided whose side to cheer for.

"I want to celebrate. We're engaged." Engaged. To engage. To interlock or mesh. He started undoing my jeans, and I let him. "I want to make love to my fiancée," he said, suddenly serious. The first time he'd used the expression *make love,* I'd thought he was kidding, until I'd seen the earnestness on his face, and realized he wasn't.

He wrapped his long body onto mine, the blanket covering us both. My roommate Lila had once walked in on us when we were "making love" and claimed she couldn't get the image of his naked, ashen butt out of her head for months. I gave the ass a squeeze. Cam took that as a sign.

Afterward, as Cam's forehead nuzzled into my neck, and the stars above scribbled across the November sky like ink from a silver marker, I raised my suddenly sparkling hand into the air. Then I followed one of the stars, the brightest star, with my index finger as it shot diagonally across the blackness.

When I was a kid in California, I used to pretend that airplanes were falling stars, and I'd close my eyes and wish that I would marry a prince, that I would win the lottery, or that my mom and dad would stop screaming at each other.

With Cam still on top of me, I continued tracing the star's path. And then I made a wish. I wished that I didn't have to choose. That I could live both lives. Stay with Cam and move to New York. Have it all. The starlight burned out and I closed my eyes. And then I drifted off to sleep.

Blowing out the candles, pennies down a well. People made wishes all the time.

How was I to know that mine would come true?

1

The Hangover

I wake up disoriented, intense light spearing my eyes like hot pokers, pain stabbing my temples.

Ow. Where? Who? What the hell? Why is my pillow stuffed with metal?

Then I remember where I am and what I've done. Kind of done. Does it count as a yes if I didn't verbally agree?

My stomach churns. Why did I lead Cam to believe I'd marry him, when tomorrow I'm moving to New York? I'm already packed! Lila has already (reluctantly) ordered office furniture for my room. An upstairs neighbor bought my double futon. True, she hasn't taken it yet, but it's scheduled to go on Monday evening. I've already ordered a mattress to be delivered to my new place in New York. I sold my car, too. On Wednesday.

It was a two-door bright blue Jetta, which I loved dearly. Which is now gone.

I feel an uncomfortable pressure on my bladder and sit up, my elbows digging into the hard truck bed. Dumb wine from last night not only made me lose my mind, but it is also irritating my bladder. I can't get married. I'm moving. Tomorrow.

I can't deal with telling Cam no. Should I sneak away? Maybe just run the ten miles home? I don't think I'll get very far with an overstuffed bladder. I'll have to sneak off somewhere and pee. With my luck I'll end up squatting over a cactus. I hate those things. Another advantage of New York. No attack plants.

What did I do? What the hell did I do?

"Morning, beautiful," he says now, his eyes still closed. He blindly reaches for me and drags me down and onto his chest. "Love you."

I am borderline hyperventilating. As if I'm trying to breathe with my face pressed against a pillow. Can't do this. "We have to talk," I say in my quiet voice. Why, oh why, didn't I say no last night? How did I get talked into staying?

Talked? It wasn't the talking that did it.

He smiles, eyes still closed. "I know. So much to plan. A date, a place…lots to do. I'm starving. Let's discuss over food."

"No. I mean *talk*." My voice cracks on the last word. I wriggle out of his stronghold, scoot backward and lean safely against the rear windshield. I reach for my jeans and struggle back inside them.

His left eye opens, focuses on me, and then his right follows. "What's wrong?"

I'm not sure how to start. This conversation is going to

be awful. Plus, I think I might be sitting on the rear wiper. "I want the TRSN job."

His shakes his head, full of supposed sympathy. "I know you do, babe. But you'll find a new job here."

He's not getting it. "You don't understand. I'm going to take it."

He continues shaking his head, not understanding. "That's not practical. How are you going to plan the wedding from New York? And what's the point of starting a job somewhere else when we're going to settle here?"

Was he always this dense? "That's what I'm trying to tell you. I don't want to settle here." I look longingly at my sparkling finger. "Can't you move with me?" I squeak.

He's shaking his head faster now, jaw clenching tighter by the half second. "You know I can't."

"Can't or won't," I say.

"Gabby, family is important to me. I'm not moving across the country. Be fair. I'm sure you'll find a good job in Arizona. I love you, Gabs, and I feel awful, but I can't."

"But I already made plans....I quit my job. Yesterday was my last day. I start my new job on Monday! Why couldn't you have proposed before I quit?"

"Gabby, I needed a minute to figure it all out. Last month life was good, and then suddenly everything was happening so fast, and you were moving and it wasn't until after I realized that you were really going that I knew how much I need you here."

"But *I* need to be there." How to say it...? I decide one fast, full vomit is best. He's tough. He'll get over it, me, eventually. "Cam, I'm taking the job. I'm moving to New York. I'm sorry."

He swallows. Hard. I watch his Adam's apple sneak up

his throat and then sliver back down. His eyes tear up and he closes them, and then opens them again. "But…what about us? The job is more important than me?"

Holy shit. Cam? Crying? We've been together for three years and I've never seen him shed a tear. I feel as if I'm hacking his arm off with a chain saw. I can't believe that I am capable of causing him pain. "You know this has always been my dream," I choke out. Which is true. It has! On our first dinner date, I'd told him I wanted to move to New York. That I wouldn't stay in Arizona forever.

A fat tear rolls down his sweet cheek. "I thought you had a new dream."

"I have to think about my career." My voice cracks. "I could never have an opportunity like that here."

"You have an amazing job here."

"Had," I remind him.

"Have, had. Whatever. You can get a new one."

"It's not the same. Here I'm a big fish in a small pond."

"There's nothing wrong with that. You'd rather be a small fish?"

I shake my head. "You're asking me to give up my dream."

"Don't make me out to be the bad guy."

We're both silent, attempting to regroup our thoughts, aka ammunition. Something I would be much better at with an empty bladder and a cup of coffee. I realize I'm too drained and hungover and tired for more talk. "I love you. But I'm moving to New York."

"Then we're not getting married."

I slip off the ring and deposit it into his palm.

"I can't believe you're doing this," he says. "You're so obsessed with that stupid Melanie Diamond scandal that you don't even know what you're doing."

This isn't about that, I want to say, but don't. Because it kind of is. "Maybe," I say. "But it's *my* call."

Instead of looking at me, he's looking at my—now his— ring. And then he says, "I'll take you home." As his voice breaks, my heart breaks along with it.

"Endless Love" is playing on the radio when Cam pulls up in front of my apartment building. It's so embarrassingly inappropriate for the moment that I almost laugh. He doesn't put the car into park. Just steps on the brake.

"Well, goodbye," he says.

I see that his tears are gone. See? He's over me already. "I'll call you when I get there," I say. "I love you, Cam. But I have to do this. For me." I open my purse and rifle through my junk for my keys. Shit. Where are they?

He shakes his head. "They're in the pocket of your jean jacket."

I feel inside my pocket. Oh. "Thanks."

A long sigh escapes Cam's lips. And then he says, "I hope it's worth it."

I hope it is, too. I open the door, squeezing my keys between my fingers, and slither out before I start crying and change my mind.

Crap. The bookshelf in my bedroom. As soon as I step into my room, I realize he was supposed to take it back. I don't want to take any furniture to New York, and I don't want to just give it to Lila along with everything else. It's not right. Cam gave it to me, he should get it back. Although maybe she'll use it. She's an accountant and is turning my room into her home office. Anyway, I should give Cam the choice.

Maybe I'll leave him a message. I pick up the phone. I pause in mid-dial. I can't call Cam. Calling him would be torturing him unnecessarily. It would be torturing myself, listening to his soft voice on the phone.

I finished most of my packing over the week so I would have every last second free to spend with Cam. Which leaves me with nothing to do for the day. My mom is in Florida and Lila is working. Lila is *always* working or reading romance novels in bed. Honestly, that girl has no social life. Even in college she was always studying or reading away. As long as I've known her, she's never had a boyfriend. She's had flings—at least four times I saw her bring home some random guy, but she always kicked him out before her day started. Musn't mess with her daily schedule. Anyway, no Lila. I'd call Melanie but she decided to take a spur of the moment road trip to L.A. She's impulsive that way.

I have officially nothing to do. Which makes me reflect on my pitiful absence of friends. What kind of a life did I even have here?

Maybe I'll call Heather and check in. I scramble through my pack of papers for her number and dial. Heather will be my roommate in the "two-bedroom, postwar, good-size rooms, hardwood floors, very generous storage space" that I'm renting. I found it on craigslist.com and my fingers are tightly crossed that my temporary roommate, twenty-something nonsmoking Fashion Institute of Technology student, Heather Munro from Long Island, isn't psycho.

After three rings, a voice yells, "I'm not hanging out with you and your little couple brigade, okay? Stop bothering me!" Heather?

Groan. Maybe I should have been crossing my toes, as

well. "Um, hi, Heather, it's Gabby. Gabby Wolf? Is this a bad time?"

Pause. "Oh God, I'm sorry. My friend Diane is driving me insane. She doesn't understand why I don't want to come over and watch her wedding video with her three other bridesmaids and their fiancés. I mean, come on! I'd rather slit my eyeball with a steak knife."

"Listen, I'm just calling because—" I stop midsentence. Is moving in with Steak-Knife Heather really my best move? I will be earning a whopping $125,000. Maybe I should stay in a motel until I can find my own place. New York has motels, right?

"Because what? Don't tell me you're going to bail. I just turned down someone else because you said you're coming. I'm not giving you your deposit back, so you can forget it," she huffs.

Steak knives aside, she does have a point about the deposit. Besides, New Yorkers aren't like the rest of us, right? They're supposed to be eccentric. Interesting. "No, I'm not reneging. I just want to confirm with you that I'm arriving tomorrow at 3:30. Will you be home?"

Long pause. "That's a relief. Although…tomorrow? I don't know if I can be home."

"Oh. Okay. Um, well, I have to get in."

She sighs. Loudly. "I suppose I can leave the keys with the doorman."

"All right. See you tomorrow. Oh, did my new bed come? It was supposed to arrive today."

"No, not yet." She hangs up. Apparently, my new roommate is not of an easygoing persuasion. I will have to remember not to borrow her butter without asking.

I spend the rest of the day on the couch, flipping

through the news channels, slowly refolding my clothes and re-squeezing them into my suitcases, and letting the excitement build and boil inside me. I catch myself singing "New York, New York" and doing a YMCA-like dance around the apartment.

"Hi, guys," Lila says from the door at around four.

"It's just me," I tell her, flipping the channel from CNN to TRSN.

I know I have at least ten minutes before she'll join me on the couch. The first thing she does every day when she gets home is change out of her suit and into her bathrobe and slippers. Then she scrubs her hands, carefully takes off her makeup, washes her face, ties her shoulder-length blond hair into a ponytail on top of her head, takes her many skin vitamins, moisturizes, stops in the kitchen for a glass of water, and then comes into the living room. She works seven-day workweeks and is very into her routine.

"Where's Cam?" she asks, post-routine, getting comfy on her white velvety couch. "Doesn't he want to spend every second of your last day with you?"

"We broke up."

Her jaw drops. "You didn't! What happened? He wasn't into the long distance?"

"Kind of. You see, he proposed—"

"What?" she shrieks and throws a pillow at me. "And you said no?"

I recount the whole story, and she stays quiet throughout. Lila has always been a very good listener. She has this way of never making me feel judged. She's a very soothing person. Like chicken soup without the salt. Almost bland, but in a good way. But Lila also thinks Cam is the best boyfriend ever. She constantly tells me how lucky I am. "Don't

you think it was wrong of him to give me an ultimatum?"
I ask. "Stay or go? Why does he get everything and I have
to give something up?"

"I suppose," she says, nodding.

"I had no choice," I say.

"I don't know about that. You had to give something up
and you did. Cam."

Gave up Cam? Is that what I did?

She sees the expression of despair on my face and pats
my knee. "You'll be fine. Really. You were never sure if
Cam was right for you anyway."

I wonder if this is true. I didn't want Cam to be Mr.
Right because I was planning on moving. But is he? Was
he?

"Finish packing and I'll order us some dinner. Pizza?"

We order, we eat, we watch TV. We rehash the whole
Cam thing. The phone doesn't ring all night. My dad lives
in L.A., although he's currently working in Australia, and
while my mom lives here, she's working in Florida these
days. There must be someone to call to say goodbye to.
Although, my social life has mostly revolved around Cam
and his family for the past year. Calling them to say farewell
might be a little…awkward. There's Bernie, my old news
director, but he's still a bit pissed off with me for quitting.

After Lila and I exchange tearful goodbyes, I retreat to
my room. Before I climb into bed, I pull down the curtain.
Okay, fine, it's not really a curtain but a dark gray sheet that
Cam found at his parents' house and helped me staple to
the ceiling to keep out the light. He nailed a hook above
the window so I could pull it up during the day. I'm not
going to bother removing it in the morning—I'm sure Lila
will get around to putting up real blinds eventually. Then

I check my Hello Kitty alarm clock (I have to remember to pack this in the morning—it was a gift from my dad when I was eight). It's eleven-thirty in the evening. The alarm is set for six-thirty, since my flight is at nine. Cam was supposed to take me to the airport. I guess I'll be calling a cab.

First I hit the radio button to make sure that the volume is on. "Like a Virgin" blasts in my ear. Then I realize I'm cold and sneak back into the living room, rummage through one of my two suitcases and find Cam's J. Crew cotton long-sleeved shirt that he left here months ago (I wear it when I want to feel warm and toasty), and slip it on to punish myself. Back in the bedroom, his smell wafts over me as I turn off the light. I wrap myself in my pink top sheet that I have to remember to pack in the morning.

Did I set the alarm properly? What if I set it for 6:30 p.m. instead of a.m.?

I sit up and check—6:30 a.m. In six and a half hours. I'm never going to fall asleep. I bet Cam can't fall asleep either. He's not a good sleeper when he's stressed. When he's working on a case, he tosses and turns and flips his pillow. Bet that's what he's doing now.

Poor Cam.

I will not cry. No, I will not—I will n—I wipe the tears off my cheeks with the back of my hand. What a baby.

How could I have broken the heart of the one person who has loved me so fiercely over the past few years? Why do I think moving to New York will be good for me? What if I'm a failure? What if I never meet another man who will love me as much as Cam does? What if no other man ever asks me to marry him, and I become bitter and bitchy and start to hate all couples and throw up at the sight of any hand holding or Valentine's Day cards?

I check the alarm. Again. I close my eyes and start to drift into a sad, desperate sleep. Cam…love you…changed my mind…

Blackness.

I wake to an intense headache. Like forks bashing into my forehead and both temples. To go along with the pain, swirls of green hot light burn behind my eyelids.

What the hell? Did I roll off my bed in my sleep? Did my lamp fall on my head?

I open my eyes slowly, intense sunlight spearing my pupils. The pain instantly dissipates. No one is attacking me. But I can't believe how bright it is in here. Weird, actually. Then I realize why. This morning, of all mornings, the staples holding my makeshift curtain must have finally given out. How appropriate.

What the—

I blink my eyes. Once, twice. Three times. I do not believe what I see.

I'm back in the desert. In the truck. Wrapped in the itchy green blanket.

In Cam's arms.

2

The Gabby Horror Engagement Show

I am going insane. That must be it. Obviously, the only explanation. How did I go to sleep in my empty bedroom,
yet wake up in Cam's truck?

Unless I'm dreaming. Yes, that makes sense. I'm still
asleep. The truck and the desert are just an illusion. How
weird is that? Normally a desert isn't a mirage—normally
you'd see a mirage *in* a desert.

When I put on one of Cam's J. Crew shirts, his scent
tortured me into hallucinations about what could have—
would have—been.

What *will* be.

In my dreamworld, I snuggle up close to him. Mmm…
feels so nice. That's it. I'm going to wake up and call him.
Cancel my move. Get married. He'll take me back. Of

course he will! I'm entitled to twenty-four hours to change my mind, am I not? I must wake up and call him immediately. Now. Wake up. Come on, you can do it! Wake up!

I have to pee. I hate when I have to pee in dreams. That means I have to pee in real life. I'm always concerned that I will pee all over my bed.

Now open your damn eyes! What's wrong with you, you lazy ass?

Cam elbows me in the chin.

This dream feels awfully real. I tenderly stroke my injured face and check out my surroundings. My very authentic-looking surroundings. I sit up in my dream, in the hope that it will wake me up in real life. But instead, I am simply sitting up. In Cam's truck.

I must admit, this is the most realistic dream I've ever had. I pinch my leg. It hurts. And the air feels so real. I take a deep breath and look up at the sea of blue. The Arizona sky always makes me feel as if the horizon goes on forever. To my left are the Superstition Mountains. They look like mounds of dirt, or children's sandcastles, against the blue. My surroundings are too alive for this to be a dream.

My heart races. Which it doesn't normally do when I'm asleep, at least, not that I'm aware of.

All right, I'm awake. This is not a dream. This is not a dream! But what does that mean? That everything that happened yesterday *was* a dream? If I'm still in the desert with Cam, does that mean that I never said goodbye to Lila? Never finished packing up the apartment? That I never told Cam no?

Does that mean—

I look down at my left hand. Sparkle, sparkle.

—that I'm still engaged?

I lean against the rear windshield to support myself. I'm still engaged! I'm getting married! I didn't ruin it all to follow some lame plan to go to New York. When my breathing has returned to its normal speed, I slither back into my spot next to Cam. I lift his arm around me and cuddle into him. His breath smells sweet. His eyes flutter open and then closed, and he pulls me against him. His stubble brushes against my cheek and I feel giddy with relief. I can't believe how close I came to ruining this. What was I thinking? People struggle their whole lives to find love like this. To find a guy like Cam. And I have him. How could I have thought for a second that a job in New York was more important? Was I crazy? Why did I want to live in the most alienating city in the world? With a psycho roommate—who's going to haaaate me when I tell her I changed my mind.

She'll live. As long as she doesn't slit her eye with a steak knife.

Hurrah! I'm marrying Cam! I hug him as tightly as I can until his eyes pop open.

"Morning, beautiful," he says. "Love you."

Hurrah! He loves me! He's in one complete emotional piece! There is no hurt in his eyes whatsoever. Officially unscarred.

"I love you, too," I say, my feelings for him overflowing like a closet stuffed with too many shoes. "What would you like to do now, Mr. Engaged?"

He grins. "Since Lila is already planning the new decor for your room, I want you to move into my apartment."

Oh. Right. That does make sense now that we're officially going to be a couple. Married people tend to live together. Cam has been asking me to move in for the past year, but I wasn't ready. You don't live with a man because you want to save money on rent. You live with a man because you want to spend your life with him. And since I wasn't sure what my ultimate plans were—staying in Arizona or hightailing it out of there—I didn't want to commit to a shared couch, or a plant, or a lease, or anything we would have to divvy up six months later. But now the decision is made. We're getting married. No need to divvy up the couch pillows. Ever. "All right. I'll move in," I say, then press my lips into his. Thank God I didn't tell him no. Who cares about a job? I'm obviously afraid of being happy. My parents have screwed me up for years and years. I pull back and look at my watch. "It's already nine. I don't know how we slept in so late in a truck bed. I don't know how we even fell asleep." I guess sleeping out in the desert was a cool thing to do. Something to tell our kids about the night we got engaged. More impressive than the How We Met story. At a friend's party in college. Boring. "What happens now?"

He rubs my two hands between his. "Now we get to tell everyone."

Fun! Is there really any better announcement than a ring-sparkling, smile-beaming, guess-what-we're-engaged one? I think not. "Who do we tell first? Should we call? Should we drop by?"

"Let's stop by my mom's. It's Saturday. We don't have anything else to do today."

Yes, the day is wide open. I don't even have to unpack—we can just move it all to Cam's place later. I kiss him again and wrap myself in his arms. Tomorrow I'll have to call TRSN to tell them I've changed my mind. Today I get to enjoy.

★ ★ ★

After showering quickly at Cam's, we drive to his parents' house in Mesa. By the happy way her arms are flailing, I can tell that Alice, Cam's mother, is already aware of the news. Cam must have told her that he was planning to propose. If it's true that you can tell how a man will treat his wife by the way he treats his mother, then I'm in for years of worship. Go, me!

She's at the truck in her flip-flops before Cam even puts it in park.

"Welcome to the family!" she sings as I open the door and she throws her arms around me. "You jerks," she says. "Why didn't you call us last night? Your father and I were waiting."

"Sorry," he says.

"Dad's inside." She winks at Cam and we follow her to the door. As I walk through the stucco entranceway, a cacophony of voices shout, "Congratulations!"

"Dad" is about fifty people. The room is filled with Cam's relatives—parents, sister, grandparents, aunts and uncles and cousins. A surprise engagement party. Sweet? Or disconcerting?

Not that a family gathering like this is unusual. We see a whole crew every Sunday night for dinner, granted not this big. Alice insists that her entire family come over. There's a barbecue in the back beside the pool. The women prepare the food, the men do all the grilling. Hello, stereotype.

Cam's sister and her brood live in Tucson, which is two hours away. For Blair to come in on a Saturday, well, that had to have been planned in advance. And even Richard, Cam's dad, is here, which is a bit of a shock. He's normally at his frame store, er, framing away.

Imagine if I'd said no? And the whole party was planned and Cam came home and had to face the entire neighborhood? Sorry, you can all go home. Nothing to celebrate. Pass the potato salad.

The entranceway is littered with family photos and cheap shoes. I hate taking off my sandals, but Alice insists. If we were somewhere that had winter, meaning slush, I'd understand. But here the closest thing we get to slush is Ben & Jerry's. Plus Alice has a white cockatoo named Ruffles that likes to pace the floor and gnaw at my pinkie toes whenever I'm barefoot.

"Let's see the ring!" Blair screams, running over to me. She's twenty-nine, only a year older than Cam, and three months pregnant. With her third. She's five foot seven and is currently nestling her hands over her swollen stomach. Her blond curly hair—Cam and Blair have Alice's golden-blond curls—is tied into a severe bun behind her head. Her face has a leathery quality to it, as if she's spent too many afternoons in the sun. Honestly, if I ran into her on the street, I'd peg her more as mid-to-late thirties.

When I show her my hand, she squeals like a twelve-year-old. Suddenly, still in the entranceway, I'm surrounded by Cam's aunts and cousins and cousins'-wives, and the questions are fast and furious.

"What's the theme of the wedding?" asks Blair.

Theme?

"Aren't you thrilled?" asks Jessica (wife of a cousin).

"When's the date?" asks Leslie (another wife of another cousin).

"Who are your bridesmaids?" asks Tracy, mother-in-law of Leslie, sister in-law of Alice.

"Are you going to change your name?" Blair again.

Even though their mouths continue moving, suddenly I no longer hear what they're saying. They seem to be on mute. The entranceway has turned into a steam room, burning hot liquid into my nose and mouth and ears, and now, not only have I gone deaf, I can't breathe.

"I need to go to the bathroom," I manage to say, pushing myself backward and tripping over a sneaker.

I steady myself and take off for a moment of privacy. I remember too late that the door's lock has been broken ever since Blair's youngest got locked inside a few months ago and Cam had to bust it open. How can anyone who has so many parties have a broken lock on their guest-bathroom door? I know this is a close family, but jeez. You have to push out your foot to barricade anyone from barging in on you.

How long can I stay inside before anyone notices I'm gone?

After doing my business, I sit on the furry orange toilet seat cover, my foot extended and pressed against the door, and try to catch my breath. The entire bathroom is orange. Alice loves orange. And brass. The two-floor split-level home is covered in gleaming brass statues, pots and massive picture frames. Since Richard owns a framing store, everyone is up on the wall. Many times. Many, many times. Everyone except me. But now that I have a ring on my finger, I'm sure to get up there. Many times.

Unfortunately, most of the brass has seen better days. The bathroom faucet is rusty, the toilet seat chipped. The orange carpet is squashed and stained. Alice fancies herself a Martha Stewart apprentice but can't quite pull it off. It's the antithesis of the übermodern houses my dad and mom used to favor. They had both been in love with chrome.

Personally, I couldn't care less about design. Whatever bedroom I occupied was usually a mess. It drove my parents—and now Lila—crazy.

I stand up. In the Windex-streaked mirror, there are deep circles under my dark brown eyes. Otherwise, I'm generally a fan of this mirror, since it's a skinny one. I look at least two sizes smaller than my size-eight frame. Almost lithe. And my skin always has a nice glow to it because of the reflection off the orange wallpaper. My brown hair is tinged red. I hold my breath and push down my shoulders, trying to imagine what I'll look like in my wedding dress. I try to smile. I've always been told I have a great smile. Two dimples, nice lips, naturally white and perfectly sized teeth. It's my best feature. And it was the best smile of my class, according to my high school yearbook.

I hadn't really thought about the whole planning-the-wedding part. All those details to work out…bridesmaids, location, ceremony…honeymoon? I'm looking forward to that part. I'd always planned on running off somewhere romantic for my wedding. Like Fiji. No muss, no fuss. Just bliss. Not that Alice would let me get away with that. Blair's wedding was the biggest event this town had ever seen. And everything, *everything,* was done by hand. They hand delivered two hundred invitations so they wouldn't get dented in the mail. Made fortune cookies from scratch with personalized messages for each and every one of her 375 guests.

Is Alice expecting us to do something similar? Do parents save money for this? Is my dad supposed to pay?

Budgets. Registries. Licenses.

Headaches.

Last year I did a story on the wedding industry and met

plenty of bridezillas. That can't be me. I don't have the time. Actually, I do have the time, since I'm currently unemployed. But I won't have the time if I'm going to be freelancing. Which I'll have to do if I can't get my job back.

Please tell me both my parents won't have to come to the wedding. After the graduation ceremony from hell, where my parents started screaming at each other in the auditorium and my mother threw a program book at my dad's head, I was hoping they would never again opt to be in the same city, never mind the same room. My mother is going to ignore him. Or throw a cake at him. It's going to be horrible. This whole wedding is a mistake. A big, fat—

The door pushes open and I make a grab for it.

"Sorry," says Blair in her nasal voice, slamming it closed. Okay, I'll be honest. I don't love Blair. Of the whole crew, she annoys me the most. She's so bossy. And opinionated. ("You don't waste your money and buy your shoes at shoe stores, do you? You should really be buying them at Wal-Mart.")

"No problem," I say.

"Is Gabrielle still in there?" I hear Alice say.

Blair: "Yup."

Alice: "Beautiful ring."

Blair: "Yes, it's nice. Pear is the latest style you know. I told Cammy he just had to get it. He was going to buy it at some jeweler in Scottsdale, can you believe it? I turned him right around, and told him to go see Stan in Phoenix."

Alice: "I told him the same thing! You know he needs a haircut. So does Gabrielle."

Nag, nag, nag. It's not hard to see where Blair gets it. Or Cam.

I lift my thumbnail to my lips and start nibbling. Oh, no. I haven't bitten since college. I should definitely not be starting again now. I take another nibble. I can't help it.

"…I don't know why she won't let me clean up her split ends for her…." Alice's voice trails off as she heads back toward the party. I can't help but study my split ends. Which I will never let Alice touch. My future mother-in-law refuses to see a stylist. She cuts her own hair, in this very bathroom. She cuts Blair's hair, too. She's always offering to cut mine, but I keep inventing excuses.

I pull myself together, shoulders down, big smile, and rejoin the party.

The group is already in the process of piling potato salad and tuna wraps onto their orange paper plates.

"There you are," says Cam, wrapping his arm around me. "Hungry?"

"Definitely." I love Alice's tuna wraps. She's a nag, yes, but a nag who can cook. She is constantly copying recipes for me. As if I could cook. Not.

"So dear, what are you thinking, a May wedding?" asks Alice as she refills the (yes, orange) potato-salad bowl. "I know how much Arizona girls love a May wedding. Perfect weather to get married outdoors."

Blair got married on May fourth. Alice got married on May thirteenth.

"I'm not really sure yet, Alice." Um, we've been engaged for less than ten hours? Can I have some time to breathe, please?

"I told Cammy that he should have proposed months ago," she continues. "So we'd have more time to plan, but did he listen to me? Does he ever? No. Now we only have six months to pull it all together."

"Mom, six months will be plenty," Cam says.

Hello? Have we picked May? Did that decision happen while I was in the bathroom?

Alice shakes her head from side to side. "Gabrielle, I tried getting in touch with your mom to invite her today. But she didn't return my call. Is she out of town?"

My mother? Here? Thank God she's out of town. I don't know what she'd make of this quasi-Brady bunch, but it wouldn't be pretty.

"She's doing some work in Tampa," I say.

I catch a look between Alice and Blair. They've never said anything outright, but I get the feeling that they don't approve of my mother's hectic career, her men, her marriages. "Ah, I see," Alice says. "Well, when she gets back, I'd like the three of us to get together for tea. We should put our heads together and start planning. When will she be back home? Perhaps we can have a girls' night this week?"

Is she kidding me? My mother? Here? What if she throws one of the brass statues? Even without my father as a target, she's always throwing something at somebody. I'm not sure how's she going to react to Alice. I can't quite picture her hand-making fortune cookies. Throwing the cookies, possibly.

"She's very busy," I say. "It's hard for her to get away." Which is true. My mother is not in the best place in her life right now. She's an entrepreneur and is always investing in the next "big" thing. Unfortunately, she loves start-ups, even though they don't always love her back. Last year, she lost a mint and had to sell her Scottsdale house and move to a small condo in Phoenix. Right now she has her eye on some business opportunity in Tampa. Which is why she didn't freak out when I told her I was moving to New York. She thinks we both have had enough of the dry heat.

Alice rubs her hands together. "I bet she can't wait to dig her hands into the planning!"

"Um…I haven't told her yet."

Up shoot Alice's penciled-in eyebrows.

When would I have found time to tell her? This kind of news takes more than the two seconds I had to myself while I was in the bathroom.

Alice fidgets with her hair. "Talk to her soon, please. We need to get cracking. I've already spoken to the church and told them to hold May sixth."

Dread sets in. My mom and I declared ourselves agnostics, but we still fast every Yom Kippur. Just in case. I'm not religious, but I absolutely can't get married in a church. And what about those wafers? Do they come in kosher? Do people actually eat wafers, or is that just in the movies? Are they carb-free? My mom is always on a diet. Oh God, my mom is going to throw the wafer.

Cam sees the panic on my face and quickly adds, "Mom, we haven't decided on St. George's. I told you that."

"Calm down, Cammy. You don't have to make a decision this second. But it is a family tradition, and it would make me very happy."

For someone not of the tribe, she sure has the Jewish guilt thing down pat. She could put my mom to shame.

"And May six is the perfect weekend," she declares. "Not that I'm pressuring, I don't want to pressure, but Aunt Zoey and Uncle Dean bought tickets in from Salt Lake for the whole family."

But no pressure.

Cam looks exasperated. "Why would she already buy her ticket?"

Alice shrugs and stares at her plate. "American Airlines was having a sale."

I don't believe this. The relatives bought their plane tickets before I even knew we were getting married. Is this normal? This is not normal. I know my own family history makes it difficult for me to understand normalcy, but I'm pretty sure this isn't it. I should tell her to back off. Step back, missy.

The words are at the tip of my tongue, but they don't come out.

"Anyway," Alice says, "let's talk about colors for the wedding. I think orange would be beautiful—"

"Let me just get something to drink," I say backing away. Vodka, perhaps. In one of Alice's orange-tinted tumblers.

"You know I'm not converting, right?"

"You don't have to convert to get married at St. George's," Cam says. We're lying in his king-size bed, wrapped in his sheets.

"I don't even know if I want a big wedding. I always pictured myself getting hitched somewhere cool. Like barefoot on a beach in Fiji. Or at a campsite in Kenya. Or a mountain in Nepal."

"My family can't afford to go to Nepal."

Bingo. "Who says our families have to come? I've always wanted to elope. So romantic."

"Watching me get married will be a huge joy for them. I can't take that away. This is the moment they've been looking forward to their whole lives."

They could probably use a hobby. I lean up on my elbow

and place my hand firmly on a patch of blond fuzzy chest hair. "Is this about them or us?"

"You know what I mean. I'm sure your family would be devastated if they weren't there. Don't you want your dad to walk you down the aisle?"

"Only if my mother is at the other end of the aisle at the time—and the aisle is five miles long."

He squeezes my hand. "What did your parents say? Were they excited?"

Oops. I knew there was something I'd forgotten to do. "I'll call them tomorrow."

His eyes cloud over. "How could you not want to talk to them? Don't you think that's odd?"

"We've been busy," I say and pull him closer. I squeeze my feet between his knees to warm them up.

"Phone them first thing in the morning. What if they hear from someone else?"

I roll my eyes. "Yeah? Like who? The *National Enquirer*? *ET*?"

"Your feet are so dry," he says, wriggling. "Why don't you use lotion? It's right by the bed."

"Because I don't feel like it." Nag, nag, nag. I pull my legs away. "Would you stop telling me what to do?"

"I didn't realize you were a fan of dry feet." He nuzzles his chin into my neck. "I'm sorry," he says, and sounds like he means it. "And we can invite whomever you want to the wedding. And dress them in whatever color you want. It's about us, not my mom. Now give me a Gabby smile."

I smile. How can I stay mad at him? "Sounds good to me." I kiss his forehead and rub my scaly heel against his calf.

He runs his fingers through my hair. "But it would mean a lot to my family if it was at St. George's."

You've got to be kidding. "We'll see." I'll deal with it tomorrow.

"Love you."

"You, too."

I close my eyes, squeezing the annoyance out like the last drop of toothpaste. I do love him. But is my whole life going to be about bowing to his mother's wishes? Did I make the wrong choice? I toss and turn, and finally drift off to sleep.

I'm awakened by blaring music, swirls of green hot light and another intense headache. Ow! What is wrong with me? I seriously have to see a doctor. My brain feels like it's imploding.

"Turn off the alarm," I mumble to Cam, wiping drool from my lips. Lovely. Head hurts. Needles in eyes.

The music is shrieking, *"Let's do the time warp again!"*

"Cam! Turn it off! It's Sunday!" He'd better not be going into work today. I'll kill him.

"Well, I was walking down the street just having a think, when a snake of a guy gave me an evil wink—"

I groan and open my eyes. Strange. My headache is gone.

As is my fiancé. The spot next to me is empty. "Cam?" I wonder aloud. Where is he?

"He shook me up, took me by surprise—"

Why are Cam's sheets pink? Am I... Is this...

I'm back in my own bed.

3

Splitsville

The alarm clock, my Hello Kitty alarm clock, says 6:30 a.m.

I stifle a scream.

I officially need to be institutionalized. What is wrong with me? I stare up at my ceiling in despair. Maybe there's someone I can call? 1-800-CRAZY? I kick off my covers and peruse my bedroom. How did I end up back here when I went to sleep at Cam's? I creak open my door and tiptoe around the apartment. The lights are off and Lila's door is shut. My two red packed suitcases are in the center of the room, mocking me.

When did I come home? How much vodka did I have at Alice's?

The apartment looks just as it did in my dream last night. After I told Cam I was moving to New York.

Am I dreaming now? As I search the apartment for some sort of sign, my gaze lands on my left hand. My now diamond-less hand.

What happened to my ring? Why am I back home? Was yesterday a dream? Did I never go to Alice's? Am I moving to New York?

I need to speak to someone. I need to speak to Cam. I race over to the living-room phone and dial his number. It rings once.

"Hi, you've reached Cam. I can't come to the phone…"

Why isn't he answering? He's supposed to be my fiancé. A fiancé should answer even if he's sleeping. I try to squash my rising hysteria. Something is wrong with my brain. I'm delirious. Maybe I have a brain tumor? I hang up and dial my mother's hotel number. And then I remember that it's 6:30 a.m. and hang up before she answers. And then I remember that she's in Florida and it's therefore 8:30. Or is it 9:30? I never remember. I call again.

"The hotel has caller ID," she says. "It's not nice to prank call your mother."

"Hi, Mom?" I sit on the couch and try to keep the rising hysteria out of my voice.

"Oh, God, Gabby, you're not going to believe the day I'm having."

"Yeah, me, too."

"Well, me first," she says. "I was woken up at four this morning by the fire alarm. I had to put on my bathrobe, and wait in the lobby. Naturally it was a false alarm, and a big waste of my time and energy. Anyway, you just caught me. I was on my way to work."

"I think something is weird with me."

"Are you throwing up? You're not pregnant, are you?"

I lie across the couch. "Does being pregnant make you stupid?"

"A little. Are your breasts swollen?"

I examine my braless cleavage. "Not so much."

"Morning sickness?"

"I don't think I'm pregnant. It's just that… Okay, I know this is going to sound weird. But I went to sleep last night at Cam's and I woke up in my own bed."

Silence. "Have you been smoking anything?"

"Mom, no."

"Booze?"

"A little. But not enough to make me go crazy."

"Moving is stressful, Gabby."

"And to top it off, Cam proposed last night—"

"He proposed? Now? What a male thing to do. He waits until you quit your job, and *then* decides to propose? What is wrong with him? With all of them? Your father always tried to control me like that. You're too young to get married anyway. You can't get married at twenty-four—"

"Mom—"

"So what did you do?"

"I'm not sure. I thought I said no. But then I went to sleep, and when I woke up I realized I *hadn't* said no. But now I'm home again. And not engaged. Is this making any sense?"

"No. You had a weird dream. You're flying to New York today. Stress is normal. Healthy, even. Or maybe you ate something funny."

"Maybe the potato salad was off." But if I hadn't gone to Alice's, there would be no potato salad. Was going to Alice's a dream? "Maybe I came home last night, after I left Cam's."

Suddenly, Lila's door bursts open. "Gabby, it's six-thirty

in the morning here. Some of us don't have to be up for another thirty minutes." She's wearing her long red silk nightgown and her matching fuzzy red slippers. Her blond hair is already tied into a neat ponytail.

"Mom, I have to go. I'll call you later." I hang up and turn to Lila. "Am I engaged?"

She narrows her eyes. "Are you kidding?"

I wish. "No. I'm serious."

"You do remember what happened yesterday, don't you?"

I remember two yesterdays. "I do, but I'm confused."

"You turned Cam down. You're leaving for New York. We said goodbye last night."

I nod, slowly. Back to single Gabby. Alice's must have been a dream. A vivid dream. More like a nightmare. I fell asleep worrying about whether or not I'd done the right thing, and I dreamed about what would happen if I had said yes. And the answer: a disaster of a brunch and a church wedding I don't want.

She studies my face. "Are you feeling all right?"

"I don't think so."

"Let me get you an aspirin."

"Okay. And then I need to get to the airport."

I watch a movie on the plane. I'm trying not to think about my crack-up, or my new job.

Am I ready for the big time? With my mental condition, I might not even be suited for the small time.

I wonder what Heather will be like. Lila and I always did everything together. Maybe I'll get lucky and have another roommate turned best friend. Maybe I'll get even luckier and Heather will have the same shoe size as me. Lila has adorably small feet—her slippers barely fit onto my big toe.

I land in New York, wait twenty minutes for my oversize luggage, another twenty for a taxi line (freezing my butt off—damn it's cold in this part of the country), have a terrifying journey into the city (both from the speed and jerkiness of the drive, and from the overwhelmingness of it all) and arrive in front of the apartment thirty minutes later. Holy shit. I'm here. I'm in New York. I'm here!

"Here you are," the cabbie says. "Thirty-fourth and Third." I do my best not to get run over as I struggle to pull my bags out of the trunk.

"Hi," I say to the doorman, I take a deep breath to steady my racing heart rate. "I'm Gabby Wolf. You're supposed to have keys for me?"

He looks behind his desk. "Nope. Nothing for you."

Terrific. "Um. Has anyone left anything at all for apartment 15D?"

He takes another look. "Nope. But I think Heather's in."

"She is?" Thank God.

He picks up his phone and dials. "Heather? You have a visitor. Your name?" he asks me.

"Gabrielle."

"It's Gabrielle," he says, nods and hangs up. "You can go up."

Why did she make such a big deal about leaving me the keys if she was going to be home? Hello, drama queen.

I roll my bags into the elevator and then off at the fifteenth floor. The carpet is a mousy yellow. It looks like a grandparents' apartment and smells like chicken soup. Whatever. I'm in New York!

I look both ways and then head to the right. A door opens and a woman is standing in the entranceway. She's shorter than I expected, about five-two. Her bright turquoise shirt-dress shows off an hourglass figure. Wide hips, and a tiny waist held in by a tight belt. Funky outfit. Her hair is light brown, curly and down to her waist. Her eyes are small and just a bit too close together.

She looks me over. "You're taller than I expected."

"Sorry?" Nice to meet you, too.

"I guess you should come in." She moves over to let me inside. She doesn't offer to help with my bags.

On the other side of the door is a plain white living room featuring a boring beige, felty, scrawny couch, a red rug, a bookshelf filled with what looks like "How to get him to notice you" self-help books, framed posters of purple flowers and a tiny TV. The first thing I need to buy is a new TV for my room. Lila was never home, so I was allowed to monopolize the one she'd bought for our living room. But I'm not sure if Steak-Knife Heather would appreciate my constant news surfing.

"This is the common space," she says and then leads me to a room off the hallway. "Your bedroom."

The room is white and grungy. Tape remnants are stuck to the wall and dust bunnies litter the scraped wooden floor. A large blind-less window looks over Third Avenue. I guess I should have brought that sheet.

Honk!

Honk, honk, honk! Holy shit I'm really in New York!

It gets quiet here at night, right?

Heather heaves the window open. The honking gets louder. "You'll need to air out the room," she says. "Leigh was a pig."

I wheel my luggage into the center of the empty space. "Wait a sec. Where's my new bed?"

Heather shrugs. "It never arrived."

You've got to be kidding. "What am I supposed to sleep on?"

"What do you want me to do? Call a mattress company."

Crap. My phone. "I forgot to pack my phone."

"Where's the rest of your furniture? Where are you going to put your clothes?"

"At the moment, I'm more concerned with where I'm going to put me." The couch did not look all that comfortable.

"It'll probably come tomorrow. Are you hungry? What are you doing for dinner?"

"I don't know. I didn't think that far ahead."

"Do you eat Italian?"

"Sure." Who doesn't? "But I'd like to unpack first, if that's okay," I say, glancing dubiously at the miniscule closet.

"Obviously. I need to make us a reservation, anyway."

At least I remembered my Hello Kitty alarm clock. I set the current time and the alarm for tomorrow. Then I pull my work clothes out of my bag and shake them out. I have no idea what I'm going to wear tomorrow for my first day, but whatever it is, it must not be wrinkled. I open the closet to find it…stark free of hangers. Wonderful. "Can I borrow some hangers?"

"I don't have too many extras."

Come on. "One? Two? I'll buy my own tomorrow."

She sighs and retreats into her bright orange room (which looks bigger than mine from this angle), and returns a few minutes later with three metal hangers, the kind you get at the dry cleaners. "I'll need these back ASAP."

I guess we won't be sharing shoes just yet.

★ ★ ★

"So what's your story?" she asks over our Caesar salads. We're at a table by the window looking onto Lexington. Every time the door opens, a burst of cold air blows through my clothes.

"Which one?"

"Men-wise."

This is one story I don't feel like rehashing. "Had a boyfriend. Now I don't."

Her eyes gleam. "So you're single."

Single. I haven't been single in years. The word feels foreign in my head, like another language. "I suppose so."

"Good. I could desperately use a new single friend. All my girls have sold their souls. It's the worst. Their men are their goddamn appendages. Tell me, why can't a wife have dinner with her friends one night a week? Will her husband starve?"

"I don't know." Cam was actually pretty good about letting me have my own space. Although who knows if that would have changed if we lived together.

"Well, I do. Women let men control their lives. They don't know how to create *boundaries.*" She draws a square in the air with her index finger. "They don't know how to keep their own individuality. At least we'll have each other. At least you didn't bail. You wouldn't believe the freaks I met trying to sublet this place. I wish I could keep the whole apartment on my own, but I'd be broke by Christmas. Leigh moving out totally screwed me, you know. What a bitch."

If Leigh was a bitch, what does that make Heather? Our server arrives with our raviolis, and I shove a forkful into my mouth in case I'm suddenly tempted to answer my question out loud.

★ ★ ★

After dinner, I'm in my bedroom, staring at the apartments across the street, my sheets covering my makeshift bed (aka the couch cushions). It's already eleven, but I doubt I'll be able to doze off anytime soon.

First of all, it's only nine my time. Second, I'm terrified of closing my eyes. I've been in denial all day, but I can't ignore that every time I go to sleep, I seem to end up in an alternate reality. And since that isn't possible, I must just be having weird dreams, right?

Maybe tonight I'll dream about something normal, like failing a test in high school.

What if I wake up back in Arizona?

No. No, no, no. Must think positively. It won't happen again! I will wake up in New York! I will…I will…I will…

My eyelids feel heavy. Yes, that's what's going to happen. I will wake up in New York. I *will* wake up back in New York. I will…

Blinding pain. Light.

"This week in sports…"

There's a fire in my head! I blink twice and open my eyes. Shit.

"Morning, gorgeous," Cam says. He's sitting up in bed, shirtless, watching TV. "You must be zonked. It's already ten."

I try not to cry. I am going mad. What is wrong with me? Why can't I tell the difference between dreaming and real life? Why is my brain playing tricks on me? I pull the covers back over my head.

"What's wrong?"

"Nightmare," I say.

"About what?"

About what, indeed. "A fire." My brain is on fire.

"No fires here," he promises.

I stay hidden until Cam eventually leaves to make us breakfast. "Omelet?" he asks from the kitchen. "Cheese and onion?"

"'Kay," I answer. I am not coming out. I am temporarily crazy, so I will remain here until it passes. Like the flu.

My stomach starts to growl as the scent of onion and bacon wafts under the sheets. Yum. I doubt Heather is making me anything this good in my real life.

"Since you won't come out for the chow, the chow is coming to you," Cam says, placing a tray on my lap. Breakfast in bed. How sweet is that? "Eat, future wife," he says. "You need your strength."

I slither out from the sheets, lean up against the headboard and dig in. A girl's gotta eat, even if she is asleep. "And why is that?" I ask, digging into my omelet.

"Because as soon as you finish, you have to call your parents. It's not right."

Yes! The man's a genius! I'll speak to my mom. She'll remember our conversation yesterday. She'll have to. Mothers know these things, right? They can sense if their children are losing their minds. I reach for the phone as I stuff another forkful of egg into my mouth. "I'm going to call her right now."

He winks, hands me a napkin and sits down on the edge of the bed beside me. "There's a good girl."

I dial her room at her hotel, but she doesn't answer. So I call her cell. "Mom? It's me."

"Oh, so nice of you to call," she snaps. Do I detect a hard line of sarcasm in her voice? "Anything you'd care to tell me?"

"What are you talking about?" I take another bite of egg.

A drop of ketchup smears onto the bedspread. Cam rolls his eyes and points to the napkin.

"Alice called me this morning."

I smack Cam's leg. "Oh, no."

"Oh, yes. Why is it that I heard about my only daughter being engaged from someone other than my daughter? Huh?"

"Sorry, Mom. I didn't have a chance to call you yesterday." *Was* it yesterday? I hear a smash and then a clang. I think she just threw the phone. "Mom?" I wait for her to pick it back up.

"I felt pretty stupid, Gabrielle. Pretty damn stupid. She called me to discuss the wedding, and I didn't even know there was a wedding! In fact I told her she was mistaken, since you were moving to New York—"

My heart races. "Exactly! Mom, I just spoke to you, remember? About the—" I lower my voice so maybe Cam won't hear "—move?" I called her yesterday. And discussed it. She has to remember—she's my mom. Moms have a sixth sense, don't they?

"Yes, just last week you said—"

Last week? No, it was yesterday! Or do I mean today? "What day is it?"

"It's Sunday. And it's been an awful day. First I was woken up at 4:00 a.m.—"

My blood runs cold. "Because of a fire alarm."

Silence. "How did you know that?"

"You *told* me! Yesterday!"

"How could I have told you yesterday when it just happened?"

"You told me. Don't joke. You don't remember?"

"How could I have told you? You're pulling my leg. Was

it on the wire? There better not have been a reporter there. I was in my bathrobe. Do you need a quote?"

"No." My head hurts. How is this possible? I spoke to my mother and she told me about the fire alarm. Yesterday. Or today. Am I living each day twice?

"Anyway, Gabrielle, I'm upset with you. How you could get engaged is beyond me. How you could get engaged without telling me is despicable."

This is way weird. My mom told me about the fire alarm yesterday. *Yesterday.* "I'll call you later," I tell her and hang up. I look up at Cam.

He's looking at me strangely. "What was that all about?"

"Nothing," I murmur. "You know my mother. Sometimes she makes no sense."

"Didn't she want to talk to me? You know? Congratulations? Welcome to the family?"

"I'll be right back." I hurry to the bathroom. I close the door firmly and press my back against the door. My head pounds.

When did this craziness start? When was the beginning of my double life? I retrace my mental steps. Today is Sunday in Arizona. I'm engaged. Yesterday was Sunday in New York. I wasn't engaged. The day before that was Saturday in Arizona. I woke up in the desert. We had brunch at Alice's. The day before that was *also* Saturday in Arizona. I *also* woke up in the desert. I told Cam I didn't want to marry him. I finished packing.

So what happened the night before that?

I shut my eyes firmly and try to visualize the night in question. The night that Cam proposed. The night we were lying in the back of the truck, watching the falling stars.

It can't be. It can't.

My wish? My wish. I wished I didn't have to choose. That I could live both lives. Stay with Cam and move to New York. Have it all.

I sink to the bath mat. It's not possible. Is it? How else can I explain what's happening? How else can I rationalize how I've been living two separate lives?

I tell Cam I need to borrow his truck to return to my place to pick up a few last-minute things.

"Like what?"

"Clothes, makeup…not that I have anywhere to put any of it."

"I'll make some space."

Instead of going to my apartment, I stop by the emergency room to see if there is something wrong with my head. Like a brain tumor. After a few hours, I finally get to see a doctor.

"Lately, I've been existing in two universes," I tell him. "Is that a psychological condition?"

He rubs his chin, looks into my eyes with a flashlight and asks me if I've been under a lot of stress.

"A little," I say.

"You look okay to me," he says. "Try to get some sleep. Do you want antibiotics?"

"No thanks." I decide not to tell him the whole story. It's not like he's going to believe me. If this is real and I'm not going bonkers, then someone else in the world must have gone through this, too. Someone who can tell me how to make it stop.

Back in my old apartment, I get comfy on the futon, laptop on my knees, and try to figure out what the hell has happened to me.

I Google *multiple lives* and get over forty-three million

hits. There are mentions of reincarnation, cats and, inexplicably, real estate. But nothing about my weirdo predicament. I try *alternative lives* and get another thirty thousand hits. Most of these are scenarios of regret. About what could have/would have/should have been. Then I land on something called *Many-Worlds Interpretation*. According to Wikipedia, http://en.wikipedia.org/wiki/Multiverse, *many-worlds* is defined as: "…an interpretation of quantum mechanics that proposes the existence of multiple universes, all of which are identical, but exist in possibly different states." Different states? Does that mean parallel universes?

I keep reading and reading and my heart pounds louder with every click, with every article. "These different states are caused by a divergence that splits the universe into two." I discover that there is a whole theory in quantum mechanics (whatever the hell that is) that believes that whenever there is a choice, or a possibility, reality splits into a new world. Therefore, there is a new independent world for every different possibility. Anything that could happen does happen. There are books and information about this theory all over the Internet. There are over twenty thousand hits on this on Google. People have done experiments on this theory. Real scientists.

Could this really have happened to me? Yes. Yeeessss. My life verged the morning after Cam proposed. I'm not crazy. I am not crazy! What happened to me has been written about! Wahoo! Perhaps there's a support group?

I get slightly nervous when one of the sites says that communication between these distinct universes in not possible, because I am, in fact, communicating with myself.

I search for another hour without finding anything specific. Not that it would help. Even though there are thousands of pages about many worlds, they're all theoretical. There aren't any real-life examples. As though no one else has gone through anything like this.

No one except me.

I keep reading and searching and end up seeing a lot of phrases like *wave function collapse* and *relative state,* which make me wish I'd taken a science class in college. I spend the next three hours searching until my eyes are tired. I type in *green light, headache* and *wish,* but still, nothing.

I close my computer and lie back. What I've learned today is that while there are lots of theories about multiple lives, no one has ever written an account of it happening. But if so many people have thought about it, written about it, and theorized about it, isn't it possible? You can't rule something out just because it can't be proven, can you? There are like a million religions and none of them can be proven!

If the many-worlds theory is true, then everyone exists in multiple universes. There are many versions of me around, right now. There are many versions of everyone around, right now. Whenever anyone has to make a choice, a new version of her or him pops up. There's a me who never dated Cam in the first place. There's a me who went away to UCLA. There's a me whose parents never divorced.

That seems a bit insane. There can't be an infinite number of mes. Can there?

As a kid, I remember asking my dad how many stars there were. Living in California, he thought I meant celebrities and asked me if I meant movie, TV or both. When I clarified that I meant stars in the sky, he laughed and said, "It's infinite."

"How can that be?" I asked him.

"They go on forever and ever."

"But how?"

"That's just the way it is," he said, playing with my hair. "Space, time, stars—they all go on forever."

If all those things are infinite, then why can't versions of people be infinite, too? Why not choices? And if so, did I somehow stumble into the ability to exist in two of these worlds?

Or maybe I just stumbled into the ability to remain conscious in two of these worlds.

At four, I hear Lila's key in the door. "Hi, guys," she says.

"It's just me!" I holler, closing the laptop. As nonjudgmental as she is, she'd still think I was nuts.

Lila goes through her cleansing/changing routine and then joins me in my room. "What happened to you? I thought your flight was this morning. Where have you been? What's going on?" she asks, sitting on the side of my futon.

I wave my bejeweled hand. "Change of plan. I'm not going to New York."

Her jaw drops. "No way. I don't believe it."

"It's true." Half-true.

"Wow." Smiling, she leans over and hugs me. "Congrats!"

"Thanks."

"But Gabby, what about the new job?"

I shrug. "A person can't have everything." Most people, anyway. Apparently, I am not most people.

She gives me a hopeful look. "Does that mean you're not moving out?"

I shake my head. "No, you're still getting your home office. I'm moving in with Cam."

She sticks her tongue out at me. "Aw. You lucky girl."

"You know what?" I say. "I might be." I'd choose lucky over crazy, anyway.

On my way back to Cam's, I'm strangely invigorated. My wish came true. It *must* have. It's the only explanation. My body feels alive and tingly. I decide not to tell Cam about my self and my other self—it's not like he'd believe it. Who would? I barely believe it myself.

I find him in the backyard, surrounded by sawdust and some sort of table with a mirror.

"What are you doing?"

"Building you a vanity table for the bedroom," he says, while hammering. "So you can have somewhere to put your makeup and jewelry and stuff. I got you a lamp, too, because I'm not sure there's going to be enough light…. Do you like it? I still have to build the bench."

I am so touched, I almost cry.

While he finishes, we return to his parents' for Sunday night dinner. Afterward, we go straight to bed and I seduce him immediately.

"That was fun," he says afterward. "Three nights in a row. Life is good."

"Yes, it was," I say, laying my head on his chest. His heart rate is beginning to slow.

"What are your plans for tomorrow?" he asks.

Tomorrow! I start work tomorrow. In New York. A fiancé in Arizona and a new job in New York. I really do get to have it all—except a job here. "Try to get my job back."

"My mom mentioned that she wants to start planning the wedding…."

"Of course she does."

"Have you given any thought to getting married in May?"

"Whatever you want, babe." Since I'm only half getting married, why not meet Alice halfway?

His eyes light up like a slot machine. "Really? And what about the church?"

Halfway does not include churches. Then again, maybe it can. If I ever get married in New York, I can do it any way I want. And to someone else. It wouldn't even be bigamy. Legally, that is. "Whatever makes you happy," I tell him with a smile. But I'm still not converting.

He kisses my forehead and promptly falls asleep.

My thoughts are too loud and crazy to let me drift off. I'm wondering how to best take advantage of my fabulous science experiment.

Should I try out different hairstyles? Go blond in one reality, stay brunette in the other? What about different diets? No carbs in one, low-fat in the other, and see which version of me loses more weight? Invest in real estate in one, stocks in the other?

Check the winning lottery number in one, choose that number in the other? Though supposedly, the two universes have nothing to do with each other. The guy who wins in the first reality might remain a poor slob in the other. But it's worth looking into.

The possibilities are endless, and I'm going to enjoy every one of them. I'm going to live it up.

Life *is* good. Both of them.

4

Lights, Camera, Action!

I'm late. How is it possible that I'm late for my first day of work? I have never been late for anything. I set my alarm for 7:00 a.m., a half hour earlier than I was supposed to get up. But it's already eight, which means the radio alarm was singing for an hour before I even heard it.

I jump into the shower, throw on my clothes (no time to debate: black pants, green sweater), flip through the news channels as I scarf down my coffee (plane crash in Bali, hurricane in the Bahamas, kidnapped girl found alive in South Carolina), grab my bag, notebook and clipboard, then run for the elevator. No time today to test out the subway. Taxi, it is. The best part of living in New York is that you can hail a cab from anywhere, unlike Phoenix, where they're as common as waterslides in the desert.

The cold air tackles me as I open the door. Damn, I really need to get myself a coat.

When I reach the street, I attempt to hail a cab, but a stream of occupied yellow taxis keeps passing me by. Hmm. How long is this supposed to take? Where are the empty ones? What if I'm here for hours and no cabs drive by and I miss my first day of work?

Oh, there's one! Hello? Hello! Why didn't he stop? How do I get them to stop? On TV, New Yorkers sometimes whistle. I don't know how to whistle.

I see one coming and I step into the middle of the street. A Honda turns the corner, almost running me over. But then I realize something. What if I die in one life? I'll still be around in the other. I think.

Just then an empty cab pulls up. He nods, and I get in. "Fifty-eighth and Broadway please," I tell him.

And away we go. He chats on his cell phone while I watch the clock. Curtis Boland, the executive producer of *Ron's Report* told me I'd be working from about ten to seven-thirty every day, assuming there is no crisis. Since Ron's show tapes at six and airs at eight, I can leave after the post-tape meeting. But today, my first day, she wants me in at nine. It's now eight-fifty.

"Excuse me, sir?"

He continues chatting.

"Sir? Can you tell me how far away we are?"

"We're here," he grunts and pulls over in front of The Gap, where a street vendor is selling Kate Spade purses (fake, I assume).

"Where?"

"Across the street."

Oh. I pay him and face the tall, gleaming chrome-and-tinted-windowed TRSN building. A news ticker is featured prominently over the entranceway, informing me about the hurricane in the Bahamas. I have to maneuver my way past myriad flowerpots (security cameras, most likely) to get to the doorway.

I pull open the heavy doors and march toward the security desk, the click of my heels echoing through the room.

"May I help you?" the security guard asks, and after I show my ID, I'm told to go up to the tenth floor. The elevator doors are about to close and I throw my purse between the sensors to stop them. A woman clucks her tongue.

"Sorry," I say sheepishly and slide inside. I slither to the back of the crowded space and accidentally elbow someone directly in the stomach. "*Really* sorry," I say.

"No worries," says a deep voice. I look up at the man I attacked.

Hello there.

The man I attacked is hot. Hmm. That stomach I elbowed was pretty hard. Muscled, I'd say. He's tall, with short dark brown hair and big brown eyes framed in black wire glasses. Like me, he's wearing black pants and a light green shirt. Now *that's* what I call fate. He's also giving me a big smile.

I feel my cheeks burn and I quickly turn away. It's too early for me to even think about other guys. Stare at the floor, missy! Think about Cam, whose poor heart you broke two nights ago. Instead I glance at the outfits of the people around me. There's a lot of black happening, I'll tell ya.

The elevator stops on the third floor. Everyone except

the hard-gut guy and me gets out. The tiny hairs on my arm stand up. Hello, sexual tension. I think. I probably shouldn't be having that elevator-tension feeling so soon after breaking up with Cam. The entire time Cam and I were together, I never even looked at another guy.

But now you're single! a voice in my head screams. Excellent. Now not only am I existing in two worlds, I'm also hearing voices.

Regardless, the voice is right. I *am* single. I'm allowed to bask in the sexual tension with other men. In fact, I should smile. It's rude not to. Turn around. Ask him if he wants to show me the building…the city…his apartment….

I'm about to open my mouth, but I freeze. Excellent. I've forgotten how to flirt.

The door opens on ten and I step off. And then at the last second, I turn around. I can do it! I give him a big smile-for-the camera grin and a Miss America wave. And before he can return it, the doors close.

Well. At least I tried. Pretty cool that I'm in the building for five seconds and I've already spotted a cute guy. I love New York! He must work for TRSN too. A coproducer? A writer? We'll both be here into the wee hours of the night and one thing will lead to another and—

I show my pass at the door, and am suddenly in the newsroom. No one except the mega-talent has offices here since it's all open space: desks and cubes overflowing with papers, computers and screaming people. I might faint. I can't believe I'm here. I made it.

What if I'm not up for this?

I walk over to where Curtis told me Ron's crew is located and spot her waving at me from her desk. "I want that interview," she says when I reach her. At first I think she's talking to me, but then I notice her mobile headset. "Throw in a book deal if you have to. Just get it. No, I don't want her talking to O'Reilly or Couric."

Curtis is wearing faded blue jeans, a black T-shirt, a brown corduroy blazer and sneakers. Her skin is ghostly pale, as though she hasn't seen the sun in months, and she's not wearing any makeup. Her dirty-blond hair is tied back in a haphazard ponytail. I'd peg her as mid-to-late forties. She told me she's been working with Ron for ten years. She's the one who discovered him and brought him to TRSN to begin with. This show is her baby.

"Get her to talk to us. Do you hear me? I want the kidnapped girl. I don't have time for your pathetic excuses...."

As she berates whoever is on the other end of the phone, I look around the room and think about how I almost didn't make it here. As a kid, I had wanted to be an anchor (my dad used to tell me I had a face for television), so I decided to major in broadcasting when I applied to Arizona State. But when I got to school, I realized that everyone wanted to be an anchor and that the real power was behind the scenes, producing, so that's what I focused on. The summer of my junior year, I interned at the NBC affiliate in Phoenix, but decided that after I graduated I would move to New York. I don't know where my obsession with New York came from. Maybe from years of watching *Law and Order*, maybe from too much romanticizing about *Sex and the City*. All I knew was that I wanted to have a zip code that started with 1. The spring before I graduated, I applied to every available and not-available entry-level job in Manhattan and flew down for informational interviews, where I was told again and again, sorry, we're hiring the interns from last year, why don't you work at a local station outside the city? When you have more experience, when you've grown your contact list, when, when, when… So I returned to Arizona, my tail nestled firmly between my legs, and took a full-time job there.

My new boyfriend Cam told me it was for the best since New Yorkers were crazy, and anyway, he wanted me on this side of the country. I jokingly warned him not to get too attached. At my graduation ceremony, I figured I would be in Arizona another year, tops. I took typical hat-throwing pictures with Lila, with Cam (who had just graduated from law school), with my mom and with my dad. (He had come even though I'd told him not to bother, not because I believed it wasn't worth the trip, but because I dreaded the fight that he and my mom would have if he did show up, which they had, and which I did my best to ignore.)

Lila and I kept our two-bedroom apartment in Tempe. (I had moved out of my mom's place in Scottsdale freshman year when Goodwin, husband Number Three, moved in. Lila's dorm room was right next door to mine. We became best friends at first by proximity, and then by habit. We moved into the two-bedroom sophomore year.) Even though I was earning decent money, I figured there was no point getting my own place, since I wasn't planning on sticking around.

I started the new job, liked the job and got promoted from assignment editor to producer eleven o'clock news, to producer 6:00 p.m. news, to executive producer 6:00 p.m. news. I was good at my job. I could smell a story. Maybe *smell* is the wrong word. When something big is going on, my mouth gets zapped dry. I don't know why, but that's what happens, that's when I know I'm onto something. My dry mouth has never been wrong. Anyway, I bought the Jetta,

Cam made me a bookshelf, and after two years, I started settling into my life. I had my boyfriend, my job, my bookshelf. I got to go into work at nine and come home at five-thirty, watch my newscast from my couch. I started to think that maybe I didn't need to move, that I could settle in Arizona.

And that was when a dark-haired Melanie Diamond, a twenty-five-year-old Phoenix elementary school teacher, was photographed leaving a hotel room with the very married, very "it's all about family values" Senator Jim Garland.

My mouth was drier than the desert.

Every producer in the country wanted to talk to Melanie. And like everyone else, I called her. I pleaded with her to tell me her story.

"I know you must be going through hell," I said repeatedly to her answering machine. "And the last thing I want is to make it worse. But until you tell the world your side of the story, it's not going to go away."

That night she called me back. "There's something about your voice," she said, sounding a little lost and overwhelmed. "You sound a bit like my sister. Like someone I can talk to. Get your butt over here."

So I got the interview. I brought a camera to her place and got her to tell her side of the story. Afterward, when the cameraman was gone, she ordered me to stay for coffee and I did. She told me about how she hadn't left her house in two weeks. How she never expected this to blow up in her face. How she can't believe what a jerk the senator turned out to be. I told her about Cam, about my messed up parents, about my dream of going to New York. And I knew that we were going to be more than interviewer and interviewee. We were going to be friends.

After the show ran, every station in the country picked up my story. My exclusive interview. The details Melanie had given me. Illicit trips to Greece, promises of marriage. A tearful, black-haired Melanie, swearing that the bald and sweaty Garland had sworn he was married in name only, that he and his pig-nosed wife Judy didn't even sleep in the same bed. I edited the pig-nose part out of my interview. I also edited out my own questions— like I always did in this type of interview. Producers stayed behind the scenes.

As the weeks passed, I became the one who listened to Melanie cry about how she would never love anyone again, and promise that she would. I found her a lawyer through Cam's firm when her school threatened to fire her for the negative publicity.

As the weeks passed, doors that had been bolted only two years before were suddenly swinging wide open. Because of my newfound notoriety as the producer who got the Melanie Diamond exclusive, job offers around the country started flooding in. Opportunity. Cash. Health benefits.

"I'd like to talk to you about working for us," Curtis said via cell phone.

I'd watched Grighton's show—as a news producer you have to watch everyone's show—and I thought he was smart, tough and intimidating. And I wanted to work for him. But most importantly, he wanted to hire a young, female producer who could deliver. Me.

And here I am.

"…Report back to me at eleven," Curtis says to whatever poor soul is on the phone with her. Then she lowers the headset to rest around her neck and stares at me. "So, Gabby, you made it. Welcome to national news."

In the next hour, I'm given a desk, a computer and a BlackBerry.

Curtis tours me around the building, barking out orders. "Morning meeting is at eleven, afternoon meeting at three, post-show meeting at seven-ten. All take place in the seventh-floor conference room. Ron hates tardiness, so don't be late. Ever. Understand?"

"Yes."

"He also detests guests who stutter, so don't book them."

"That's fine." N-no p-problem.

She shows her pass to the security guard and we enter a small puke-green room. "The green room. Obviously."

In Arizona, the green room, where the guests wait to be interviewed, wasn't actually green. But I always thought that was kind of lame. This one has a watercooler, a coffee brewer, a loaf of banana bread, a TV and VCR, and a blue leather couch.

"If he catches a grammar mistake in the script," Curtis says, "he'll think you're illiterate. Watch out for sloppiness. And always get your facts right. He's known as one of the most trusted newsmen in the nation for a reason. Us."

"Got it."

She presses her finger against her lips. "Control room," she mouths and opens the door.

No one looks up as we sneak inside. Jane Hickey's morning show is filming.

I love control rooms. I always feel like I'm in the center of the world. Two rows of producers at their computers face a wall of television monitors. The center monitor shows the two smiling blondes, Cameron Diaz and Jane, discussing Cameron's new movie. The monitor beside her shows the police chief in South Carolina, the one who found the kidnapped girl. As soon as Jane finishes her interview with the movie star, the feed will switch to the police chief. Built into the side walls are fifteen television monitors showing the news on every other news station in the country.

"You'll be working here," Curtis mouths, pointing to one of the desks, which a tall, lanky man now occupies.

She motions me back toward the door.

When we're back outside, Curtis continues growling orders. "Ron's ratings are highest when he gets a good debate going, so don't book any wimps. Make sure the guest can stand his ground."

"No problem," I say.

"And make sure to know who else the guest is talking to. If he appeared on Larry King last night, we don't want him tonight. Ron won't be happy with you. He won't be happy at all."

"Got it." Butterflies are anxiously flying around my stomach. If I was intimidated by Ron before, I'm scared shitless now. What if Ron doesn't like me? What if he thinks I'm some sort of hack? What if he thinks I'm illiterate?

"And remember," Curtis says as we step back into the elevator, "he's very happily married. And we want him to stay that way."

I try to keep the shock from my face. What exactly does she mean by that? Does she think I'm going to try to sleep my way to the top? Or is it my responsibility to keep guests from hitting on him? He's not exactly a rock star. I can't exactly imagine screaming teen girls pressed against the tinted windows flashing him their panties. "I understand," I say.

"Good." With a glance at her watch she adds, "It's time for the morning meeting."

My hands are shaking. I've moved them under the conference-room table so nobody notices, but there doesn't seem to be anything I can do to make them stop.

Curtis, the reporters and the associate producers are all chatting among themselves. Ron is expected any minute and I can't get my hands to stay still. Ron will probably think I'm some sort of crack junkie. Just as I'm about to try putting them on the table again, so I can use the right one to take notes, he enters the room.

"Good morning, you guys!" he sings.

"Hey, Ron," everyone chants back.

Ron looks exactly like he does on television, only taller. He comes across as the ideal dad: smart, trustworthy, handsome and in control. His hair is short, dark gray and parted to the side. He's wearing beige pleated trousers and a navy collared sweater. He places his steaming mug of coffee at the head of the oval table and sits down.

"Everyone excited for today's show?" he asks, scanning the table. His gaze rests on me. "You must be Gabby. Welcome to the team."

My cheeks flush when he says my name. I'm not surprised he knows who I am, but the familiarity of my nickname catches me by surprise. "Thanks, Ronald," I say, trying to sound smooth and praying I don't stutter. "It's a pleasure to be working for you."

He smiles, and I'm surprised to see that he has two

dimples. "How do you feel about the cold, Arizona? No dry heat here, is there?"

He's so sweet. And what a cute new nickname. "It's a bit of a shock to my system."

"Wait till January. You'll be wanting to get on the first plane back to Phoenix."

I don't need a plane for that. I just have to fall asleep. "I doubt that," I say, smiling. I am bantering with Ronald Grighton!

"Wow, what a great smile," he says.

My smile gets even bigger.

Curtis rustles through her portfolio. "Welcome to *Ron's Report*, Gabrielle. Now let's get started on today's show. Since we can't get the kidnapped girl—I just heard she's talking to Paula Zahn—"

Groans from the table.

"—I think we should stick to our program. We'll do the segment about the elections first. Then the hurricane in the Bahamas. We have the director of the National Hurricane Center and the governor-general scheduled. Then we're supposed to go to—"

Suddenly my bag begins to vibrate. What the hell?

In a split second, everyone at the table whips out his or her BlackBerry, apparently the cause of said vibrating.

"They lost the Cookie Cutter," Curtis says.

Murmurs around the table. The Cookie Cutter is Jon Adams, heir to Cookie Creams, the chocolate-chip dynasty, who was arrested for raping and fatally stabbing three women in Spanish Harlem. "How did that happen?" asks Michael, an associate producer. "He was in custody."

"He jumped bail," she reads. "We have to run a story on this today."

Ron sips his coffee. "Who can we get to talk?"

"The district attorney is doing a press conference at noon," Curtis says. "We'll need to cover that. Let's speak to someone from the defense team. Do you think the Adams' parents will talk to us?"

This all happens so fast, I barely have time to think. I need to add something. What can I say? "What about interviewing the victims' families?"

Ron grins and taps his mug on the conference table. "Definitely."

Wahoo!

Curtis continues flicking through her BlackBerry. "The mothers are Puerto Rican and Dominican. Who speaks Spanish?"

"I do," I say quickly. You don't live in Arizona without learning the lingo. Some of it, anyway.

"Good," says Curtis, nodding. "Go to it."

My hands stop shaking. I'm going to do fine. No, I'm going to do great.

"The chicken pad thai," I order at the Thai restaurant counter. "To go." I'm starving. All I had for lunch was coffee, coffee and more coffee.

What a day. What an amazing, incredible, exhausting, overwhelming day.

The show went smoothly. My segment went perfectly. I called the mothers and convinced them (in Spanish) to come on the show, where I got them a proper translator. Both Curtis and Ron praised me for a job well done.

When my meal is ready, I return to my apartment. My doorman informs me that my mattress and frame are waiting for me. Micha, the porter, helps me carry them up to my apartment. I give him a twenty and then sink into the couch, turn on the news and dig into my chicken.

Heather is in her room, chatting on the phone, and doesn't come out to say hello. If I weren't so damn tired, I'd be insulted.

A picture of the kidnapped kid flashes across CNN and I feel a pang that she went to Paula Zahn and not us. My BlackBerry buzzes a few times, but it's only sports scores. When I'm done eating, I strip off my clothes, wash off my makeup, replace the couch pillows, make my bed and then climb underneath the sheets. Tired and happy, I think about potential stories for tomorrow. Maybe the defense attorney will be willing to speak to us. Maybe someone will find the Cookie Cutter. What will happen with the hurricane? I cannot wait to chase these stories.

Crap. Tomorrow—maybe I should call it re-today?—I won't be doing any chasing. More likely, I'm going to be getting chased. By my future mother-in-law.

My Mothers, Myself

Considering how abnormal my life is, the next few days (actually several for me, a few for the rest of the world) pass by in a relatively normal way. Note *relatively*.

First, on Monday in Arizona, my mother calls at eight (yes, eight) to tell me that she's still mad at me. I grovel until she's satiated, and then just when I fall back to sleep, Alice calls. Groan. Both mothers on my first official day of being unemployed. Fate can be cruel.

Though, my mother, I can handle. My mother, I can tell off. But the Number One rule in any book of practical etiquette is "Don't piss off your future mother-in-law." In other words, wait until after the wedding to tell her, for instance, you will not be hanging that lovely portrait of her on your bedroom wall. Otherwise an argument might ensue, and what if your fiancé sides with Mommie Dearest? You get to be the queen only after you ascend to the throne. So when Alice calls me on Monday morning at nine (yes, nine), demanding that my mother and I come by that afternoon so we can all "get our heads together," I remain composed.

My mother does not do the let's-get-our-heads-together thing. At least, not well. "My mom doesn't get back until tomorrow morning," I explain, trying to keep the exasperation out of my voice.

Alice sighs. Loudly. "All right, Gabrielle, but don't blame me if we can't get everything done on time and your wedding is a huge disaster."

"Why don't we just meet tomorrow." I pull the comforter over my head in the hopes that she'll go away.

She sighs again. "Fine."

"Let's meet at night so Cam can come, too."

She laughs. Shrilly. "No. We don't need Cam."

"Really? I think we kind of do."

"Trust me, he's not going to care. He doesn't want to be bothered with the small details. Let him worry about work, and we'll worry about the wedding. I'll see you at four tomorrow." She hangs up.

I call back my mother and ask if she'll come with me to Alice's.

She groans. "Do I have to?"

"Mom! It's my wedding."

"I know, but I don't want to go to Alice's. She sounded so…Martha Stewart. But without the good taste and prison stories. She made me want to throw up a little."

"Hey, you're talking about my future mother-in-law."

"I'm sorry, I'm sorry. But she does."

"Mom."

"Fine, I'll come. My plane lands at eleven. Should I meet you there?"

"Yes. At four." I tell her the address and wait as she types it into her planner.

"Done," she says. "Wait. I don't have to bring anything, do I? Like freshly baked cookies?"

This whole situation is making me want to throw up a little, too. "No. Just come."

Once I'm up, I call the person who bought my car and ask him if there's any way, if it's at all possible, if I renege on the sale. "I'm really sorry, but I'm not moving now and I really need my car—"

"No," he says flatly through the phone.

"Oh. Um. Pretty please?"

"No. Sorry. But have a nice day," he says and then hangs up.

Fantastic. I decide to wait until after I've had my coffee before calling both Heather and my old boss (to beg for my job back). When I'm fairly well caffeinated and thus prepared to face another phone call, I get Heather's voice mail ("I'm really sorry but—") and then reach Bernie. He tells me he's already hired my replacement.

That was fast. So much for being indispensable.

"I'm sorry," he says, "but let me know if you're interested in freelancing."

Nothing is worse than going from a full-time producing gig to freelance producing. It's like going from teaching to substituting, or full-time girlfriend to 2:00 a.m. sex buddy.

Guess I'll try to find myself a new car.

★ ★ ★

Nothing says early November like postelection coverage and, with a full day of airtime to fill each day, TRSN has been doing it to death. Without a major federal election this year, Tuesday's brainstorming session becomes a contest to see who can come up with the strangest story angle. There's the standard surprise winners and losers, the perennial favorites being tracked as possible presidential candidates and of course those oddball stories from the "flyover states" (I visibly grimaced when Curtis used that expression) like the dead guy elected mayor.

I send out some e-mails, and by the afternoon meeting I know I have a winner.

"Listen to this," I say after the room gets quiet. "Apparently in a small six-hundred-person Colorado town south of Denver, a group of college students got a mayoral candidate on the ballot from a new, unknown party called the Progressive Democratic Party. They won by campaigning on a premise of promising to reduce the smell and noise from cow herds—I'm guessing a hot-button issue in town. But I have it on good authority that the party's real goal is to legalize marijuana."

Many of the people around the table groan. TRSN is even more old-school than CBS, and I suppose the politics of the newsroom might not be that progressive, either.

"Can you get the story for tomorrow's show, Arizona?" Ron asks.

"Already on it," I answer. I really don't know what I was so worried about.

On Tuesday night, I go shopping. My heels just aren't going to work at the station. I need a pair of cute flats like everyone else's. Even as a producer, I am not above running tapes from room to room, and appropriate footwear is definitely needed.

I also need to lose ten pounds. Everyone here is absurdly skinny. The reporters. The cameramen. The doormen. The lunch lady.

Heather retreats from her room to flip through my purchases. I voice my weight concerns and she recommends I try the Pilates studio down the street from our apartment. I think she might be onto something and book an appointment for tomorrow night. She also recommends a therapist, but I'll hold off on that one for a while. At the moment, I'm preferring denial to certain institutionalization, thanks.

On Tuesday morning in Arizona, I drop off Cam at work and head over to the Barnes & Noble in the truck. I hate driving the truck. But thank goodness Cam spent eighteen hours last summer teaching me to drive stick or I'd really be stranded this week. Until I find a new car, anyway. I buy Ron's autobiography, *My Report: The Lessons I've Learned by Ron Grighton*, and my first bridal mag. Since I don't want to let Alice bulldoze me into getting everything she wants, I feel I should arm myself with some info before I get to her place. Then I order myself an iced mocha something, find an empty seat and flip through the glossy pages.

By page ten, I am exhausted. It seems that there are many, many things one has to do to have a wedding.

Set a date! Alice wants May. May is fine. I have nothing against May. See? I can be conciliatory.

Create your budget! Who's paying for this circus, anyway?

Decide if you want premarital counseling. Maybe we can use Heather's therapist.

Decide if you need a prenup. Don't even joke about it.

Have you thought about your Bridal Lingerie? No. I have not. Flip.

Dream dresses to die for! If the preparations don't kill me first.

Get into shape! If my Pilates class in New York whips me into shape, will I be thin in Arizona?

Pick the perfect bridal bouquet! What do I know about flowers?

The ultimate wedding registries! That I can do. Shopping. What do I need? New sheets…for my New York apartment. Boo. This is going to suck. I hardly need anything in Arizona, yet I need everything there. If only Pottery Barn shipped to alternate universes.

Choose the lucky members of your wedding party! Do I really need a wedding party? Maybe we can skip the bridesmaid/groomsman thing. It's kind of degrading. You are my handmaiden. Now look fat and ugly so I look even more beautiful.

I call Cam from my cell. "Do we have to have groomsmen and bridesmaids?" If I had a sister, maybe I'd feel differently.

"Very funny," Cam says. "I'm planning on asking Dan, Joshua, Matt of course, and Jer and Rick."

Dan and Joshua are his friends. Jer and Rick are his cousins. Matt is his brother-in-law. That sounds like an awful lot of people. "Five? Does that mean I need five bridesmaids?"

"If you want even numbers."

I nibble on my thumbnail, and then my index finger, and

make my way right through both hands. All this wedding talk has turned me back into a nail biter. "Does it matter?"

"Probably."

"Who am I going to ask? I don't even know five people."

"You're crazy. My sister, Lila…you can ask Jessica and Leslie. I'm sure they'd love to march for you."

He thinks I'm asking his cousins' wives to be my bridesmaids? "I barely even know them."

"They're going to be your family."

I notice that I somehow managed to acquire a two-inch coffee stain on the sleeve of my white shirt. Fantastic. "If I'm going to include cousins, they should probably be mine."

"You have cousins?"

"Cam! You know my mother's brother has three kids. And my father's sister has two."

"I forgot."

True, he's never met them. And I haven't seen them in five years. I just recently skipped the bar mitzvah of one of my cousin's whiny offspring. What was the name again? Darryl? Jacob? Still…why does Cam assume that his family is more important than mine? "Maybe you'll meet them all at the wedding," I tell him. Maybe *I'll* meet them all at the wedding.

My mom is a half hour late.

By the time she arrives, Alice has already tsk-tsked, and glanced at the clock above her two matching ovens seventeen times.

When the bell finally rings, I leap to the door.

"Hello, Ms. Engaged," my mother says, enveloping me in a hug.

"Alice is waiting in the kitchen," I whisper. "She has binders. And clippings. Lots of clippings. I'm afraid."

My mother raises her perfectly arched eyebrows and follows me into the house. She's looking extra thin in straight-legged gray linen pants, a crisp white shirt and black leather sling backs. In the past ten years, my mom has become slightly obsessed with her weight. She took up jogging and actively limits her carb intake.

I grimace. "You have to take off your shoes."

She scowls in protest, but I give her a pleading look and she sighs and slips them off. "You owe me," she hisses. "And what's up with all the photos on the wall?"

"Just be polite," I murmur.

"Hello, hello," Alice says, some sort of banana loaf in hand. "It's wonderful to finally meet you, Sherri."

"Same here," my mom says, eyes popping at the platters of homemade chocolate-oatmeal cookies, sun-dried tomato feta dip and freshly baked pita piled on the table and counter.

I probably should have mentioned my mom's carb phobia to Alice.

"I hope you didn't go to too much trouble," my mom says, automatically patting her hips.

Alice places the banana bread beside the cookies and dismisses the comment with a wave. "Oh, it's my pleasure. Would you ladies like some homemade lemon-strawberry iced tea?"

How does one make homemade lemon-strawberry iced tea, exactly? "Sounds great," I say, sitting down on a hard plastic chair.

"Thank you," my mom says in her oh-so-polite voice. Before she sits, I catch her frowning first at the carb-fest and then at her bare feet. I can deal with a frown. She can't throw a frown.

"Plate?" Alice asks.

A plate she can throw.

My mom hesitates. "Sure. Thank you."

"You'll have to try the cookies," Alice says, passing the platter over the table. "They're my special recipe. Delicious."

"I'm sure they are," my mom says, ignoring the platter and turning to me. "Let's get started. Gabby, you're not going to make a big fuss about this, are you? Of all my own weddings, my favorite was at the Four Seasons in Nevis. You should do something like that. Small, intimate."

Alice's knuckles, which are still holding up the platter, are now white. "Don't even joke about something like that, Sherri! That would be awful! Now *take* a cookie!" She shoves the plate closer to my mother's face.

Oh, boy.

My mother whips her chair back and a scraping sound echoes through the kitchen. "I don't *want* a cookie. Thank you."

Alice frowns, then shoves the plate toward me. "Gabrielle wants one. She *loves* my cookies."

After I take two cookies to keep the peace, Alice whips the platter away and hands us each white binders. "I've made us wedding binders. It helped us stay on top of Blair's wedding, and I know it will work for us."

I cannot believe what I am holding in my hand. On the cover, in calligraphy, it says The Wedding of Cameron & Gabrielle, May Sixth. I'm too shocked to speak. I said okay to May, but when did I agree to the sixth? Did I agree to the sixth?

"You're getting married on May sixth?" my mom asks.

"Apparently," I say, flipping open the binder to discover orange plastic dividers. With labels: Ceremony, Favors, Flowers, Invitations, Music, Notes, Tables. All in alphabetical order.

My mom gingerly touches the binder as though she's afraid it's contagious. With her free hand, she picks up her glass of iced tea. Probably to quench her annoyance.

"Oh yes," Alice says. "Gabrielle thought it was best to have a May wedding. And I've already booked St. George's—"

The glass of tea comes crashing back to the table. "Excuse me?"

"St. George's. The church on—"

My mother glares. "Yes, I know where it is, but there's not a chance in hell my daughter is getting married in a church."

Uh-oh.

Alice looks bewildered. "But she wants to!"

"No she does *not*," my mother snaps. I place my hand on my mother's plate to make sure it remains on the table.

"Yes, she does!" Alice insists.

Yes, this is going splendidly. "Actually—" I say.

My mom: "We're Jewish, Alice. Jews don't get married in churches. They just don't."

Alice: "They can if they want to! And Gabrielle wants to!"

The both stare at me.

Alice: "Gabrielle?"

My mom: "Gabby?"

I don't know, I don't know. I hate making these kinds of decisions. I look at my mom and then at Alice and then back at my mom. Slowly, I shake my head. I know I promised Cam but… "I don't think I can get married in a church. I'm sorry, Alice. I know how much it means to you, but I don't believe it's appropriate."

My mom smirks. "Ha."

"Well," Alice says with a humph. "Cam is certainly not getting married in one of those temple things."

Oh, yes, she's very respectful of my religion.

"Look," I say. "I'm willing to keep May sixth, as long as it's okay with you, Mom. And my dad, of course. But I think it's best if Cam and I get married somewhere non-denominational. We could even have the ceremony and reception at the same place. Save money."

"I suppose we can have the ceremony here as well as the reception," Alice says.

"What?" My mom looks around the overcrowded orange house. "You're planning a reception *here?*"

Alice looks surprised. "Of course I am! We landscaped the backyard specifically for Blair's reception. It was beautiful. Blair and I made the tent, and Cam built the pool covering so we could convert it into a dance floor. Since we still have the tent and the covering, we can save a lot of money this time around. Oh, this is perfect! They can get married here under the tent, and then we can have the party!"

I don't know how the five million people they invited all fit in the yard, but that's beside the point. I don't want to get married under some macramé-like tent.

My mother, thankfully, agrees with me. "I think we should rent out a hall at a hotel," she says.

Alice scowls. "Why pay for a hotel when we have a perfectly good space here?"

My cheeks burn. And so it begins. The discussion of money. "We should talk about the budget," I say slowly. A compartment that Alice has left out of the binder. How interesting.

My mom nods and whips out a calculator from her purse. Not sure why she carries one around with her, but it does seem like something she would do. Now that we're talking cash flow, she's in her element.

"I've looked over my finances and I can kick in fifteen thousand," she says. "What about you, Alice?"

My mom has fifteen thousand just sitting around? I'm about to thank her for her insane generosity when Alice says, "Me? I'm not kicking in anything."

My mom looks confused. "Your husband then. Whatever."

Alice purses her lips. "Richard will not be kicking in anything, either."

Huh? "He won't?" I ask.

"The groom's parents do not have to contribute to the wedding, dear," she tells me.

"Why not?" my mom asks.

"Because that's the way it's done."

"That's crazy," my mother says. And then…throws her calculator. Shit. Luckily it lands on the floor, and not on Alice.

Without missing a beat, Alice picks up the calculator and places it back on the table. "It certainly is not. It's tradition."

I can feel a real fight brewing. "It's all right, Mom. Thank you for your generous offer. Cam and I can pitch in a few thousand, and I'm sure Dad will give us something, too."

"You and Cam will certainly not put in any of your own money," Alice says.

"Why not? It's our wedding."

"The bride's parents are supposed to pay for the wedding. Period. You can't go draining your real-estate nest egg."

Huh? Are Cam and I buying a house? We've never even discussed buying a house. We moved in together only five days ago. "We'd be happy to put some money towards our own wed—"

"No," Alice says. "You'll have to ask your father. Of course, if he can't afford to contribute, Richard and I will be happy to have the wedding here. That would certainly be easier to afford than some *hotel*." Emphasis on *hotel* as if it's a dirty word.

The unpleasant conversation then jumps to bands, to colors, to themes, to floral arrangements, and finally to regular meeting times.

"We are not meeting once a week," my mother says, responding to Alice's comment that we'll reconvene next Tuesday.

"I agree," says Alice. "It's important for the three of us to be in constant contact. We should meet twice a week. How are Tuesdays and Fridays for you?"

My mom's jaw drops. "Every Tuesday *and* Friday?"

"At least. It's obvious you've never planned a wedding before." Alice stuffs a third cookie in her mouth.

"I've planned several weddings," my mom protests.

"I'm talking about *real* weddings. Not your weddings. Thousands of details need to be worked out."

My mom snorts with laughter. "That's what a wedding planner is for. We're hiring a wedding planner. I hired one two weddings ago and it worked out perfectly. Well, not the marriages, but the weddings."

Alice waves dismissively. "Don't be ridiculous. We're not

going to waste money for someone else to plan the event when we can do it ourselves."

"You've made it clear that it's my money being spent, so it's my money to spend as I want. You're the one being ridiculous. I wholeheartedly support hiring a professional when necessary. When you want your hair cut, you go see a stylist. When you want to plan a party, you hire a party planner."

Right. I probably should have mentioned Alice's haircutting philosophy.

"I will not hire a wedding planner. Absolutely not." She scribbles away in the Notes section of her binder. "That has to be all for today, ladies. I need to get back to work."

"I didn't know you had a job," my mother says in surprise. "What do you do?"

"My *job* is to create a warm and loving home. And at the moment, I need to prepare for tomorrow."

My mother stands and stretches her arms above her head. "What's tomorrow?"

Alice looks at her as if she's clearly on crack. She pauses to see if my mom is joking. When my mother's oblivious expression doesn't change, she says, "It's Thanksgiving."

"It is?" my mom says. "Already?"

"I don't know how you can forget Thanksgiving."

My mom shrugs. "Holidays don't mean much to me."

"Obviously. Does that mean you don't have a place to go? You're welcome to come here tomorrow night with Gabrielle."

"Oh…um…uh…" My mother's expression tells me she would rather shoot herself in the head than come back here for Thanksgiving.

"She's going to be out of town," I down-and-out lie.

Grateful smile from Mom.

Dubious look from Alice. "But you just got back. Today."

"I'm a frequent flyer," my mom says, looking guilty. "But I'll be back next week, and we'll catch up then."

Alice looks back at her notes. "So your job, ladies, is to brainstorm the names of hotels. Then we can all go see them on Tuesday."

Hurrah! Mother and daughter score on that point!

"Yes, we should go see them in the next few weeks," my mom says.

"Not the next few weeks. Tuesday. The clock is ticking."

The only thing ticking is my mother. Any second now she will explode.

We thank Alice for her hospitality, I cringe as I watch my mother and Alice exchange strained goodbyes, and then my mom and I take off faster than race cars. We crack up as soon as the front door is closed.

"That woman is insufferable," says my mother, heaving with laughter. "Are you sure you want to marry into that gene pool?"

I'm beginning to wonder. "I warned you, didn't I?"

"Not really. Thanks for getting me out of Thanksgiving hell. I can't think of anything more awful."

"Come on Mom, she's not *that* bad."

"Yes, she is."

"You're right. She is."

She unlocks her car door with a beep. "You have to call your father tonight and ask him for money."

"I know, I know." He'll help us out, won't he? He'd better. I climb up into the truck and roll down the window so we can continue our chat.

"He's going to ask you what I'm giving, so tell him thirty."

"I'm not lying to him, Mom."

"Yes, you are. You know he's going to match whatever you tell him I'm giving you. And you also know that he's only going to actually give you half of what he promises. If you want fifteen from him, tell him I'm giving thirty. Trust me."

Unfortunately, I know she's right. And I need to raise this money.

Otherwise…hello, macramé tent.

6

A Stomachache Is a Stomachache Is a Stomachache

When I rehash the budget conversation with Cam, I'm surprised by his lack of surprise regarding who should pay for the wedding.

"Isn't it normal for the bride's family to pay?" he asks, all innocent eyed.

"I'm sure it happens. But it's a little old-fashioned."

"My parents paid for the entire wedding when Blair got married."

"So now my parents have to suffer because Matt's parents are cheapskates?"

He cocks his head to the left. "Are you calling my parents cheapskates?"

Yes. "No," I answer. "I'm just concerned about what will happen if my father doesn't give us enough money."

He wraps his arms around me. "Why don't you ask him first? If he says no, then we'll worry about it. And I'm sorry about my parents. They get so set in their ways sometimes. But I'll see what I can do."

"Thanks. Hmm. What about our savings? I have about fifteen thousand in investments."

He grimaces. "I'd rather not use too much of our own money on the wedding."

"Why not?"

"Because we're going to need it for the down payment."

"What down payment?"

"For our house."

I wonder why everyone seems to know we're buying a house except me. "Oh. I didn't know we were looking."

"Of course we're looking. I know how much you want to have a home Gabby. You told me how important it is to you that night in Mexico." He squeezes my hands.

My heart rate speeds up as I realize what he's referring to. For our one-year anniversary we had gone down to Rocky Point for the weekend. Walking on the beach, I had told him about how tough the moves had been for me as a kid. How I always dreamed of the day when I would have my own home. "But…" My voice trails off.

"We have the money."

I've never point-blank asked him what his accounts look like. "We do?"

"I have about seventy-five thousand dollars worth of investments."

My jaw drops. "You do? Impressive."

"Not I do, we do. We will, that is. As soon as we go to the bank and combine all our accounts."

Wow. I had no idea. "So if we *have* to, we can contribute

our own money for the wedding. Not that I want to chew away at our nest egg, but if we *have* to—"

"If we have to, yes. But every dollar spent is coming out of our future abode."

I raise my hands to look like a scale. "Living-room curtains or wedding cake."

"Exactly," he says, smiling. "But let's worry about missing furniture and appliances after you ask your dad for money. I don't think he's going to say no. You're his favorite kid."

Cam gets a kick out of my dad's use of hyperbole. Every place he goes to is the most incredible place he's ever been. Every restaurant is the absolute best.

"But she's your only kid," Cam said, the first time he heard my dad call me his favorite.

My dad's response: "Even more reason why she's my favorite."

Even so, asking my dad for wedding money is going to seem to come out of nowhere since he doesn't even know I'm engaged.

My dad is a Hollywood producer. He's no Steven Spielberg, but he does have a few credits to his name, though nothing that would get your fishnets in a twist. He's worked on a few movies for Fox and a couple for Universal, but it's not as if he's a bigwig. At the moment, he's an associate producer on a movie that's filming in Brisbane, Australia. Which means it's not so easy to get in touch with him.

I call his hotel, but get his voice mail. I'll have to put it off until tomorrow. Okay, not my New York tomorrow, but my Arizona tomorrow… Although it's already tomorrow in Australia….

My brain hurts.

★ ★ ★

"I've never denied that I support the removal of criminal penalties for the use of marijuana—responsible use by adults that is," says Mayor-Elect Tom Fields on-screen.

It's Wednesday and I'm in the control room in New York manning my show. I switch the screen back to Ron.

"But you did mislead your town, didn't you?" Ron asks, reading from my script. "You campaigned on a premise of promising to reduce the smell and noise from cow herds. Without mentioning your ulterior motive."

Tom, the four-hundred-pound, gray-bearded, soon-to-be mayor of Renkin, Colorado, shrugs. "I would have mentioned it if anyone asked. I don't see what the big fuss is about. Government shouldn't limit individuals' rights. It's our body. Our right."

"For comment, let's go to Michael Simpson, the chairman of the National Anti-Marijuana League in Colorado."

I patch him in.

"Hi, Ron. Hello, Tom," Michael, a fortysomething tiny man says.

"What do you think about all this?" Ron asks.

"I think Tom is living in a dreamworld. We don't have the right to do anything we want with our body. You can't walk around naked, can you? If you're strolling around downtown in your birthday suit, you're going to get arrested."

I type furiously into the script. "But you can walk around naked in your own home. Tom, aren't you advocating marijuana for private use only?"

"But you can walk around naked in your own home. Tom, aren't you advocating marijuana for private use only?" Ron asks.

By the time the show finishes, I'm left on a high. A natural one, of course.

★ ★ ★

When I show up at the Pilates studio after work, I find that it disturbingly reminds me of an S and M shop. Not that I've ever been to one, but I have a pretty active imagination. The studio is filled with wooden machines you lie on and strap your legs into. It's practically medieval.

"The accent has to be on your spine," my instructor tells me while I am in a rather compromising position. "Everything must come from your core." I have no idea what she's talking about. I'm too busy wondering if it's pointless to work out in one dimension when it won't pay off in the other. It's like giving one sick identical twin a placebo and the other a miracle drug. The further weird thing about working out while existing in two dimensions is that you don't feel the pain for two days. Talk about a delayed reaction.

On Wednesday, I wake up in Arizona muscle-ache-free. Although not headache-free, since I still have to phone my dad and beg him for money.

I call him from the living room while Cam watches *Law and Order* from bed.

Static and then, "Hello?"

"Dad!"

"Gabs!" My dad is always cheerful. Always. This is partly because he's a happy guy, and partly because he smokes a lot of pot. Maybe he should move to Renkin. I didn't know about the pot when I was a kid, of course. I found out when my mom made an offhand comment about the fact that he used to grow marijuana in our backyard in Malibu. She believes that maybe he could be the next Steven Spielberg if he stopped the puffing. I don't disagree.

"Dad, I have some news!" I try to make myself comfy

on Cam's black leather couch. I hate this couch. It's so stiff. I feel like I'm in the waiting room of a doctor's office.

"You're coming to visit?" he booms.

"Actually, I'm engaged."

"Hey! Congratulations! Way to go, you two! Where's Cam? Put my man on the phone." My dad is a typical Hollywood guy. Best friends with the world. Tells everyone how fantastic they are. Always has a huge project on the go.

You know the expression *believe half of what you hear?* It was made for my father.

"Cam, pick up the extension!" I holler.

I hear a low grumble and then Cam's voice. "Hi, David."

"Cam, my man!" My dad always calls Cam *my man.* I can hear Cam smiling through the phone. He thinks it's hysterical. "That's some news you two have!" my dad says.

"Thanks. We're pretty excited about it."

"You're going to treat my favorite kid like a princess, you hear?"

"I wouldn't dream of treating her any other way."

Now I'm smiling.

"When's the big day going to be?" my dad asks. "Not too soon, right? I'm not back till March."

"We're planning it for May, Dad. That good for you?"

"Yup. Phenomenal. You two should honeymoon out here. It's amazing. The most incredible place I've ever been."

"Movie's going well?" Cam asks.

"It's amazing. Honestly, it's going to be huge. I'm talking Oscars here."

"Sounds terrific," Cam says wryly. "Great speaking to you, David. I'll let you guys catch up. Enjoy the koalas."

"So, Dad," I begin, once Cam has clicked off the phone. I realize that my hands are suddenly sweaty. I hate asking for money. I haven't asked my dad for money since I was eighteen.

"Yes, hon."

"Since I'm getting married, well, I need to make a budget. I'm wondering…" I hate this. What if he says no? Will I really have no choice but to get married on Cam's pool? Or will we be forced to live in a trailer park?

"Yes, hon?"

"I'm wondering if you've set aside any money for my wedding. Or if you want to contribute. Anything. Please."

He laughs. "Of course! You're my favorite kid! What do you need?"

I feel like I'm at a job interview. They want to know what my salary expectations are and I want to be paid as much as possible without pricing myself out of the market. Who knows? Maybe he'll happen to mention that he has fifty thousand dollars from that movie he did with Johnny Depp, fifty big ones he's been saving for just such a rainy day. And that he wants to spend it all on one day, all on me. Yeah, right. Johnny Depp. As if.

I've decided not to take my mom's double-it advice. I'd rather leave the question open-ended and let him come to me with an answer. Pressuring someone for money just makes me squeamish. "I'm trying to get a ballpark of what I have to work with. So if you could tell me what you're thinking of giving—if anything—I'd really appreciate it."

"What's your mother giving?"

Sigh. "Thirty thousand." Okay, my mom has a point. I have to listen to half of what he promises.

In a way it makes sense, since only half of me is getting married.

He whistles. "That's a lot of moola, Gabs. But if that's what your mother is giving, then that's what I'll give, too."

I smile. "Really?"

"Of course. You're going to have a beautiful wedding, honey."

"Thanks, Dad."

Then he laughs. "Your mother isn't planning the wedding, is she?"

"She's helping. Cam's mother loves this kind of stuff, so she'll probably do most of it."

"I figured your mother would want nothing to do with it. She barely had anything to do with our wedding. Her mother planned the whole thing. And didn't she elope for the other four?"

"Other two. And she only eloped the last time."

"Right." He laughs again.

"Anyway, thanks so much. So—" back to the money part "—are you going to send me a check? Is that the easiest way?"

"Oh, already?"

"We'll have to start booking stuff soon, and there will be deposits…." I hate this. I hate having to ask for money. It is so out of my comfort zone.

"Oh, sure. No problem. But you don't need the whole thing right away. How about I start you off with five gs? And then you'll tell me when you need more."

Something is better than nothing, I suppose. I sigh. It looks like I won't be back in my comfort zone any time soon. At least not in Arizona.

On Thursday, I wake up in New York with a stomach-ache. It feels like that new flu strain that my BlackBerry just buzzed me about.

"What's wrong with you?" Heather asks as I gasp my way to the bathroom.

"Core. Hurts. I hate Pilates."

"It's worth it," she tells me. "Wanna go for a speed walk in the park?" She's already dressed to go, in skintight Lycra pants, brand-new Nikes and a fitted parka.

I clutch my stomach. "I can barely move."

"Trust me, it'll be worth it. You have to take advantage of the weather while it's still good."

Good? It's forty-eight degrees out there! How bad does it get? "Fine," I answer. Maybe if I'm too busy thinking about how cold it is, I'll forget about my stomach. And I wouldn't mind getting to know Heather better.

"You should come with me to my parents for dinner tonight," she says forty-five minutes later, as we swing our arms and legs past the Great Lawn. With every step we make, we hear the crunch of yellowed leaves. It looks as if we're walking down the yellow brick road. Even though I've been to the park on an earlier visit to New York, I still can't get over the place. The honey-colored autumn trees that look straight out of an Impressionist painting, the skyscrapers perched in the background. Honestly, it's cooler than the Grand Canyon. Okay, maybe not cooler, but almost.

As sweet (and shocking) as I think Heather's invite is, I politely decline. I mean, come on, I have to go to Alice's tomorrow. Two Thanksgiving dinners in a row? I'm no glutton for punishment.

Crap, I'm going to have to do everything twice. Double the dentist appointments. Double the gyno. Double the bikini wax. Not that I have any reason to get a bikini wax in this reality. So only one bikini wax then.

I lift my hand to take a bite out of my pinkie nail, when Heather slaps my hand away. "What are you doing? You have nice nails. Don't ruin them. And anyway, you cannot bite your nails in New York. Absolutely not. This city is way too dirty. Unless you want to pick up hepatitis or that flesh-eating disease."

Gross. I drop my hands back down beside me. I don't want my renewed nail-biting habit from Arizona to spill over here. "Okay, I won't bite."

After lunch, I spend the day shopping online, admiring my not-bitten fingers as they tap on the keyboard. I buy a flat-screen TV for my bedroom. (Which leads me to mention one of the plusses in living a dual reality. Think of all the time saved by not watching so much TV. Once I've seen an episode in one reality, why see it in another? I've never been one for reruns.) Then I order groceries from this site called FreshDirect. How crazy is that? Heather claims you can get everything delivered right to your apartment. Groceries. Pot (not from the same place, of course). The wash. Heather sends all hers out. Since there's no washer and drier in our apartment, we'd otherwise have to do the wash on the fifth floor (at two dollars a load!), but Heather says it's practically cheaper to pay someone else to do it at seventy-five cents a pound. I don't know about cheaper, since I have never weighed my loads, but it sounds far easier. Not sure how she affords it as an FIT student, but it's not my issue.

I add orange juice to my online FreshDirect shopping cart. Then I click on cereal bars. I can eat those on my way to work. So far I've put eighty dollars of food in my basket. It's so easy. Avocados! Bananas! Carrots! Chicken breasts! Shrimp!

"I'm off to Long Island," Heather says, popping her head into my room. "Last chance to come along. My mom's a great cook. You won't regret it. You'll get to be grilled by my entire family about why you're still single." She reconsiders. "Can I stay home with you?"

"You're welcome to. I'm planning a wild night of Chinese takeout. I wish I had known about this FreshDirect thing before. I could have cooked us a real dinner."

"You cook?"

"Not really. But I'm planning on learning."

She shifts her overnight bag to her other hip. "Sure you don't want to come?"

"Honestly, I'm fine. But thanks."

"Suit yourself. I won't see you in the morning, since I'll probably take a midday train. What are you up to tomorrow night? Will you come with me to a party? Jeff—that's Mindy's husband—is having birthday drinks uptown. Are you working tomorrow?"

"Yeah. And I don't know what time I'm going to get out. I was looking forward to just coming home and crashing."

"Please? There might be some eligible guys there. You never know."

Am I eligible? "I'm not sure I'm ready to date yet."

"It's time for you to meet some new people."

"I'm meeting new people every day. At work."

"Come on. I really don't want to go alone." Her eyes look big and needy. "It will probably be all boring married people."

"Sounds tantalizing. Where do I sign up?"

"Pretty please?"

I want to say no, but she looks so desperate. I hope I don't regret this tomorrow. "All right."

"Thank you! You're the best. It's at the bar in the Bolton Hotel uptown. Meet me there at eight," she says and then closes the door before I can change my mind.

Sigh. I guess it's a good thing to explore the non-work side of the city. That was my plan. To go out and have fun. To laugh and flirt. To drink Cosmos and eat pâté.

I wonder if I can order pâté online.

What is pâté, anyway?

I find it and add it to my basket. Because I can.

Happy Thanksgiving (again) to me! Happy Thanksgiving (again) to me! Happy Thanksgiving (again) to—

"Surprising, really. Since Gabrielle is so quiet."

Since Alice is obviously talking about me to Blair, I pause outside the kitchen before bringing in the salad plates.

"Did she bring you anything?" Blair asks.

I heave a sigh of relief. Even though Cam said it wasn't necessary, I brought flowers.

"Nada, can you imagine? I put out a whole spread for that woman, and she brought nothing. It's not every day you meet your future in-laws for the first time. It wouldn't have killed her to pick up a little something."

My relief, obviously, is short-lived. They're talking about my mother. We might not be all that close, but no one, absolutely no one, gets to knock her except me. Hell, I don't even let my father bad-mouth her.

"How rude," Blair says.

I back away from the kitchen, feeling as if I've been slapped. And they call my mother rude. I eat here once a week! Isn't that enough? My mom has to pay her dues, too? Anyway, I told my mom not to bring anything.

"What's wrong?" Cam asks, coming up behind me and nuzzling his chin into my neck.

"Nothing," I say, embarrassed. I pull away and pass him the plates. "Here, take these in for me."

"Everyone ready for turkey?" Alice hollers from the kitchen. "It's coming out of the oven."

I'd like to put *her* in the oven. Isn't that what Gretel does to the wicked witch?

"Hey, Cam, have you guys seen the new complex out in north Scottsdale?" Rick asks us from across the twenty-person table. "Each home has a two-acre lot. And what a view."

Anyone under fifty always sits on the left side, the over-fifty crowd on the right. Next to me and Cam we have Rick, his wife Jessica, Jeremy, his wife Leslie, Blair and Matt. Next to Matt is the kids' table.

"Are you two looking to buy?" Jessica asks, reaching over for her glass of wine.

As she sips, I hear an audible sigh from her mother, Tracy, Alice's sister-in-law, on the other side of the table. Tracy's daughter-in-law, Leslie, has been married for more than a year now, and Tracy is not happy that the union has not as yet produced an heir. Leslie either doesn't hear the sound of her mother-in-law's anguish or has decided to ignore it.

Oh, God. Am I going to start getting those same sighs as soon as we're married? Probably. Except with Alice, they're more likely going to be jabs. I take a big gulp of my wine.

Cam squeezes my knee under the table. "We just started looking."

We did? When? I know we discussed the house thing briefly, but did I miss something?

"Would anyone like more stuffing?" Alice asks, circling the table. Then she adds, "Why don't you look at houses here in Mesa?"

I almost spit out my wine. Sure. Why don't we buy the place next door? Wouldn't that be swell. We can be the Arizona version of *Everybody Loves Raymond*.

"We'll see," Cam says.

"As long as you don't move all the way out to Tucson, I'll be happy," Alice says, looking pointedly at her daughter.

In case Blair missed it, that was a shot.

Blair rolls her eyes. "Mom, I know, I know, I've ruined your life by moving to Tucson."

"I didn't quite say that, dear," Alice says. "But you can't deny that it's not exactly next door."

"Which is why we make the drive back to see you once a week."

"Once a week is very nice, dear. Tracy, how often does your daughter come and see you? Gabrielle, you didn't touch the turkey. Take some turkey, please."

"I had some. I'm full," I say. I'm not eating. I'm secretly protesting how she bad-mouthed my mom.

"I babysit the grandkids twice a week, and then there's dinner Friday nights, and…I don't know, about three to four times a week," Tracy answers.

That is insane.

Alice shoots Blair an accusatory look.

"Mother, I live in Tucson. I can't come by four times a week. Think of the gas."

"Gabrielle," Alice continues. "You didn't have any stuffing. You're insulting me by not eating."

The witch is trying to fatten me up.

"Mom," Cam says, spooning stuffing onto my plate.

"Blair didn't move to Tucson to spite you. Matt's practice is there."

"And why can't he be a dentist here? Mesa doesn't need dentists?"

As usual, Matt decides just to stay quiet. He and Blair met when she was a senior at the University of Arizona in Tucson. He's from Tucson and had opened his practice two years earlier. I'm sure he's thanking his lucky stars that he doesn't live in the same area code as his crazy mother-in-law. Actually, lucky for Alice. No telling what would happen if he had her in his dental chair, with a lethal weapon in her mouth.

"At least Cammy is going to buy in the Valley," Alice says. "He won't desert his mother. Families have to stay together. Always. Right, sweetie?"

"Right, Mom," Cam answers, while stuffing his mouth with sweet potato.

For some reason, I look up at Alice and see that she's looking right at me. Is that a smirk on her face? She's daring me to challenge her. She's warning me. She knows that I had the job offer in New York. She knows that Cam wouldn't come with me. She knows that she won. Alice = 1, Me = 0.

Cam gives my knee another squeeze. "While we're all here, Rick and Jer, I want to ask you two a question."

"Shoot," Jer says.

"You've always been like brothers to me. And I'd like you both to march at our wedding."

What? I nearly drop my empty fork. Again, I know we talked about it, but when was it decided? Aren't the bride and groom supposed to make the decision together? A cumulative *aw* comes from everyone in the room. I try to kick Cam under the table, but it's not so easy to kick sideways.

"Sure, man," Jer says.

Rick high-fives Cam across the table. "Of course."

"Who are your other groomsmen?" Jer asks.

"Dan and Joshua. And Matt is my best man."

An even louder *aw* floats through the room.

Matt smiles shyly.

I'm too taken off guard to react.

Reading my mind, Cam says, "I asked him earlier."

Would have been nice if he'd told me.

Alice leaps out of her chair and throws her arms around Cam's shoulder. "I'm so happy! That is so wonderful!"

It would have been nice if he'd warned me that he was going to pop the big question tonight. I slump into my chair. Please don't, please don't, please don't—

"And who are your bridesmaids, Gabrielle?"

Crap. "Oh, I don't, um, I haven't, um…"

"It would be nice if the groomsmen could walk down the aisle with their wives. You should ask Leslie and Jessica."

No, she didn't. My future mother-in-law didn't just tell me I should ask Cam's cousins right in front of them.

Cam squirms in his chair. "Mom, let's not put Gabby on the spot. She can ask whoever she wants."

"And why wouldn't she want to ask Leslie and Jessica? They'll be beautiful bridesmaids."

I don't believe this. I really don't. I peek over at Leslie and Jessica who are also slumped in their chairs, looking equally horrified. All sound has been sucked out of the room. I want to tell Alice to go to hell. But I don't. Instead, I say, "Leslie and Jessica, would you two like to be my bridesmaids?"

Silence.

"Sure," Jessica croaks out.

"Great," squeaks Leslie.

Silence.

"Wonderful," declares Alice. "And what about your maid of honor? I'm assuming you're going to ask Bl—"

"Mom," interrupts Cam. "Leave it alone. Dad, pass the cranberry?"

Richard passes it to him, clearly ignoring us all.

Jessica lets out a nervous laugh, and all I want to do is put down my head, fall asleep and go back to New York. Instead, I carry on with my secret hunger strike.

When we get home, I have a killer stomachache. I'd like to blame my ailment on the Pilates class, but we all know that's impossible.

7

The Skeleton in Your Closet Is Ringing

It's eight-thirty Friday night, and I've completed an entire workweek in New York. Granted, I had one day off for Thanksgiving. But still.

As I wait for the elevator to open to the TRSN lobby, my eyes, fingers, legs, feet and brain are exhausted. But what a day. Hurricanes. Bird flu. Crazy kidnappings. And I'm at the center of it all. Okay, not the center obviously, since then I'd be wet, in isolation or missing, but at the center of the reporting of it all. I can't believe it took me so long to get to New York. What was I thinking? I should have moved here years ago.

Ding!

The elevator door opens and I step into the lobby. Crap. It's raining outside. And, of course, I don't have an umbrella.

I wish I didn't have to go for drinks. I just want to go home, get into my new bed and relax. Not that I'm in a rush to fall asleep and get back to Arizona, but I desperately need some shut-eye. I live twice as much, so I guess it's expected that I'm twice as tired.

I push through the glass doors and press my back against the outside wall to avoid getting drenched. This isn't rain. This is a falling swimming pool. I was supposed to be at the Bolton Hotel a half hour ago. Not only am I late, but I have to meet all of Heather's friends looking like a wet mop.

Cab! Wahoo! Damn, someone's in the back. Another one...no lights...someone's in it. Another...also taken. If it weren't pouring, I could just walk, since it's not that far. There's one—and his lights are on. Which means he's free, right? I jump into the middle of the street and wave frantically. He whizzes by.

I creep back onto the sidewalk, cursing.

"He's off duty," a voice beside me says. Suddenly I realize an umbrella is shielding me. I turn to see who my mystery umbrella-man is, and it's the hot guy from the elevator on Monday.

Hello there.

But instead of an exuberant yet sexy *hello there,* I offer a restrained, "How can you tell?"

"The two side lights mean he's off duty. See how they say 'off duty'?" He points to a passing cab. "You want only the center light to be on."

"Got it, oh, cab guru," I say, hoping the rain hasn't made my mascara run down my cheeks. I can't believe it's him. Not that I've been looking for him or anything. Okay, fine, I've been keeping an eye out.

Shit, that sounded sarcastic. Why can't I flirt properly? I must be out of practice. Being engaged will do that. "I appreciate your advice," I add, smiling brightly as a measure of precaution since sarcasm just won't do.

He looks at me oddly. Do people not smile brightly in New York? "Right," he says. "Don't worry about it."

"I'm Gabrielle." Oh, God, did I just introduce myself? He didn't ask for my name. Now he thinks I'm some clueless loser who not only doesn't know how cabs work, but also goes around introducing herself to random people.

He juts out his free hand. "I'm Nate."

Hurrah! His shake is strong and warm. I have a feeling mine is limp and cold because of the rain. You know, like shrinkage. "You can call me Gabby for short."

"Nice to meet you, Gabby-for-short. You're a producer?"

"Yes. You?"

"Sales."

"What floor is that?"

"Thirteenth." He leans in close and I notice that his glasses have fogged up.

"Isn't that bad luck?"

"Good luck for me."

Since thirteen is good luck in the Jewish religion, I deduce that he might be of the tribe. Funny, I've never dated a Jewish guy. Not that I wouldn't (if I weren't already engaged, that is—but wait! I'm not engaged, at least not here). Fact is, I never met many Jewish guys in Arizona. They exist, of course, my school even had a Hillel, but the Jewish guys at ASU always seemed so…short. What can I say? I like my men over six feet tall. I'm sure Arizona has tall Jewish guys somewhere; I just never met any. And none of them looked like Cam. Then again, Nate here doesn't look like Cam, either. He has dark hair for one thing, and even though he's just as tall, he isn't as built. Not that he's scrawny. He's just leaner. And I've already confirmed his taut stomach....

"Where you off to tonight?" he asks.

"Meeting friends at the Bolton. A half hour ago," I add, glancing at my watch.

A cab passes by with its off-duty lights flashing, but Nate waves it down, anyway.

"Where to?" the driver grunts.

"Which way are you going?" Nate asks me.

I smile hopefully. "Times Square."

"Get in," the cabbie says.

Now I'm totally confused. "But I thought the lights meant—"

"The rules only apply to newbies," Nate says with a wink. "Have a great weekend." He holds the door open. A gentleman.

"Do you need a lift?" I ask. Do you want to come? I can't ask him out. Can I? Why not? I'm single now. Half-single, anyway.

"I'm good, thanks. I'm going to grab the R downtown."

I slip inside the cab. Nate waves from under his umbrella as we drive away.

I might be only half-single, but I'm totally disappointed.

I get to the bar about ten minutes later. It's packed with a crowd of hipster twentysomethings whose wet jackets and umbrellas make them far less hip. The walls are all mirrored and the ceiling is covered in spotlights, making the room seem exceptionally bright for a bar. I peek at the faces, looking for Heather, but can't find her. Excellent. I try her cell. "Where are you?"

"I can't find a cab."

Groan. "What am I supposed to do until you get here? I don't know anybody!"

"Get a drink," she orders and then hangs up. That girl is always ordering me around and then either leaving or hanging up. I don't think I'm ever going to get the last word in.

I inch my way to the bar, find an empty stool and order a vodka cranberry.

"—such an asshole, I don't know what she sees in him—"

"—thinking of spending a few days in Carmel next month to get away from the weather—"

"—told me his wife is frigid—"

As I catch snippets of conversations, I feel a wave of loneliness. There are so many people in this city, and everyone here is a stranger.

I scan the room and wonder which group I'm supposed to be meeting. The two women sitting beside me having the asshole discussion are wearing tight, low-slung pants and draped, metallic blouses. Those women maybe? No, their left hands are ringless. Not the party of couples that Heather is dreading.

I gaze at my own ringless left hand. In this life, anyway.

At the other side of the bar, on the other side of the door, there's a cluster of people that seems to be a group of couples. Four couples, to be exact. And one single guy. Hmm. Cute. Tall, broad, short reddish brown hair, chocolate-brown pants, beige untucked button-down shirt. As I'm looking at him, he looks back at me. And smiles.

I quickly turn back to the bar and my drink. The men in this city are so friendly. Who would have thought? I always assumed New York men would be cold and pompous. Banker types. But now everywhere I go, I spot cute ones. All I have to do is relearn to flirt, which can't be that hard. Besides, this guy looks harmless. Any guy who looks like Archie, from the comic book, has to be relatively undangerous. Who doesn't want to cuddle with Archie? A sexier, broader Archie no less. All I have to do is look back up and smile. I look back up. And smile. Too late. Archie is no longer looking at me.

By nine, I'm on my second drink and, since I haven't eaten all day, feeling a few degrees north of tipsy. Heather *finally* walks in.

"So nice of you to join me," I snip as she pushes toward me.

"Sorry about that. Clothing crisis," she says, folding her soaking wet jacket over her arm. She's wearing an off-the-shoulder black lace shirt, skintight camel leather pants, and a cluster of beaded necklaces around her neck that remind me of Mardi Gras. But somehow she pulls it off in a funky way. Guess you learn how to do that in fashion school.

"I thought you couldn't get a cab."

She shrugs. "That, too. Ready to meet the couple brigade? I'm going to need a drink first. Apple martini," she orders the bartender. "What a day I had. What a fucking day. I think my mother needs to be institutionalized."

"Whose doesn't?"

After she pays for and downs her drink, she grumbles, "Let's get this over with, roomie." She leads me toward the big group in the back, the one I spotted earlier. The one that once included Archie. Who has somehow and unfortunately disappeared.

"Hi, everyone," Heather says. "Happy birthday," she says, kissing the guy I'm assuming is Jeff, aka the birthday boy, on the cheek.

"Heather!" screeches the woman clinging to Jeff's arm. "We haven't seen you in ages! Where have you been?"

"Out," she says and then rolls her eyes at me. "Everyone, I want you to meet my new roommate, Gabby. Gabby, this is Mindy and her husband Jeff, Lindsay and her husband Peter, Dahlia and her husband Jon, and Amy and her husband Erik."

I shake everyone's hands. And then suddenly Archie is back and standing in front of me. He's even cuter up close—he has a big smile, two dimples, the bridge of his nose is covered in tiny freckles and his cheeks are flushed pink. And those shoulders are awfully broad. "Hi," he says. "I'm—"

"Brad!" Heather shrieks, throwing her arms around him. "What are you doing in town?"

Brad untangles himself from my overstimulated roommate. "I'm on a project in the city."

"How lucky for us!" she says, still gripping his hands. Is that Heather…flirting? She's even worse than I am. At least I don't attack the men I'm interested in. Either I call them gurus or totally ignore them.

"Who's your friend?" Brad asks, looking me over.

"What friend?"

Thanks, roomie.

He cocks his head in my direction.

Heather dismisses me with a flip of her hand. "Oh. That's just Gabby."

"Hi, Gabby," he says, leaning in closer. "Nice to meet you."

His eyes are big and green and laughing. And suddenly my fear of flirting is thwarted and I smile. "You, too," I say. Fine. Not the most risqué of responses, but after three years, it's a start.

Heather scoots herself over so that she's between us. "So how long are you in town?"

What looks like annoyance clouds his face. "I'll be in and out of town a lot in the next year."

"That is *amazing*," she says. "Why didn't you call me? I told you to call me any time you come in." She runs her fingers through her hair. "Jeff should have told me you were going to be here tonight."

"Jeff didn't tell me that *you* were going to be here tonight, either."

Jeff perks up at the sound of his name, and I catch Brad jutting his chin out at him, which I assume is his "save me" look.

The night is definitely starting to get interesting. Apparently, Jeff had a reason for not telling Heather that Brad was in the city. And another reason for not telling Brad that Heather would be here. I brilliantly deduce that both reasons are connected.

"Excuse me, ladies," Brad says, shaking free of Heather's grasp. "Can I get you something to drink?"

Heather downs the rest of her martini. "I'd love one," she chirps. "I'll go with you."

I don't know what the backstory is here, but Heather is being so obvious. She re-grabs hold of Brad's wrist like a handcuff and pushes him toward the bar, leaving me staring awkwardly at the group of strangers.

So.

All four couples stare at me. I sit down in an empty, cold, black metal chair.

Cough. Sip. Cough, cough.

"Gabby," Jeff finally says. "How long have you and Heather been roommates?"

"About a week."

"Where did you used to live?" asks one of the others.

After chitchatting for a few minutes, I start to feel almost at ease, but then the conversation turns to people they know, and I obviously don't, and I end up sitting there, drinking, feeling like a cardboard doll. I hated the bar scene in Arizona. Why on earth did I think I would like it in New York? I'm dying to bite my nails, but I can only imagine how grimy and diseased my fingers are, so I refrain.

Finally, Brad (with Heather trailing behind him) returns to the table. He deposits some sort of clear drink onto the table in front of me as Heather excuses herself to the ladies' room. I figure she must really have to go, or she wouldn't leave him alone for a sec.

"Thanks," I say with a smile. Not what I normally drink, but a nice gesture.

Brad lifts his beer and clinks it against my glass. "So, Gabby. You have a great smile, you know that? What do you do?"

"Thanks. I'm a producer."

His eyes light up. "Movies?"

"No, news."

"Even cooler," he says, smiling. "I'm a news junkie. What network?"

"TRSN."

"Cool. Maybe you'll give me a tour one day."

Is he flirting? He's flirting! "Maybe," I say. I take a sip of the drink. Whoa, it's strong. "And what do you do? And I'm not talking about work," I add smoothly. Hey, I'm flirting! I'm doing it! It's not so hard, after all. But was I too subtle? I don't want to be obvious. Flirting is an art. Although I should stop flirting with the guy Heather likes. Immediately. Bad roommate. Bad.

His forehead nearly touches mine when he says, "I like picnics. Boat rides in the park. Romantic moonlit walks on the beach."

"Interesting." Even I know that was a line. Why am I talking to him anyway? This is wrong. I should excuse myself and join Heather in the bathroom.

"Not really. Just trying to butter you up. Is it working?"

As I'm about to answer, Heather, who has magically re-appeared, plops herself onto his lap, wrapping her arms around his shoulders. "Tell me, good-looking, what have you been up to? Did you miss me?"

Brad's cheeks turn even redder. "Uh…yup."

I return to my drink. And then get another. And another.

By ten o'clock, the room is slanted and my eyelids feel heavy. I wonder what would happen if I fell asleep right here. I make a fuzzy mental note to try taking an afternoon nap sometime. Just to experiment with the time zones.

Heather is still talking to Brad, but he looks like he's trying to keep himself from falling asleep, too.

"Heather, I'm getting kind of tired," I say, but she ignores me. Whenever Brad tries to talk, she interrupts him with a high-pitched giggle, a squeeze to his shoulder and a toss of her hair. He keeps stealing glances at me, as if he'd rather be talking to me. But even though I'd like to, I really can't go after the guy Heather so obviously has a thing for.

One of the couples leaves, and then another. "I'm going home. I'm wiped," I say. "Nice to meet you, Brad."

"Bye!" Heather sings.

Brad stands up, basically pushing Heather off his lap. "It's late for me, too. I'll walk you out."

"All right, all right," Heather says, putting on her rain jacket. "I guess it's time for bed." She gives him a look and another nails-on-a-blackboard shrill giggle.

Outside, we discover it's stopped raining. "Wanna share a cab?" Heather asks Brad.

"No, but thanks. I'm staying here at the Bolton."

A rush of headlights illuminates Heather's face as she breaks into a smile at the news. "You are? And you walked us out anyway? You're so sweet. Look, I know how lonely it can get at a hotel. If you ever want a home-cooked meal, you should come over. I know you have my number. I gave it to you this summer."

"We could have an indoor picnic," he says, grinning at me.

Whoops. Okay, he's definitely flirting with me. I hurry into the street to hail a cab. Heather shouldn't waste her time with all those "how to get guys to notice you" books. She should start reading "how to not scare the hell out of them" books.

When we're finally in a cab, Heather is humming to herself. I'm humming, too. Not because of tonight, which turned out to be annoying, boring and embarrassing, but because the streets are bright and lively, I have a great job, I live in the best city in the world, and I'm drunk. I peer out of the open window and see stars twinkling over the towering buildings. "I thought you couldn't see the sky in this city!"

"Isn't Brad gorgeous?" she asks, also drunk, in her own dreamworld.

"He's cute." I wonder if I'll have a hangover in Arizona.

"I've always liked him. But he never seems to get it."

Oh, yes, *that's* the problem.

I wake up on Friday in Arizona hangover-free. Wahoo! I still have the reality-switching headache of course. Nevertheless, when Cam asks me if I want a mimosa, I decline. One round of drinks a day is plenty for me— even if a day does consist of forty-eight hours. Since he has another day off, we spend it watching movies in bed, scanning the automobile section in the *Arizona Republic,* all the while ignoring the ringing, and ringing, and still ringing phone. Not for one second do we have to wonder who it is.

"I should probably call her back," he says at around four.

"I'm sure your mom can go one day without hearing from you," I say, lying my head on his stomach so he can't get to the phone. I'm still annoyed with her for railroading me into asking Cam's cousins to be bridesmaids. Cam apologized to me later, but he didn't seem to think it was as big of a deal as I did.

Leslie and Jessica both pulled me aside after dinner and told me they felt awful, and they were not holding me to making them bridesmaids.

"No, I want you two to march for me, really," I lied. Sweet

of them to give me an out, but it wasn't as if I could take it.

Five minutes later, the phone rings again. And rings. I hate her. Really, I do. Once it's stopped ringing, I grab the cordless from the night table, click it on, march out of the bedroom and stuff it in the linen closet under a pile of towels. I wait for the annoying yet muffled "If you'd like to make a call" message to end before I return to the bedroom and announce, "I want one day of no phone calls from your mother. One day. Please?"

"Whatever makes you happy. Now bring that hot ass back to bed."

We watch more movies, fool around, make dinner. As we're loading the dishes into the dishwasher, I take a moment to appreciate the blissful quiet.

When the phone rings.

"How is that possible?" I shriek. "How does she do it?" She is a witch.

Cam looks bewildered, but before I can stop him, he picks up the kitchen phone and says, "Hi, Mom." He smiles at me sheepishly and mouths, "Sorry."

Not sorry enough.

I slam open the closet, dig for the phone and try to turn it on. It's dead. The goddamn phone needs to be recharged. I want to hurl it to the floor and watch it shatter, but because I'm basically nonviolent, instead I plop down inside the closet and pull the door closed. I need a time-out.

Alice, two. Me, still zero.

Too bad it's only a little after four in the afternoon. Now would be an excellent time to call it a night.

8

Deliver Me from Annoyance

I wake up on Saturday morning in New York in pain. No, not mother-in-law pains. Severe hangover pain. Feel sick. So. Goddamn. Unfair.

I stagger into the bathroom, gobble down a handful of Tylenols and climb back under my covers. My Fresh-Direct order, however, arrives at ten, ruining my plan to die in bed.

Not that I entirely mind. All these fresh ingredients look yummy. I don't need Alice to cook for me. So there. I can cook all by myself, thank you very much. After I organize my side of the fridge, I collect my dirty laundry and send it out. Except for the hangovers, isn't New York life wonderful? If it weren't for work, I would never even have to leave the apartment.

Now what should I do? I need to start doing some research for wedding locations in Arizona, but surely that can wait until I'm back there. I hear Heather in the shower and decide to prepare brunch with all my new ingredients.

Ten minutes later, she peers over my shoulder. "Smells delicious. What are you cooking?"

"I'm making us omelets." Trying to anyway.

"You are so sweet!" She dances over to the fridge and pours herself a glass of juice. "So what did you think of last night?"

"Your friends seem nice."

"They're not. But what did you think about Brad? Isn't he adorable?"

I was hoping she'd forget about Brad. I drop the egg yolks into the pan, pretending to be deeply involved in my cooking so I don't have to look her in the eye. "He's all right."

"Just all right! You shall not speak ill about my future husband."

How could she not have sensed that he wasn't interested?

I've never seen her in such a good mood. I've also never seen her butt look so good. She's wearing a pair of low-slung tight black pants. She has the best clothes.

"We had fun together at Jeff and Mindy's wedding. I knew we could have something together, but he's not into long distance."

Aha. "The drunken one-night wedding stand."

"I didn't *sleep* with him. We just had a connection. I could sense it. Couldn't you feel the electricity last night?"

Sure. Except he was plugged in to me. I admit I felt a little spark, but I'm no potential-boyfriend stealer. Just an ambitious heartbreaker. "I was exhausted. I wasn't paying too much attention." Like I'm not now. I put all my energy into attempting to grate the cheddar. This isn't as easy as you would imagine. I think I just grated my finger.

"He couldn't take his eyes off me."

"Yeah?" Maybe because you wouldn't get off his lap.

"I know he's going to call."

I sprinkle the cheese into the pan. My eggs aren't looking so good. "I hope so."

"But I'm not sure I want a long-distance relationship. It's tough. Isn't that why you broke up with your guy back home?"

Her allusion to Cam catches me off guard and I almost drop the spatula. "It's more complicated than that."

"It always is," she says, and steals a piece of cheese.

When I wake up Saturday morning, in Arizona, first thing I do is straddle Cam.

"And good morning to you," he says. After a quickie, I roll over and he disappears to the shower.

"What are you going to do today?" he calls.

"Relax."

"We relaxed yesterday. Today, I have to go to work."

"Ca-am," I whine. "It's Saturday."

"But I have a big case. Don't you have wedding stuff to do?"

"No," I lie. I don't feel like researching hotels. Bor-ing. Although I am concerned that if I show up to Alice's meeting on Tuesday empty-handed, she'll say we have no choice but to have it at the house.

"Do you think you can do the laundry then? I've run

out of boxers. And maybe clean the bathroom. We need some Drāno—your hair seriously clogs up the drain. I just showered in a pool of water. And it would be great if you could pick up some groceries."

"No problem," I say, wishing I could order food online and send out our laundry.

After showering in a pool of water (I do need to get some Drāno), I do two loads of laundry, go to the grocery store and clean the apartment, all the while not answering the ringing phone.

She. Is. Out. Of. Control.

I need someone to talk to about this. Jessica and Leslie seemed sympathetic to my plight and I'm sure they have their own mother-in-law stories, but I don't fully trust them yet. I call Lila and invite her out for lunch. Also, I want to ask her to be my maid of honor before Alice asks Blair.

"I'm working," Lila says. "How is almost-married life?"

"Good. Come on. It's Saturday. And I have to ask you something important."

"Sounds mysterious. Okay, for you I'll ditch work. Where do you want to meet?"

"The Mexican place on Mill."

"Gabby, there are two thousand Mexican restaurants on Mill."

"The new one near the bookstore."

"Fine. See you in twenty."

Twenty minutes later, she's begging, "Let me see the ring again."

I chomp on a tortilla chip, then wave my adorned hand under her nose.

"So gorgeous. Can I try it on?"

"Of course," I say and slip it off.

She admires her new look. "Wish I was marrying a guy like Cam. Lucky bitch."

"I know." I finish chewing and say, "Big question coming up. Will you be my maid of honor?"

Her eyes widen. "Really?"

"Of course. You've been like a sister to me." As I say it, I wonder if it's true. A sister? Really? If we were that close wouldn't I have called her at least once from New York? I should so e-mail her from there. Anyway, even if she's not a sister, she's still my best friend. We've done everything together since freshman year.

"I'd be honored," she says. "Wow. Thank you. It's a big job."

I chomp some more. "It shouldn't take too much time."

She takes a big sip of her water. "Perfect. Did you set a date?"

"May sixth."

She coughs her water. "Are you kidding?"

"No, why? Is there something else that day I've forgotten about?"

"No, but it's so soon. You can't plan a wedding in six months!" She peers at me closely. "Are you pregnant?"

"God, no."

"So what's the rush?"

"It's Alice. She insisted."

"Whose wedding is it, exactly?"

Good question. "An excellent lead-in to the second subject I want to discuss with you. My crazy future mother-in-law."

After I relay my wedding struggles, Lila says, "She sounds horrendous. At least Cam's worth it."

"He is," I say uncertainly. "He is."

Since I now have two bridesmaids and one maid of honor, I figure I might as well ask the others and go for the whole circus. I call Blair first. She gives me a courtly thank you and then makes a lame-ass excuse to hang up. I mean come on, water her cactus?

Next, I search through my Palm for Melanie Diamond's number.

"Hi," she says in her extra-breathy voice. "How have you been?"

"I've been getting engaged." I wriggle into Cam's uncomfy couch, trying to make myself comfortable. "And I'm not moving."

"No way—congratulations! I'm so happy for you."

"Thanks. How have you been?"

"Oh, all right. I'd be better if the tabloids stopped running that horrendous ugly picture of me—"

"You don't look ugly." Granted, it doesn't capture how gorgeous she actually is, but she definitely doesn't look unattractive. It's very difficult to make Melanie look unattractive. You'd have to draw a mustache over her lip or something.

"Anyway, I'm thinking about writing a tell-all book."

"Oh God, no."

"Why not? You only live once."

Or twice. "I suppose…"

"I might as well take some risks."

Maybe I should learn to take more risks. Without

keeping a back-up life as a safety net. "Listen, I want to ask you a question. Will you be a bridesmaid?"

"Me?" She sounds surprised.

"Yes. I know we've only known each other a few months but…okay, this is going to sound cheesy—"

"You feel like we've been friends since high school?"

"Exactly."

"Well, then I'd be pleased to. Awesome. Sounds like fun."

I smile into the phone. "It'll probably be a pain, actually, but thanks."

"What do I get to wear?"

"Not sure yet. Something pink and horrible."

"Super."

"I'll make sure to take a picture for the tabloids." The call-waiting beeps and I excuse myself. "Hello?"

"Hey, it's me," says Cam. "Come outside!"

"Now? Why?"

"It's a surprise."

I stuff my bare feet into my flip-flops and hurry outside. And see Cam. Driving my Jetta. He honks twice and then backs into a parking spot. I can tell it's mine since it has the scrape on the fender from last year's parking-lot incident. I run over to him, clapping my hands. "Hurrah! How did you get it back?"

"I'm Superman," he says, stepping out of the car and smiling broadly.

I plant a kiss on his lips. "Seriously. How?"

"I reasoned with him."

"That's it?"

"I'm a very good reasoner. And I know how much you loved this car."

"I see that. I guess law school was good for something."
I throw my arms around his waist as we walk back to the
apartment.

"Love you," I say.

"Love you, too," he says, kissing me on the forehead.

I spend Sunday afternoon in New York brainstorming
stories. I spend Sunday afternoon in Arizona brainstorming hotels.

At Sunday night dinner, Alice asks me how my research
is coming and gazes longingly at her backyard. I do my best
to ignore her.

Monday in New York is tough and exhausting but
still fun. I keep my eyes open for Nate aka Elevator Boy,
but don't see him anywhere. I pick up sushi for Heather
and myself on my way home from a place called Sushi
on Third. Not too many places in Arizona where you
can get good sushi. Mexican, yes. Japanese? Not so
much.

When I get back to the apartment, I see that Heather has
uncorked a bottle of wine and set the table with wine-
glasses, two sets of chopsticks, two plates and two…steak
knives? I did tell her we were having sushi.

"What's the deal with the knives?" I ask, opening the
plastic container and digging in.

"Huh?" She takes the steak knife and slices her California roll in half.

"I've never seen anyone cut sushi before."

"I have lockjaw," she says. "I have to be very careful with
my mouth. If I open it too much, it hurts."

The way she can go on and on, life must be a constant

source of pain. "I see. Can't you stretch the muscle?" I make wide-mouth expressions, partly kidding.

"It's not a joke. It's a medical condition. I can't give blow jobs."

Not quite ideal dinner conversation. "Interesting," I say, pick up a full roll with my chopsticks and insert it into my mouth.

"Guys understand. I tell them the truth. It's a condition."

A condition as in *disease,* or a condition to their relationship?

We polish off the bottle of wine. After dinner, I decide I need a long, hot shower. I wish I could take a bath, but the bath here isn't deep enough for a baby. I'm pretty sure if I sat down in it, my boobs would pop over the top and they're not even that big. Tomorrow I'm definitely taking a bath in Arizona.

As I rinse, I notice a brown-and-blue bruise on my upper thigh. What is that? I notice another one on my calf, and then another one on my elbow. What is wrong with me? Did I have some sort of accident and not even know it? Maybe jumping realities is causing physical damage.

When I'm done, I wrap myself in a fuzzy towel (brand new and recently ordered online) and open the door. And walk straight into a pissed-off-looking Heather.

"What's wrong?" I ask her.

"Nothing," she snaps.

"Okay." I try to step around her, but she blocks me as if she's a quarterback.

"Oh, there is one thing. Brad just called. He wants you to phone him back."

Pow. Brad? Called me? Ouch. I imagine the look on Heather's face when Brad asked to speak to me. Glad I was in the shower for that. "Shit, Heather, I'm sorry."

"Why? He likes you. Nothing to be sorry about. You should go out with him."

"I don't want to go out with him." I mean he *is* cute. And a date or two would certainly help me get over my fear of new men. But he's not worth sacrificing my relationship with my still-new roommate.

She crosses her arms. "You think you're better than me?"

"I didn't mean it like that."

"I don't want to go out with him," she mocks, using a squeaky voice. "You think you're better than me."

"I do *not* think I'm better than you."

"Oh, I think you do. The guy I like isn't good enough for you. Well, fuck you. I think he's good enough for you. I think he's too good for you. I don't want any of your pathetic pity. You will go out with him. Or else. You *will* go out with him!"

I cling to my towel in alarm. She's gone crazy. My first instincts were right. My roommate is a nut job. Totally psycho. "Heather, I'm not dating the guy you like."

She wags her finger at me. "You will. You'll either go out with him or move out. Capisce?"

What, is she channeling the Sopranos now? I hope she's put away those steak knives. "Heather—"

"Here's his number." She hands me a sticky memo, the number written on it and underlined multiple times. "Call him back. Tonight."

I grab it from her, stomp into my room and slam the door. I think I need to get a lock for my room. I put on my sleep T-shirt and hang my towel on the edge of the bed. I am so not leaving my room tonight. Or ever.

I don't want to call back Brad, but I don't think I have a choice. I have to tell him I can't go out with him. I'll tell Heather—what? That the reason he'd called in the first place was business-related? Come to think of it, he never did tell me what he did for a living. I crawl under my covers with my (new) cordless phone (this one has a longer battery life than my cordless in Arizona), squint to see the underlined number in the dark, and I dial.

"Hello!" he shouts into the phone. He sounds like he's at a bar. Do people in Manhattan ever sleep?

"Brad?" I whisper. No need for Psycho to hear me.

"Hello!" he shouts again. "Anyone there?"

I raise my voice slightly. "Brad?"

"Anyone there? I don't think anyone is there," he says to someone else.

Crap. "Hi, Brad, it's Gabby."

"Hey! Good to hear from you."

"You, too." Please don't ask me out.

"It was great meeting you last night."

"You, too." Pretty please don't ask me out. If you don't ask me out, then I can tell Heather you didn't ask me out and she won't have to kill me. Sorry, Heather, I called him back, but he didn't ask me out. No, he's taking a trip to Phoenix and wanted to know what to pack.

"Wanna see a movie on Saturday?"

"Um…" Now what? Was Heather testing me? Am I supposed to say no? Or will she really kick me out? It's getting seriously hot under the covers. I have to wrap up this conversation before I suffocate.

You know what—screw her. I don't need mind games. He's cute. I'm single. She told me to go out with him. I'm going to do it. "Sure."

"Cool!" he shouts. "My friend Jono offered me tickets to a some artsy premiere at the Angelika."

Funky. My first date, and it's a cool New York event. "Sounds good."

"I'll come by and pick you up. Where do you live?"

I give him our address and insist that I meet him downstairs. No need to risk him and Heather coming into contact again. I also make him promise that from now on he'll only call me on my cell. After I hang up, I sneak out from under the covers and stare at the ceiling. I think I'm excited. Am I excited?

There's a knock on my door. You've got to be kidding. "Gabby."

I don't answer. Maybe she'll think I'm asleep.

"Gabby," she says sweetly. "I want to come in."

Hmm. Perhaps she wants to apologize for being crazy. Should I let her know I'm awake?

Suddenly, she throws open the door. I'm too shocked to fake sleep. The light from the hallway illuminates her silhouette, and she looks as if she's surrounded by a ring of fire. Heather might be the devil.

"Ha!" she shrieks. "I knew you were awake. Faker. Tell me you're going out with him."

Gulp. One of her hands is hidden behind her. She could so have the steak knife back there.

Oh, God. I'm going to die. At least I'll still be alive in my other life. Maybe. Sure, I'll have the full-time mother-in-law from hell, but it beats being dead. I think.

I contemplate lying to Psycho, but then remember that she asked for it. "Kind of. He invited me to some movie thing."

"And…"

Please don't kill me. "I said yes."

"When are you going out?"

"Saturday night."

"Bullshit. He asked you out for a weekend?"

"Yes. Why?"

"Guys don't ask women out on weekends for their first dates."

I hug my pillow into my chest as a protective shield. "Apparently, some do."

Silence. "Fine. Whatever." She slams my door.

I need to find a new apartment pronto.

Once I hear Heather settle in her own room, I try to convince my heart rate to slow down, but it won't listen. I have a date. What will I wear? I need something fabulous. I guess asking Heather to borrow her good-butt pants is out of the question.

"Don't get mad," my mother says into my cell phone. It's Tuesday in Arizona and I'm on my way to Alice's to discuss locations.

"About what?" I ask, making a left into Alice's cul-de-sac.

"I'm in Florida."

She's got to be kidding. "Mom! You're supposed to be at Alice's in ten minutes!"

"I know, but I couldn't—"

A loud honk drowns her words as I almost cut off a green Taurus. "Couldn't what?"

"Couldn't stand being around Alice?"

"Thanks for your support."

"I'm sorry, all right? I sent over a surprise to make your life easier."

I turn into Alice's driveway. "What, exactly?" I ask warily.

"You'll see."

I kill the ignition and bang my head against the steering wheel. I'm going to kill her. How am I supposed to battle Alice on my own? As I step out of the car, a white Mercedes convertible pulls in front of the house and then stops. The driver, a petite blonde in a fitted mauve Chanel suit picks up a briefcase from the back seat and strolls toward the house.

Does this have something to do with my surprise? I catch up to her before she gets to the door. "Hi, can I help you?"

She gives me a big, toothy smile. "You must be Gabby. I'm Tricia, your new wedding planner."

"You could have told me," I growl into the phone. I'm in the restroom at the Marriott, biting my now-raw fingers. Talk about plush. Even the sinks are marble. The way I'm feeling right now, I don't care if we decide to have the wedding in the bathroom.

"It was a surprise," my mom answers. "What's she like?"

I glance at my watch. I don't want to be gone for too long in case Tricia and Alice begin World War Three. "Organized. Blond. Chirpy. Has lots of folders and schedules."

"Good! She's the best in the business, you know. I asked around."

"But you shouldn't have hired her without talking to us."

"I had no choice. I need her there to protect my—and your—interests."

"How much does she charge?"

"Don't worry about it."

"I have to worry about it! That's coming out of the fifteen thousand you promised!"

"It's my fifteen thousand, and I can spend it any way I want."

I want to hurl the cell phone into one of the fancy-shmancy, tushy-plushy toilets. "Goodbye, Mom. I have to get back. This is the fourth hotel we've seen, and Alice isn't liking any of them."

"Don't let her boss you around," she says, with no trace of irony. "Wait, just tell me. What did Alice say when she met Tricia?"

I sigh. "She slammed the door."

"No, she didn't!"

"Yes, she did. I had to call from outside, apologize for you and explain."

"You did not!"

"Yes, I did. Mom, you *hired* a wedding planner without talking to her. Or me."

"So? She chose a date without talking to me."

I shake my head. "I have to get back. I'll speak to you soon."

I square my shoulders and return to the ballroom. Alice isn't happy about the new hire, but there's nothing she can do, as my mother already signed a contract and made a deposit. It goes without saying, the mood at Alice's when we all met was definitely hostile. Tricia had set up appointments for this afternoon, so now we're a hostile team on the go. Alice insisted on driving, and the three of us, wedding binders and brochures in hand, set off to see hotels. Alice dismissed the first one with "It's too small," the second one with "It's too big." When she nixed the third one with "It's too hot," Tricia muttered something about Goldilocks, except she didn't use language appropriate for a children's story.

Alice is sitting on a velvet couch in the corner of the ballroom, her arms crossed, a sour expression on her face.

I clap my hands. "So? Just right?"

"Too dark," Alice says.

I catch Tricia snarling. "Next," she says, and motions us back to the car.

My, what big teeth she has. Except this is no fairy tale—this is a nightmare.

Back in New York, on Wednesday, I'm watching the news after work when Heather waltzes in. I consider bolting to my room to avoid another psycho confrontation, but I know she's seen me.

"Helllllllo!" she sings. "How are you, sweetie?"

Sweetie? Heather might have multiple personalities. "Fine. You?"

"I had the best day. The *best*. I met the cutest guy in the library."

Ah. I see that her moods depend entirely on men. I hope she didn't come on to Library Lad as strong as she did with Brad. Otherwise, her happy mood is going to be very short-lived.

"I'm starving," she says, and disappears into the kitchen.

"Take some of my food," I offer. I think I might have over-ordered. I bought all this fresh stuff, but on my way home from work, I realized I was too tired to cook and picked up more sushi. Next time, I'm only ordering non-perishables.

She plops onto the couch with one of my apples, my block of blue cheese and her favorite utensil, the steak knife.

I whip my legs into the lotus position. If I'm not careful, she'll not-so-accidentally drop the knife and take a pinkie toe with her.

Heather slices the apple into small cubes, and asks, "When was the last time you had sex?"

Hello, dinner conversation. "Excuse me?"

"Come on, you can tell me. We're roomies."

"I…um…" Last night with Cam when he got back from work? Not sure she'll understand. "Before I left Arizona."

She layers a cube with a piece of cheese and pops it in her mouth. "With your boyfriend. Cam."

"Yes."

"Why'd you not want to try long distance?" She steals the remote from behind my leg and changes the channel to Comedy Central. "Don't you get bored of watching news all the time?"

"I don't get bored, it's my job. And Cam and I are complicated. He proposed. I said no."

She waves the knife in the air. "Why?"

Still in a lotus, I wriggle my body farther down the couch. "Because I wanted to move to New York."

"Did he have a ring and everything?"

"Yup."

"And you said no? What was wrong with him?"

"He wouldn't move here, for one thing. And he sometimes tried to be controlling…and he's a bit of a mama's boy."

"Then why'd you stay with him for so long?"

"Because he's smart. And loving. And gorgeous."

"And he proposed. I don't know. Maybe there's something wrong with you."

I wonder. "Maybe."

"Don't you want to know the last time I had sex?"

Not really. "If you want to tell me."

She pops another apple-cheese combo into her mouth. "When I was twenty-three."

"What?" I give her a closer look. Maybe she's only twenty-four? No way. I see a few lines around those eyes.

"Yup. Four years ago."

"You haven't had sex in four years?"

"Nope."

"Why?"

"I'm not sure if that's any of your business," she huffs, and turns back to the TV.

What? Then why did she bring it up? I sigh and shake my head. "I'm going to take a shower." At least the bathroom door has a lock.

When I'm out of the shower, there are two steaming mugs on the coffee table. "I made us herbal tea," Heather sings.

I think she might need to be medicated.

"All right," I say. "Let me just get dressed."

Perhaps this is just her way of saying sorry. She can't actually say the words, so instead she apologizes with hot beverages. Hopefully this means that I don't have to look for a new apartment just yet. Just in case, I Black-Berry my mom: *In case I die tonight, Heather poisoned me. Love you!*

I'm still mad at my mom for the disappearing act she pulled in Arizona, but I can't hold her accountable here. Anyway, I'm secretly pleased to have Tricia around. She was just as annoyed as I was by Alice, after Alice rejected seven, yes seven, different hotels. "More to see on Thursday," Tricia chirped, trying to keep my spirits up.

Over tea, neither Heather nor I bring up her sexual history. Or Brad. We talk about Cam. Funny how she maneuvered the conversation back to him. Or maybe it was me who did the maneuvering. After tea, I climb into bed and think. Not about whether I should be looking for a new apartment (haven't turned blue from the tea, but I did get a nervous e-mail from my mother), but about Cam. And what he's doing now. I wonder if he's thinking of me.

I pick up the phone and dial his number. My number when I'm in Arizona. His number here.

He answers on the first ring. "Hello?"

"Hey," I say.

"Gabby?" his voice sounds scratchy and familiar.

"It's me." I draw my comforter up to my chin, so I have something to cuddle.

"How's New York?"

"All right." There's a deep silence. "How are you?"

He laughs. Bitterly. "I've been better."

"Oh, Cam. I'm so sorry."

I used to tell Cam that he had a horseshoe up his ass. Everything came so easily to him and nothing traumatic had ever shaken his world. No death. No move. No divorce. Secretly I wondered if some traumatic event in his past would have done him more good than harm. Made him more sensitive. Perceptive. Reflective. Now, I can't help but wonder if me leaving him is the trauma in his life, the trauma that will make him into the ideal husband for someone else.

"Sorry enough to come home?" he asks.

Sadness swells up in my chest like a balloon. "This is my new life."

"Then why are you calling?"

"I still care about you. I want to make sure you're okay. You know. Moving on."

"Gimme a break. It's only been a week and a half."

I feel a wave of guilt for my upcoming date with Brad. "I know. I just meant…you know." Why is this conversation so awkward?

"No, I don't know. Have you moved on already?"

I take a second to think about my answer. A second too long.

"There's someone else," he spits out. "That's why you said no."

"No, of course not. There was never anyone else."

"But you've met someone there."

"It's just a date, okay? Someone asked me out and I said yes."

"Who is he?"

"You don't know him."

"I might."

I almost laugh. Even in my wildest dreams I cannot think of a connection between the two of them. "You don't."

"Tell me his name. Did you sleep with him?"

"I haven't even gone out with him yet! His name is Brad."

"Last name?

I pause. "I don't know."

"You have a date with someone whose last name you don't know?" Now it's his turn to pause. "How am I going to do a background check?"

I let myself laugh. "Come on."

"I can't believe you're already dating."

"I'm not dating. I just have one date."

"How would you feel if I had a date?"

"I'd hate it," I say, rolling over. "But I'd know it was for the best."

"I guess I just thought…I was hoping you'd realize you made a mistake. That you miss me. And that you'd call me and say, I changed my mind, I want to marry you. And then you'd come home."

"That isn't going to happen," I say softly.

He sighs. "I'm realizing that."

"I think we were just wrong for each other. I need a different kind of guy. You need a different kind of girl. You know? Someone who remembers where she puts her keys. Someone who remembers to pay the phone bill. And I need someone who is willing to follow me anywhere. To make me number one."

"Maybe I need someone who would follow me any-where," he says.

In the silence that follows, I wonder if that's true. What does Cam need? I mean really, really need?

"I spoke to Lila yesterday," he says. "I'm stopping by this weekend to pick up my bookshelf."

"I figured you'd want it back. You should have it."

"Yeah, well. I gotta go. I'm meeting up with Dan and Joshua."

"Now don't go picking up any loose women."

He laughs, sadly I think. "Now that sounds like fun."

I get a sour taste in my mouth. "Cam—"

"Don't worry, they'd never replace you."

"Never?"

And then he says, "Not in this life."

It's Friday night in Arizona, and I'm unloading the dish-washer and thinking about my two existences. How can I marry someone in one life who I think is wrong for me in another? How is this even happening to me? Maybe I am crazy. Suddenly I notice a sheet of white printer paper propped up on the stove. Written in red marker on said sheet of paper is this: FIRE!!!!!!!!!!!!

"Um, Cam?" He is watching TV in the living room.

"Yes, honey?"

"Why is there a sheet of paper that says Fire on the stove?"

"Eee! Eee! Eee!" Cam says, running over to me.

"What are you doing?"

"Eee! Eee! Eee! It's a fire drill. Eee! Eee! Eee!"

My fiancé has lost it. "What am I supposed to do exactly?"

"Eee! Eee! You may want to get the fire extinguisher. Eee! Eee! Eee!"

"Where is the fire extinguisher?"

"Think, for a second, you see it every day. Eee! Eee! Eee! This is something you should know." He taps his watch. "Time is ticking."

I might kill him. "Why are we doing this exactly?"

"Because you had that nightmare about fires, and I don't want you to ever have nightmares again."

"Interesting." I vaguely remember mentioning that I had a nightmare about fires. I should have kept my mouth shut. I try to remember if in fact I have ever noticed a fire extinguisher. I might have spotted one in the linen closet. "Is it in the linen closet?"

"Maybe. Eee! Eee! Eee!" He taps his watch again.

I open the linen closet and start rummaging through the towels.

"Eee! Eee! Eee!" He points his chin at the middle shelf.

Oh, there it is. A First Alert kitchen fire extinguisher. I pull it out of the closet. "Do you want me to actually use it on the paper?"

"No, just tell me what you'd do."

"I'd pull off the top. And then..." my voice trails off until I spot the instructions on the bottle. "I'd hold the unit upright. Then I'd aim at base of fire and stand back six feet. Then I'd press lever and sweep side to side." I go through the motions as I read.

"Well done!" He kisses me on the forehead. "Although it took you too long to find the extinguisher. It also took you forever to notice the fire—"

"You mean the piece of paper."

"These are things you should know."

"Things I should know," I repeat. I have to admit that Cam's behavior is a bit...weird. He's always been a bit pedantic, but there have never been drills before.

"Yes. If it had a been a real fire, you would have suffocated"

"But it wasn't."

"Tomorrow it could be."

No, it can't. Because tomorrow I'm going to be in New York, on a date with Brad.

9

Four's a Crowd

The sun is shining when I wake up the next morning in New York. I feel a vague sense of nervousness I can't quite place, and then I remember that it's Saturday. Date night.

I'm going out with a man who's not Cam.

I pull the covers back over my head. I can't do this. I am not ready to go out with anyone else. Someone who doesn't smell like Cam. Someone who doesn't laugh like Cam. Someone doesn't wear the same brand of underwear.

It's always weird to find out what kind of underwear a guy sports. I like Cam's low-key boxers. Although some of them are so old, it's embarrassing. I discovered one seriously bent-out-of-shape pair when I was doing the wash. I'm talking frayed elastic, two holes on the crotch part, Cardinals design long-faded. "How old are these?" I'd asked.

"I bought them my last year of high school," he admitted with a sheepish smile.

"Eleven years. I think it's time to toss them."

"Never," he said, stealing them back. "I was wearing them the night I met you."

Aw.

What if Brad wears tighty-whities? Not that I'm planning on seeing what kind of underwear he's got on. Not tonight. I can barely imagine holding his hand, never mind seeing what he's got on underneath.

Speaking of clothes, what I really need is a new outfit. I have no idea what constitutes a good first-date outfit these days. Skirt? Dress? Black pants and a sexy top? My wardrobe is not quite date ready. I need to go shopping.

The butterflies are a'fluttering.

I wonder how Heather's feeling this morning. For all I know, she crept into my room while I was sleeping and shaved off my eyebrows. Or wrote all over my face. I always hear her slithering around the kitchen in the middle of the night. I jump out of bed and check myself in the mirror glued to the door, which was left by the roomie who lived here before me. If I'm lucky, I won't see my current roomie all day. Maybe she's at school, or the library. I place my ear firmly against the door to check for sounds. Nada. No TV. No click-clacking of her shoes.

I wait a few seconds and then, full of hope, I slowly creak open the door. Her room appears to be empty. Her door is open, her light turned off. The bathroom door is in the same unoccupied state.

Could it be? Could I be so lucky that she has already left the apartment? Perhaps she's forgotten about my date.

Perhaps she's so enthralled by the new guy that she's run off to make mad, passionate love to him behind the library stacks.

What are stacks anyway? Are they anything like shelves? People are always talking about hooking up behind them. Does FIT have stacks? Does FIT have a library?

"Good morning!"

The greeting is hurled at me from the living room. Damn. I whip my head to the left and see that she's already dressed in a white seventies-style velour pantsuit. "Looking for me?" She's sitting on the couch, a glass of orange juice in one hand, *Vogue* in the other.

"Hey, Heather. I didn't hear you."

"I'm not very loud. I can really sneak up on people."

Er. "Sleep well?"

"I'm not much of a sleeper. I'm an insomniac. Excited for your big date?"

Maybe she's a vampire. I make small steps toward the bathroom. "Looking forward to it."

"What are you going to wear?"

"Don't know yet. Planning on doing some shopping today."

She nods. "I thought so. I'll take you."

Hmm…an entire day with Psycho. Not sure that's the best plan. "Don't worry, I'll be fine on my own. I'm sure you have better things to do than hang out with me."

"Of course I do, but I'm willing to help." Then her eyes narrow and she throws her magazine onto the coffee table. "Unless you're too good for my help."

"No, I didn't mean that. It's just…" My voice trails off as I contemplate worst-case scenarios. She could throw me in front of a cab. She could steal my clothes and purse while

I'm trying on a dress and then bolt, leaving me broke and in my Skivvies.

"I don't understand why you don't want me to come. I study fashion."

Because maybe you'll purposely steer me wrong and I'll end up looking like a contestant on *What Not to Wear*. I sigh. I don't feel like arguing. Besides, I don't have to buy what she suggests. And it's not as if she'd really try to kill me. Not in broad daylight. "Sure. Show me around. If you want."

"Oh, thanks," she says, her voice dripping with sarcasm. "You're doing me a real favor."

What does she want from me? My firstborn child? "I want you to help me, Heather. Really. I appreciate your expertise."

She leaps off the couch. "Good. We should really hit the pavement by ten. We'll start in NoLita, move our way through SoHo, the West Village, and then back uptown. Have you given any thought to your outfit?"

Slow down there, Seabiscuit. "We don't need to go crazy. All I need is a new top to go with my black pants."

"That's what you're planning on wearing? Your boring work pants? The baggy ones?" She shakes her head.

"Is that bad?"

"Not if you're forty. You need to be wearing jeans."

"I have jeans."

"Not good ones."

"I'm not sure I want to wear jeans on a date."

"Don't be stupid. Of course you do. You're not going to the prom. Do you want my help or not?"

It's true that I know nothing about fashion. And let's face it, living in Arizona did nothing to heighten my fashion consciousness. Sure, there's the Biltmore Fashion Park and let's not forget Nordstrom, but I confess, my high-couture experience ended at Tar-jay. Maybe having Heather around isn't the worst idea. She's certainly more stylish than I am, and she is studying fashion. She must have picked up some tips, white seventies pantsuit notwithstanding. "Yes, yes, I want your help," I say. Who wouldn't want an FIT student as a personal shopper? And what's the worst that could happen? If she starts acting crazy, I can always jump in a cab.

If she doesn't push me in front of one first.

At a cozy store called Sude, Heather unfolds a pair of low-cut James jeans that would maybe cover a quarter of my butt cheeks, appraises them, then hands them to me. "Try these on," she orders.

"Are you crazy?" Unfortunately, I already know the answer to that.

"Just try them on. This, too," she says, tossing a brown blouse at me.

I get into the changing room, strip, and then sigh when I unfold the jeans. They are gorgeous. They look perfectly soft and worn, like they've spent many years in the drier, even though I'm sure they cost over a hundred and that they're never supposed to see anything but a dry cleaner.

There is no way these are going to fit. No way! Is she insane? I point my toe and squeeze the first leg in. This is never going to work. She didn't even ask for my size. I squeeze the other leg in and heave the jeans over my hips. I suck in my breath and zip them up. No way. What a waste of time and—hey, they fit! I look in the mirror. They're low, yes, but they look great. It must be the Pilates. I've been going twice a week. There's no way these would fit on me in my other life.

I pull away the curtains and twirl. "How did you know?" Okay, so maybe I misjudged her. Maybe she really does have the hots for Library Lad and wants it to work for me and Brad.

She's rifling through another rack and has two more shirts in hand. "It's my job."

"I love them," I say and do another twirl. My ass looks terrific.

"Now put on that blouse."

"Anything you say, my fashion guru."

I try on the blouse. It's tight and frilly, and I love it. "Perfect!" I sing, stepping out of the changing room.

She looks me over. "No. Take it off. That color is awful on you. You look like an albino. Do you know you have a big head?"

"What?" I examine my silhouette in the mirror. "I do not."

"Yes, you do. Compare it to mine." She squashes her face next to mine. "See?"

She's right. Apparently, I have a massive head. Jumbo sized. "Maybe that's why I'm so smart."

She rolls her eyes. "Maybe."

By the end of the excursion, I've found a second pair of jeans, two pairs of shoes, a new tight silky pink top to wear tonight and a pair of crazy gold feather earrings that I would never have looked twice at on my own. Heather buys a new pair of jeans and a tight V-neck gold dress.

We stop at one of the five hundred nail salons on the way home.

A bell chimes as we step inside the small shop. There

are at least ten women at tables in the midst of having their nails done.

"Manicure?" asks the Korean woman at the desk.

"Two," Heather says, then turns to me. "This place is the best. Cheap, clean and good."

I look at the prices on the wall, and read Manicure, Seven Dollars. That is cheap. "Pick your color," the woman at the cash tells us.

"I'm getting a French," Heather says.

We walk over to the rainbow wall of polishes. I hate this part. Red or clear? I've always liked cherry-red, but it's so much. What about a light pink? That's pretty. Or should I just get a French? When I was a kid, I used to love to paint each of my fingers a different colors.

I shuffle through the many shades of pink and finally pick a clear one.

"Ready?" asks my manicurist. Her name tag says Annie. She's wearing her dark hair in a tight bun, and a clean white smock over a pair of tight dark jeans and stiletto heels.

You know what? I really want red. I pick up the bottle and pass it to her. "Yes, thanks."

I take a seat at Annie's station and dunk my hands in a warm bowl of water. Heather is already sitting next to me soaking and chatting on her cell.

My own cell rings as my fingers are soaking.

"Hello?"

"Hey, Gabby, it's Brad." He's screaming again. What is it with him and cell phones?

"Hey." After all this, he better not be canceling.

"Listen, my friend's date just bailed on him for tonight. Does Heather want to come along?"

What? Does my roommate who wants to steal my date want to come on my date? Probably. I'm debating what to say when I notice Heather watching me. She for sure heard his question. "Let me ask," I tell him. "Brad's friend has an extra ticket to the movie. Do you want to—"

"Yes!" she shrieks clapping her hands and smearing her polish. "Careful," she tells her manicurist.

"She's in," I say to Brad. Guess she's not quite saving herself for Library Lad.

"Okay, he's going to meet us there, but I'll swing by your place at seven."

"All right, see you then." I flip back down the phone and Heather returns to her phone call.

As my nails are pruned and filed, I try to make sense out of what just happened. I don't get it. Brad acted like he wanted nothing to do with Heather at the hotel, so why is he inviting her along now? Can't his friend find another date?

As Annie applies the base coat, I decide that he must just be a really nice guy, who doesn't want my roommate to feel left out. Which is quite sweet when you think about it. Annie takes out the red and begins painting. First my thumb, then my index finger, and then—

"Wait," I say, my heart rate speeding up. "The color is *so* red."

"Yes, cherry-red," she says, smiling and nodding.

My fingers look like lollipops. "Too red?"

Her forehead furrows with concentration. "You don't like? I can take off."

"I don't know." I tap Heather, who is still chatting on the phone, on the elbow. "Do you like the red?"

"Mindy, hold on a sec. What did you say?" she asks me.

"Do you like the red?"

"No. Too madame," she says and then returns to her conversation.

I have no idea what that means. "Sorry?"

"Too...oh, hold on. Mindy, I'll speak to you later." She flips closed her phone and deposits it on her table. "It's trying too hard. And anyway, you bought a pink top to wear tonight. Use a champagne color."

"Do you have a champagne color?" I ask Annie.

She nods, pulls a beigy pink color from her drawer, and removes my polish with a cotton ball.

I feel Heather looking at me, and turn to her. "Yes?"

"You're not very good with decisions, huh?"

I laugh. "Not personal ones."

"You're different at work?"

"They don't stress me out in the same way," I say. It's weird actually. At the station, when I'm working on a show, I usually have about four seconds to choose a direction, and I never look back. But I am a bit of a stuttering freak when it comes to my personal life. Red or pink? Chicken or pasta? Too many choices make me want to pull out my hair. (One strand or two?) Or bite my nails. Or get married and let Cam make all my decisions for me.

"You need to relax," Heather says.

"You want ten-minute shoulder massage?" Annie asks, while painting my thumb for the second time.

"Oh, I don't know...."

"Do it. I'll have one, too," Heather says to her manicurist. "You guys always get me on the up sell."

"You want lip wax, too?" Annie asks me.

Yikes. "Um, no thanks." I turn to Heather. "Do I need a lip wax?"

She peers at my face. "It wouldn't hurt. And an eyebrow wax, too. You're starting to look a bit Bert-ish."

"Yes," says Annie pointing at my brow. "Like *Sesame Street*."

Excellent. I'm so glad they all agree.

After an hour of intense pain, I agree, too. My nails are gorgeous, my eyebrows sculpted, and my upper lip, hairless. Heather might be my new BFF. Back at the apartment, I drop my bags onto the floor of my room and notice that I only have an hour to get ready for my date. I'm about to step into the shower when I realize that Heather has beaten me to it. Damn her. It was my date first—I should so have shower priority. My upper lip is stinging a bit, so I check out my appearance in the hallway mirror. Fantastic. I have a red mustache-like line from the lip wax. Perhaps my new BF only encouraged me to have my hair removed to make me look weird so she could steal my date.

When Heather is finally out of the bathroom, I jump into the shower, quickly dry my hair and then apply my makeup. Thankfully, my red mustache has disappeared and my skin looks pretty good, so I don't need much. Maybe Heather isn't trying to sabotage my date after all. Unfortunately, I only have seven minutes until Brad gets here. All I need is my new top. Where is my new top? Where is my damn—

Beep!

Shit.

"Hello?" says Heather, pressing the intercom. "Brad's here," she calls to me.

"Tell him we'll be—"

"Let him up!" she tells Charlie, the Saturday-night doorman. "Shall I entertain him while you're getting ready?" she yells at me.

I'm sure that's not all she'd like to do. I don't want him to come up—my room is a mess. Shoes and socks and sweaters all over the place and my bed isn't made. I wanted us to meet him downstairs. "I'll be two secs!" I slip on my new shirt. "Heather, can you do this up for me?"

"Absolutely," she says, joining me in my room.

Hello, there. She's wearing her new low-cut gold dress and a ton of makeup. Sure she tells me to wear jeans, yet she's dressed to the nines. I don't get it. I told her I wouldn't go out with him if she didn't want me to. Instead she's going to hit on him during my date? "There you go," she says. "Let the games begin."

Weeeeeeeeeeeeeeeeeeird. I'm going on a date with a guy and the girl who likes him.

Ring!

"Let's go," I say. I zip up my boots, grab my purse and run to the door.

Brad is looking faux-James Dean, in faded jeans and a black leather jacket. He gives me a big, dimpled smile. "Hey. You look great."

I give him a big smile back. "Thanks, so do you."

"Hi, Brad," Heather says. She's leaning over provocatively, lacing up her boots.

Brad's gaze flickers over the exposed cleavage. "Hey."

You've got to be kidding. "All right, kids," I tell them warily. "Let's get a move on."

We stand outside and try to hail a cab. Finally, I flag one, we get inside, and I scoot over to the window seat. I'm expecting Brad to follow me, but Heather climbs in next.

This is getting weirder and weirder. There is going to be another guy meeting us, right? Brad's not on a date with both of us? "What's your friend's name again?" I ask.

Brad roles down the window and a burst of cold air floods the cab. "Jono."

"What kind of a name is Jono?" Heather asks, leaning into him.

Brad shrugs. "Short for Jonathan."

"That's the dumbest name I've ever heard," she says, shaking her head.

We pull up in front of the theater, and Brad hands the driver a ten.

"There's Jono," he says, pointing to a short, stocky, balding guy smoking and waiting at the front of a line of about thirty people.

I catch Heather's scowl.

"I'm freezing," his friend says as we approach.

Nice to meet you, too.

Brad introduces us all, but I can tell that Jono and Heather are not a match made in blind-date heaven. For one thing, Jono is paying more attention to his cigarette— puffing and sucking and then puffing some more—than to Heather. And instead of trying to talk to Jono, Heather is standing beside Brad and me in line, leaving Jono to wait by himself.

"You're wearing great jeans," Heather says to my date. "Where did you get them?"

"Macy's."

"No way."

"Really."

And just when I'm minding my own business, examining the ground, someone walking in the other direction smacks right into me, slamming my already bruised shoulder.

"Sorry," I say without thinking twice.

"What the hell?" says Heather, and charges after him. "You just knocked into my friend and didn't even apologize."

The beefy-looking guy turns around and squints. First at Heather and then at me. "Oh. Excuse me."

My face turns red and it's not from the cold.

"Watch it next time," she responds, hands on her hips. She nods, satisfied, and then returns to the line. "What were you saying sorry for? He bumped you."

I shake my head helplessly. "It just came out."

"Well, it shouldn't," she snaps, and then turns back to Brad. "So, have you spoken to Mindy this week?" She then launches into a ten-minute conversation with Brad about all their mutual friends while I stand by, now examining my hands.

I don't know why I apologized. It just poured out. If I'm going to live in this city, I'm really going to have to toughen up. And I can start right now by stopping Heather from monopolizing my date.

Unfortunately, Brad doesn't seem to mind that he's only spoken to Heather since he picked us up. I keep expecting him to cut her off, or to try to engage me in a tête-à-tête, but he doesn't. He just keeps talking to my roommate as I stand in line, bored, feeling very untough and wishing I were back at home. Or back in Arizona. What am I doing dating, anyway? I have Cam. Cam would never ignore me on a date.

"The line is moving," Heather tells us. "What are we seeing anyway?"

"Some low-budget independent movie," Brad says.

"Thanks again for inviting me," Heather coos.

He didn't—Jono did. Although technically, I guess it was Brad who did the inviting.

"Anybody want to share a popcorn?" Brad asks.

"No thanks," I say. Popcorn always makes me a bit nauseous and this date is already making me queasy.

"I do," says Heather. "I want to get a drink, too. Jono and Gabby, you guys get the seats."

This is ridiculous. She forced me to agree to go out with him, but now she has hijacked my date.

As we exit the theater, Heather says, "Who's up for drinks? Let's go to Safari Bar on Mercer."

I don't think so. The last two hours were two of the most annoying of my life. First of all, Heather would not shut up for one second to let us watch the movie. We were seated Jono, Heather, Brad, then me, and Heather kept trying to engage Brad in random conversations: about the actor on-screen, the friends they had in common, anything. Brad would nod while continuing to stare at the screen, giving her what I assumed was the brush-off, but she did not take the hint. Instead she would pipe up with a new topic of conversation. Jono actually shushed her twice. Brad seems like a decent guy. He's cute and he's sweet, and if it were possible, if we existed in another universe perhaps, I would like to get to know him. But Heather is obviously never going to let that happen. She likes him, and she wants to date him. And I don't care enough about him to put up a fight. I have Cam. My night is ending right now. "Thanks," I say. "But—"

"Sounds good," says Brad, while zipping up his coat. "Okay, Jono?"

Huh? If Brad actually liked me, then wouldn't he want to spend some time alone with me?

Jono shrugs his okay and lights up a cigarette as the gang starts walking toward Mercer.

"You guys go ahead," I say. "I think I'm going to pass."

Brad stops in his tracks. "I'm not going if you're not going."

"No really, go ahead, I don't mind," I say. "I'll just grab a cab home."

"Absolutely not," he says. "You're my date. We can take a rain check on drinks."

Heather swings around. "Come on, guys. Please? One drink. They make the wildest martinis." She gives me a pleading look.

Yes, I want to go home. But Heather really, really likes Brad, and this is her only chance to work her nonexistent charm on him....

"Fine. One drink."

I stick to my one-drink suggestion. Unfortunately, Brad does not. Every time he says he's had enough, Heather orders another drink for him. Four Jack-and-Cokes later, his cheeks are flaming and he's dancing in our brown leather booth.

At least the bar is cool. The tables are thick planks of lacquered wood, and the walls are painted bright blue and decorated in African masks. I take another tiny sip from my Mango Mozambique Martini.

"You are so hilarious, Brad!" Heather shrieks, leaning over the table giving him another peek down her dress.

He ignores her, continuing instead to bop up and down to the thumping African music. With every drumbeat, he inches closer and closer to my side of the booth, until his thigh is pressed smack against mine. "You're really hot, you know that?" he whispers, his breath reeking of booze. "Sexy smile."

I try to squeeze myself into the wall. "Er, thanks." I doubt I've smiled once all night.

Across from me, I catch Jono rolling his eyes.

"Why don't we get another round of drinks?" Heather asks.

"Good idea," Brad says. A trail of drool dribbles out of the corner of his mouth. He wipes the drool, then gives me one of his boyish smiles. He raises his hand and waves down our leopard-halter-top-clad curvy waitress.

"What can I get you?" she asks, flicking her long blond hair off her bare yet glittering shoulder.

"Another Jack-and-Coke for me and—"

"Shots for the table!" Heather suggests.

"Maybe you'll join us for a round?" Brad asks the waitress with a flirty wink.

She laughs, but shakes her head. "My boss will kill me."

"It's already one-thirty—he won't care. Come on, gorgeous, live a little."

She laughs again. I squirm. Heather glares. In addition to quasi-flirting with my roommate, my date is now full-on flirting with the waitress.

A moment later, she returns with five shot glasses. The four of them clink their drinks together.

"Come on, Gabby, you, too," Heather orders.

I pick mine up reluctantly and clink it against theirs. Then all five of us down them. Yikes, that's strong. I put mine down halfway as I feel my throat close up. I notice Heather wincing—I'm not sure if it's from the drink or from watching Brad hit on the waitress.

Ten minutes later, Jono stands up. "I need a smoke, and

to get me home." He deposits two twenties on the table and says, "Excuse me, Helen."

"It's Heather," she says with a scowl. She scoots out so Jono can get out of the booth and then scurries back to her seat.

Brad burps. "Yup. I guess it's time to go."

Heather squeezes the edge of the table in apparent panic. "You should come over. For a nightcap."

Is she insane? I kick her under the table. Heather is flirting with Brad, Brad is flirting with me (and the waitress), and I want to go home. Alone. Now Brad thinks he's being invited for a drunken roommate threesome.

"Sounds like a plan," he says, downing the rest of his drink. "Let's go to it, ladies."

Oh, yeah, he's definitely getting the wrong idea.

Tell him no, my inner voice says. *Tell him to go home.*

My mouth stays silent. I hate being the party pooper. And anyway…Heather obviously thinks she's getting lucky tonight. Maybe I can just sneak off to bed and leave them to it.

Somehow I end up paying the remainder of the bill. Annoying, yes, but not the biggest deal. Once outside, Brad pretends he's surfing on the sidewalk. Jono salutes us goodbye and starts walking downtown. I hail us a cab. I climb in first, and then Heather and then a slightly paler Brad. "You sure you don't want to go home?" I ask him. "You don't look so good."

"I'm fine," he says. "Yup. Perfecto. Picnic time!"

Heather giggles, not getting our private joke. I sigh. Loudly. When we pull up in front of the apartment, the two of them climb out, while once again I get stuck with the fair.

I try to squash the anger bubbling inside of me.

I slam the cab door and race to meet them in the elevator. All I want is for this night to end. I won't make a scene. I'll just sneak into my room.

Back at our apartment, I unlock and open the door.

"Do you want a glass of wine?" Heather asks him en route to the kitchen.

"Yes, yes, yes," he says, tossing his coat toward the coat tree but missing. He laughs and then holds on to the wall. "You know, I don't feel so good."

I take off my own coat and then unzip my boots. "What's wrong? Do you want a glass of water?"

"Dizzy," he says. And then he clenches his stomach. "I think I'm going to puke."

Oh, God. He is looking a bit green. "Toilet. Go." I point to the bathroom and watch as he scurries over and pulls the door closed.

I flop onto the couch in despair as Heather emerges with two glasses and a bottle of chardonnay.

"What did you do to him?" she asks.

At this point, I don't appreciate the hostility in her voice. "I sent him to the bathroom. He's not feeling well."

"Oh. Is he all right?"

"No, he's not. He's drunk and he should be in his own house, not in my bathroom."

Heather pours herself a glass. "Our bathroom."

Something inside me snaps. "Heather, it might be our bathroom, but he was *my* date. We invited you along, but he was there with me. Not you. If I'd wanted to invite him over, I would have invited him myself. Next time you want to hit on my date, do it on your own time." There. I said it.

"Excuse me," she huffs and storms down the hallway, into her bedroom, and slams her door.

I spend the next few minutes with my arms crossed, staring at the peeling paint on the ceiling.

I hate that I hurt her feelings. But it had to be done. I have to learn how to put my foot down.

A little bit later, Heather's door creeps open. "He's been in there a long time."

"Yes, he has."

"I hope he's conscious."

I glance at the clock. It's been sixteen minutes. It is two in the morning and a guy I didn't want at my place to begin with has moved into my bathroom. I push myself off the couch and knock softly on the bathroom door. "Everything all right in there?"

Silence.

"Hello?" I hope I'm not going to have to call an ambulance.

"Yup. I'll be out soon," he answers.

"Do you want some water?" I ask.

"Sure."

I head to the kitchen, fill a glass with tap water and hurry it back to him. When he opens the door a crack to grab the drink, I spot him kneeling on the bath mat, hunched over the open toilet seat.

Heather follows me back to the couch. "I'm sorry," she says. "I shouldn't have usurped your date."

I wrap myself in the knit throw blanket and look at her. She seems genuinely apologetic. "It's all right."

Heather kicks her heels up onto the coffee table. "Wanna watch a movie while your date throws up in our bathroom?"

Sure, *now* he's my date. "No, thank you. As soon as he's

done, I'm going to bed." And forgetting this entire evening ever happened.

Suddenly sounds of heaving echo through the apartment. Heather flicks on the TV. I close my eyes.

Twenty-two minutes later, I'm awoken by the flushing toilet. The door opens and out comes Brad, face extra splotchy. "Um, you have a flood in there."

"Sorry?" I squeak.

"A flood. In the bathroom. The toilet overflowed. Do you have a plunger?"

I'm going to cry. I turn to Heather. "Do I have a plunger?"

"No, but Fred has one."

"Who's Fred?"

"The super."

"Can you get it?" Brad asks.

"It's the middle of the night," I say. I can't ring the doorbell of a super I've never met in the middle of the night.

Heather jumps off the couch and smiles sweetly at us both. "I'll run over to the Duane Reade and pick one up."

"Thank you," I say with relief, and then turn to Brad. "Are you okay?" I creep over to the bathroom to check out the damage.

"I wouldn't go in if I were you," he says, retreating to the living room.

Despite the warning, I peek inside and find the entire floor flooded. I try to stop the nausea from overflowing and ruining my new shirt. The smell is…indescribable. No one should ever have to smell what I am currently smelling. My gag reflex kicks in, as if something were just rammed down my throat. I step away from the door and try not to breathe. Tears spring to my eyes.

Now I know why Heather left. She wanted to get as far away from this debacle as possible. I figure Brad must be watching for my reaction, so I attempt to compose myself. He must be horrifically embarrassed. I should try not to make this worse for him. Surely, now he's going to go home, tail nestled between his legs. I order myself to wipe the disgust off my face and return down the hallway to the living room. "How are you feeling?"

I find him sprawled on his belly across the couch. "Much better, now," he says. Then he reaches over to the coffee table, picks up Heather's wine and finishes it.

I don't believe it. "Don't you think you've had enough?"

He sits up and then pats the spot next to him. "Why don't you come get comfortable."

Oh God, he thinks we're making out now? He hasn't even brushed his teeth. *Be nice.* "I'm all right, thanks. Can I get you something? More water? Pepto?"

He smiles. "How about that picnic?"

"Um, not tonight."

He shrugs. "Wanna go to bed then?"

Finally, he gets it! "Yes, that is what I'd like to do."

He rubs his hands together. "Cool. Is Heather going to join us?"

Or not. I try to keep my voice composed. "Actually, you're going to bed in your own apartment."

"But I'd rather stay here," he whines and then, to my horror, unbuckles his belt.

"What…are you doing?" Now I'm going to be sick.

Out come the boyish dimples. "Getting naked."

Stay calm. Stay calm. "Yet another thing you can do in your *own apartment!*"

He gives me the same exaggerated wink he used on the

waitress and pulls down his pants, exposing checkered green-and-brown boxers and freckled knees. "I don't want to get naked alone."

That's it. I've had enough. I storm over to the door and fling it open. "It's time for you to leave."

"Why? Aren't we going to have sex?"

"No. We are *not* going to have sex."

"Ever?"

"We are never going to have sex!"

"Maybe Heather wants to have sex? She's looking kind of cute."

I pick his coat off the floor and throw it at him. "Get out."

He steps outside, jeans still rumpled around his ankles, and tries to win me over with a big grin. "Are we going out again next week?"

"I don't think so," I say and firmly close the door.

I am never going on a date again. I'm so relieved he's gone, I'm almost laughing. I mean, come on. My first date as a single girl and this is what happens? As my laughter turns to shudders, I buzz Charlie downstairs. "Will you do me a favor? I just sent a guy to the lobby. Can you put him in a cab, and tell the cab driver to make sure he gets to the Bolton Hotel?"

"No problem."

"Thanks."

The night finally over, I retreat to my room and change into sweats and a T-shirt.

A few minutes later, I hear Heather's return to the apartment and meet her in the living room.

"I got it," she says, plunger in hand. She looks around the deserted room and frowns. "Where did he go?"

"Home. At last."

"What?" she shrieks. "Why?"

"Because he was drunk and gross." To be honest, I'm feeling pretty proud of myself. I wanted him out and I kicked him out.

"But…but…you had no right to do that! He was finally warming up to me!"

"You've got to be kidding. Anyway, he was my date, and I wanted him out."

She narrows her eyes and then hurls the plunger at me. Apparently apologetic Heather is long gone. "Since he was your date, you can do the cleaning."

Shit. I forgot about the state of the bathroom. I put on flip-flops, strip down to my underwear and a ratty tank top and wish I had a nose plug. I plunge (ew) and plunge (ew) and plunge some more until our toilet is back in working order. Unfortunately, I now need a mop. I step back into the living room. "Do we have a mop?"

"No," she says.

I'm hoping she'll offer to return to Duane Reade, but she doesn't. Instead she says, "Use paper towels. And open the window. It stinks in here."

"I don't think it'll work," I say, my voice cracking. "It's too wet." Trying not to cry, I open the window, and then pull out one of my new towels from the closet and get back to work.

"Are you almost done?" Heather asks peeking inside. "I have to pee."

That's it. I've had enough. "You could help me, you know. You were the one that invited him over."

"But he was your date," she mimics.

"Don't give me that. I would have ended the date hours ago."

"Your date, your problem." Then she shrugs. "But I'll assist."

"Fine." Better than nothing.

When I'm done with the towels, Heather holds open a garbage bag as I cram them inside. After tossing the bag into the garbage shoot outside, she returns with the Comet and liberally tosses it over the tiles, toilet, shower, door handle....

Then we scrub and scrub and scrub some more until our new manicures are long gone. And then she showers. And then I shower. By four-thirty, I'm starting to get concerned that if I don't get to sleep soon, I might get stuck in this New York life. Exhausted, and finally on my way back to bed, I smash my knee against my new dresser. Ow. Ow, ow, ow!

This room is so goddamn small. What was I thinking getting a queen-size mattress for this little tiny-ass room? I can barely fit in here.

Ah. That is why I have all those bruises. It's from this crowded city. The room, the apartment, the streets...everything is so damn crowded. I bet I don't have any bruises in Arizona. I bet New Yorkers statistically have more bruises than anyone else.

Emotionally and physically bruised, I get under my covers and pick up the phone. I need to call Cam. I dial his number, but I hang up before it even rings.

I can't call him. It's not right. I broke his heart. I have to let go. No more phone calls. No more jokes. No more Cam. Not in New York, anyway.

"You missed a spot!" Heather hollers from the bathroom.

"Just clean it!" I scream and then cover my head with the pillow.

"I love you." I murmur into Cam's ear in the morning. I cradle my forehead into his neck.

He pulls me in closer.

10

The Search Is On

In Arizona, I spend my days looking for a place to hold my wedding that doesn't involve a tent or pool covering. I spend my evenings ordering take-out Chinese or pepperoni-and-pineapple pizza (Cam's favorite). I spend my nights cuddling with my fiancé.

In New York, I spend my days working, my evenings picking up sushi and my nights cuddling with my Black-Berry. It buzzes at least every twelve minutes. *Disease. Death. Is starlet too skinny? How skinny is too skinny?*

I wipe the bad date with Brad clean from my mind. It's not as if I have time for dating, anyway. I'm always working. I'm in the office by 8:00 a.m., out by 9:00 p.m.. When I'm not at the station, I'm in the apartment watching the news.

I order everything I need online, so I never have to venture too far from a television screen.

This obsession seems to be working. Except when I ask my Pilates instructor if she minds turning on the news in her studio while I work out, and she suggests that Pilates might not be the right exercise for me. So I join the gym, where I can plug my headphones into the StairMaster and watch CNN.

But the most important news happens on December eighth in Arizona. This is when we book the location for our wedding.

Tricia shows us around the Sunset Hotel. It's hotel Number Twelve. It's not as nice as the last eleven, but Alice seems to be a little less nasty about it, since one of her friend's kids got married here. Personally, I liked number eight, where the terrace overlooked the Camelback Mountains, but Alice didn't like the look of the manager.

This hotel can host the ceremony outside, on the lawn. The ballroom, where we would have the reception, features a stage, a large circular wooden dance floor and a nice crystal chandelier. It's pretty, the price is right, and Alice doesn't hate it. Sold.

"Not as nice as my backyard. But it'll do," Alice says, eyeing the chandeliers suspiciously, as if they could fall and squash her like a bug at any moment.

I'd better be careful what I wish for. In my universe, wishes come true.

"Do we have a winner?" Tricia asks, clearly exhausted. Whatever my mom is paying her, it should have been more.

"It's fine," I say. Not my dream location, but I don't care anymore. "Done."

Alice hesitates. "I'm not a hundred percent sold…."

"Yes," I say. "You are." I can feel a showdown coming, but this time I'm not backing down.

We face each other and stare into each other's eyes. Her eyes look like Cam's but older. And colder. I'm not blinking. This is it. It's my wedding and I'm not giving in.

She's staring, staring, staring…and she blinks. Ha! She looks away and shrugs. "If you want to get married here, get married here."

"Good. I want Cam to see it, and if he likes it, it's settled. Let me call him and see if he can sneak away."

Cam is fine with it. The four of us are sitting in the hotel lobby waiting for the manager to bring us the papers to sign.

"I'm so happy you finally picked a place you like, dear," Alice says, patting me on the knee. She makes it sound as if I were the problem. As if I were the one holding us back. Maybe I was. Maybe I should have put my foot down after hotel Number Two.

Cam winks at me. "Good find, Gabby."

"It's a very popular hotel to get married at," Tricia assures us. "Everything's coming together. Next biggies are the band, the photographer, the invitations. And, of course, the color scheme."

"I know what color you should choose," Alice says.

"And what color is that?" I ask. Wonder what she's going to say. Could it be orange. I think it might be orange? Is it orange?

"Rust," she says, tugging on her sweater sleeve. "Like this."

Looks orange to me. "Maybe."

"You shouldn't take too long to decide," Alice continues. "The bridesmaids have to order their dresses. And we need to get matching ties for the ushers."

"There is no way," Cam says, "my ushers are wearing orange ties."

"Not orange," Alice corrects him. "Rust."

I stop myself from laughing. "We don't have to order the bridesmaid outfits just yet. I haven't even started looking for a wedding dress."

Alice shrugs. "Whatever you think is best, Gabrielle. But Blair's dress took nine months to come in. Wedding dresses have to be ordered in advance. You need to go for multiple fittings. Tell her, Tricia."

Tricia nods. "It helps. You don't want your time line to influence your choice."

I'd have nine months to find my dress if Alice hadn't insisted I get married in May. "Okay, I'll go soon."

"Blair and I had a ball shopping for gowns. The three of us should look for yours."

"Maybe." Please, God, no.

"Perhaps Lila can join us, too." Alice coughs. "Cam tells me she's your maid of honor."

"Yes," I say, keeping my voice strong. "We've been friends for a long time."

"Yes, friends. Not family though. You'll learn as you get older that friends can't always be trusted. Not like family. Not like my Blair."

Oy. "Blair is still going to be a bridesmaid," I explain.

"You know," Alice says while pointing a finger in the air, "many brides have a maid of honor and a *matron* of honor."

Is she kidding me? I've never heard of that. "I think it's one or the other."

"Nope, my friend Rose's daughter had both. Maid of

honor and matron of honor. I even asked Tricia about it, and she agreed."

"It does happen," Tricia admits with a guilty smile. Traitor.

"I would think you'd want to honor two people if you could. It would really mean a lot to Blair if you made her the matron of honor. She was hurt that you chose a friend instead if her."

I don't answer.

"It would make Cam very happy," she presses on.

My fiancé turns a nice shade of pink. "Mom—"

"I'm sure you'd like your sister to be the matron of honor," she insists. "Since her husband is the best man."

I feel myself caving in. I scored a point on the hotel; why not give in on this? It doesn't hurt anyone…. "All right, Alice, I'll ask Blair to be my other maid of honor."

"Matron of honor. *Matron*."

"Whatever. Matron."

She claps her hands together like a little kid. "Oh, I have something for you." She reaches into her purse, pulls out a folded piece of paper and shoves it into my hand.

"What's this?"

"Cam's favorite recipe. It's for coconut shrimp."

"Oh. Thanks."

"Cam mentioned that you guys have been ordering a lot of takeout lately."

I shoot Cam an accusatory look.

"So I thought that you might want to cook a little something for him. It's much cheaper to make dinner than to order in. Of course, it's not an easy recipe, but you don't need to be Albert Einstein to cook, dear. I'm sure you'll get the hang of it eventually."

"Thanks," I mumble, stuffing the recipe into my pocket. Leave it alone, I warn myself. Just leave it alone. Besides, I've always liked coconut shrimp. Then I remember the shrimp I ordered from FreshDirect. The fresh shrimp that's surely bad by now. Too bad I can't e-mail the recipe to myself in New York. That way I could practice on Heather first. But I know what I *can* do. I can memorize it. My brain, it seems, is the only part of my body that can transcend time and space. So there, Mr. Einstein!

That Sunday, Cam wakes me up to say that he wants us to spend the day looking for houses.

"Can't it wait until after the wedding?" I mutter, still half-asleep.

He's sprawled across his side of the bed on his stomach, sifting through the classifieds. "I would rather buy something now. So we could move in the day after we're married."

I tickle his side. "You're going to carry me over the threshold?"

"What about this place?" he asks, tapping a listing with his pen.

"Where is it?"

"Chandler."

"As long it's not Mesa."

"Hmm?" he asks, still tapping, but on another listing.

"I said, as long as it's not in Mesa."

He stops tapping to look up. "What's wrong with Mesa?"

"It's probably not too healthy to live next door to your parents."

He laughs. "I'm not going to rule out a property just because it's in Mesa. There are some great deals there."

"Let's just try."

"I am. This place is in Chandler. I'm going to shower and then we'll check out the open house."

"Cam, I'm really busy this month. You know. With wedding stuff. I need to find a dress, a band, a photographer—"

He does some sort of dance move with his hands. "Can I help find the band?"

"Really?"

"Yeah. That would be cool. What would I have to do?"

"Just listen to them. Then choose. And hope they're not booked."

He takes off his T-shirt and boxers and tosses them at the laundry basket. Score. "Yeah, I'm in."

Not only is my fiancé a great shot, he's a sexy great shot. "Why don't you come back to bed?" I try out my best femme-fatale voice.

He wags his finger at me. "Houses. Real estate. Agents. Then dinner at my parents."

Boring.

We don't like the house in Chandler. It's small and grungy.

"The bathtub is New York–sized," I complain.

"When have you ever taken a bath in New York?"

"It's an expression," I say, ducking back into the doll-sized master bedroom.

Oops.

A few days later, we see a house in Tempe. It's on the first floor of a condo. It has two bedrooms and a gorgeous dining room and a shared pool.

"Nice," Cam says, eyeing the wood-burning fireplace.

Smash.

The noise is coming from upstairs.

Clunk. Boom.

"They have six kids," the broker tells us. "Adorable, all of them."

"Loud," says Cam.

"Sweet," says the broker.

"No thanks," say I.

That Sunday, we fall in love with a house in Scottsdale. Unfortunately the price doesn't fall in love with us.

On Monday I begin my search for a wedding dress. Cam's at work, and I tidy up and then hit the road. I know Alice would have been overjoyed to come with me, and as much as I would have liked her to come along (the way I enjoyed getting my lip waxed), I fear that such an event would be detrimental to the state of my engagement, as surely, I would end up killing her. So I ask Lila instead, who graciously agrees to meet me at the boutique, after my many telephone calls and e-mails begging her to accompany me.

"I can't just take two hours off work," she complained. "I'm behind on my billing. Can we do it after six?"

"Snow White closes at four."

"What is it with these places? Most brides-to-be work. How else can they afford these weddings? Bridal boutiques are worse than banks."

"Please?"

After enough begging, I can usually convince Lila to do things my way. She's dependable that way. She sighed loudly and agreed to come during lunch.

I park on Scottsdale Road and see Lila locking her car.

"Hey stranger," she says, kissing my cheek. "How's the lucky bride?"

"Fine. Excited. Nervous."

"You know," Lila says, "we should have turned this into a girls' trip and gone for the weekend to New York. That would have been fun."

I wonder what would happen if I went to New York in this split. Could I run into my other self? "Too tough. I'd have to go back for fittings."

The heat in the boutique is on full blast. Which is crazy. It's almost seventy degrees outside. "Excellent, there's nothing like trying on dresses all sweaty," I say.

"Hello, hello, you must be Gabrielle," says a white-haired, frail-looking woman in a heavy woolen sweater. "Congratulations!" She looks at Lila. "And you're the sister?"

Lila giggles. "Friend. Maid of honor."

I'm going to have to mention at some point that she's sharing said honor.

"We're pleased to have you here on this joyous occasion. I'm Aurora, and I'm here to help."

Aurora? You've got to be kidding. At least that explains the boutique's name, Snow White. It does not, however, explain the heat wave in here. Maybe the owner has a thyroid problem. My mom has one, and she always thinks it's cold out. I think that's why she insisted on moving to Arizona in the first place. That and because she couldn't stand my dad. Anyway, I swear, we're standing in a sauna. A circular, mirrored sauna. Off to the side, I see rows and rows of dresses and, on the other side, I see two massive pink cushioned changing rooms.

"Let's get started," Aurora says, making a smacking sound with her lips. "Now tell me. What are you looking for?"

I don't have a clue. "A white dress?"

"Right. Yes. Well. Do you want something traditional? Princessy? Modern? Sophisticated?"

"Yes," I say, turning to Lila. "What do you think?"

"Close your eyes," Lila says.

Weird. But okay. I do as I'm told.

"Now, imagine this. You're at the Oscars. The announcer says—"

"Who's the announcer?"

"Denzel Washington."

"Oh, I like him. What a great smile."

"Good. But shut up and listen."

"Sorry."

"Denzel lists the nominations. Julia Roberts. Judi Dench. Gabby Wolf."

"Wahoo!"

"And the winner is…"

I cross my fingers and wave them in the air. "Is it me? Is it me? Please let it be me!"

"Gabby Wolf!" Lila shrieks.

"I don't believe it!"

"Keep your eyes closed, Gabby, or this won't work. All right, you kiss Cam, squeeze his hand and float to the stage."

"I want to thank all the little people!"

"Yes, but here's the question. What are you wearing?"

"I'm wearing the dress Julia Roberts wore when she got her best-actress award. The black-and-white Valentino gown." I'm lean and tall in my imaginary world.

"Oh, good choice. So you like vintage dresses."

Do I? "No, wait. I just remembered that I like the dress Angelina Jolie wore. Remember the halter cream satin? Gorgeous."

"So you like slinky and modern."

I open my eyes. "Yes, definitely. Although I think I'll pass on the accompanying dragon tattoo. Wait! I just remembered another dress I loved. Remember the one Halle Berry wore when she won? The red full skirt and the embroidered flowered top."

"Something princessy then. A showstopper."

"Exactly. Except—"

Aurora clears her throat. "Why don't you girls look at some dresses and show me what you like."

We start walking around, pulling out gowns. One with a puffy skirt. One with beading. One that's straight. "I like them all," I say.

Lila shakes her head. "But you can only have one."

Not if I meet someone in New York I want to marry. Then I get to have two.

I finger a pretty puffy one. "How much is this?" I ask Aurora. I got my dad's first check yesterday. And it's going straight to my dress.

"This one is Vera Wang."

"How much is Vera Wang?"

Aurora looks at her clipboard. "Nine thousand eight hundred."

Lila whistles. I start laughing. "Are you kidding?"

"It's Vera Wang," she huffs.

"Pricey. I'm looking more for dresses in the three-thousand-and-under range."

"Let me see what I can find in a size ten," Aurora says.

"I'm not a size ten," I say quickly.

"Wedding dress sizes are different than regular sizes," she says, ushering me into the massive dressing room. "Now get down to your bra and panties, and put on your heels while I find you dresses."

Lila sits down on a cushioned bench. I strip then step into the shoes I was told to bring when I made the appointment. I can't help but stare at my pale flab in the mirror. I might be a size ten here, but I'm a six in New York. Except for the lack of bruises here, I look much better in New York. This is not good at all. I turn around and check out my butt. I think I'm going to need one of those big puffy dresses.

Aurora enters with one draped over her arm. She unzips it and says, "Now step in carefully."

I try not to topple over as I slip into the dress. Since it's strapless, she pulls it over my bust line, heaves it closed, then pins it so it fits snuggly.

Man, this baby is heavy.

"What do you think?" she asks me, trying to read my expression in the mirror.

White. Lots of white. Pretty.

"Gabby," says Lila. "Do you like it?"

Pretty. White.

"Maybe it's too tight," Lila says, looking worried. "Hello? Anyone home?"

I snap out of it and smile. "I'm not used to seeing myself in a wedding dress. I'm overwhelmed." It's ivory with a tight bodice and a princess puffy skirt. Rows of small crystal beads run along the top and on the low waist.

"You look beautiful," Lila says.

I feel choked up. "Thanks."

Lila reaches into her purse and takes out her camera. "Smile. You can send it to your mom."

Aurora blocks the camera with a karate chop-like

move. "No photos. We have a sign at the front. Absolutely no pictures."

"It's for her mother!" Lila says, annoyed.

"Her mother should have come then," Aurora says, shaking her head. Yes, my mother should have come. I didn't even think of inviting her. Maybe I would have if she hadn't pretty much wiped her hands of the whole wedding.

"It's okay," I say. "Let's focus on the dress. What do you think?"

Lila puts her hand on my bare shoulder. "I love it."

"Yeah? I like it a lot, too. But let me try on some others."

Aurora undoes me, and then I step into dress Number Two. And then Three. And then Four. Number Two has capped sleeves, Three is tight and hugs my curves and Four is straight and covered in taffeta. And I like them all (except for Three, which makes me look like a bloated mermaid).

"Which do you like best?" I ask my audience.

"The first one. Definitely," says Lila.

"What do you think?" I ask Aurora.

"I prefer the last one."

"Yeah?" I look them over again. "How do I know which one I like the most?"

"I think you just know," Lila says. "It's like finding a husband. As soon as you meet the man you're supposed to marry, you know. As soon as you try on your dress, you know."

"That is so dumb," I say. "I didn't know the moment I met Cam. Hey, can I ask Cam for his opinion?"

"You can't show Cam your dress!" Lila shrieks.

Aurora shakes her head. "Absolutely not."

"Why not?"

"It's bad luck," Aurora says.

"Says who? Anyway, I'm buying the dress for him, right?"

"No," Lila says. "You're buying it for you."

"No, I'm buying it so when he sees me in it, he gasps. I want him to think I'm the most beautiful woman in the world in the dress."

Aurora starts unsnapping my back. "He will."

I need another opinion. If I can't ask Cam, it has to be someone who has good taste in clothes. Someone like Heather.

"How was your day?" Cam asks. I hear honking in the background. "Hold on, I'm just switching lanes."

I'm exhausted after an afternoon of dress shopping and so I'm back at the apartment, back in my pajamas, watching the news. It's too time-consuming watching it all in New York, so in my downtime, I catch up here. Whether I watch it in New York or Arizona, it's the same news, right? I think of it like instant replay. "I went wedding dress shopping," I tell him.

"Did you find anything?"

"No. There are too many choices. What kind do you think—"

"Hon, I heard of a great property today in the Valley."

"You mean to buy?"

"Of course, to buy. It's a steal. Two years old. Four bedrooms. Pool. Three bathrooms. I think we have to take a look. There's an open house from five till seven."

"Why do we need four bedrooms?"

"We don't need four bedrooms this second. It's for the future. For when we have little Gabbys running around."

"Very funny."

"I want a house full of Gabbys. Adorable little girls with your big smile."

Aw. "Aren't we going to have any boys? Don't I get any little Cams?"

"I'd think you'd be sick of one of me by now."

"Never." I hope not, anyway.

"So what do you think? Should we take a look? It's a great deal."

"All right."

"Good. I'll pick you up in five."

"Now? But I'm watching the news!"

He laughs. "Honey, you're not working, remember? There'll be plenty of time later for the news. Right now your top priority should be our house." *Honk!* "Gotta go. See you soon. Love you."

Before getting dressed, I stretch out my back. Trying on all those dresses took its toll. Those things are heavy. Who needs the Pilates? Maybe the gym should add a new class— wedding dress try-on.

I quickly change into clothes and meet Cam outside. "I'd like some more information about this house," I say as I fasten my seat belt.

He kisses me on the forehead and we drive off. "What do you want to know?"

"How much they're asking, for one thing."

"Three-fifty."

I start coughing.

"We don't need much for a down payment. We'll take out one of those pay-only-the-interest mortgages. It would be nice to start our marriage with a new house that we own together."

I did a story on those mortgages and I'm not sure

they're so smart. "Those mortgages are too risky, and we'd be using our entire savings. And how would we furnish this so-called house?"

"That's what wedding registries are for. Which we have to do. Soon. My mom keeps asking me about that."

"I don't know if I'm ready for this." Buying something here means we're never leaving. I'm not sure if I'm ready to put down roots in Arizona forever.

I catch him looking at me sideways. "We can always sell, Gabby. Look, let's just see what the place looks like. We don't have to make any decisions today. Unless there's another buyer," he adds.

"Where is this place, anyway?"

"Mesa."

Groan.

When we finally reach the property (only four blocks from his parents, whoopee!), I'm already miserable.

I heave lots of sighs and make lots of unflattering I'm-annoyed faces as Cam signs us in, introduces us to the broker, holds my hand and pulls me from room to room. The worst part is, the house is beautiful. Hardwood floors, high ceilings, two floors. The kitchen has all new appliances. The master bathroom has a Jacuzzi. I can already feel the jets on my back. Ah. That's the spot. Oh, yeah.

"What do you think?" Cam asks.

"It's nice."

"It's a steal," he says. "Apparently the owners are divorcing and trying to get rid of the property fast. That's the only reason they're willing to sell. I think we should make an offer now."

"Today?"

"I want to go home and check the numbers, but yes, let's

do it. Let's make the offer." He takes my hands between his and squeezes them together. "Let's buy you a home."

The thing is, when I used to dream about a home, I used to imagine myself coming home after a long day at work at my fabulous job. "I don't know," I say, my voice shaking.

"Gabby, this is us building a life together." His cheeks flush and his globe eyes dart around the room. "You and me," he continues. "I can already see you lazing by the pool, while I barbecue lunch. The kids will be kicking around a soccer ball back and forth, and the dog will be barking and chasing them. At night we'll relax in the Jacuzzi and then drink wine by the fire…." Instead of continuing, he pulls me into him.

I feel my body melt as I breathe in his soapy scent.

"Don't you see it? I love you so much," he whispers. "And we can have it all. The whole dream."

"I love you, too," I say softly. We can have it all. And in my other split, I can have whatever *else* I want. Like the fabulous job.

"All right," I say. "Let's buy it."

They're Fake and They're Spectacular

"Heather, what are you doing Friday night?" I'm standing in my New York living room, brushing my teeth. Talk about multitasking. I'm simultaneously watching the news, getting ready for work and solving my wedding-dress crisis.

"Going home for Christmas Eve."

Oh, right. "Does that mean you don't want to come shopping with me?"

Her eyes light up. "What do you need?"

"A wedding dress," I mumble through a foamy mouth, and then return to the sink to spit and rinse.

She follows me into the bathroom. "Excuse me?"

One more rinse and then I do my best to quasi-explain, "Not to buy, just to try on."

"You want me to come with you to try on wedding dresses?"

"Yup."

She eyes me suspiciously in the mirror. "Why?"

"Because I've always wanted to."

"For no reason?"

"Not for no reason. For fun." She is just crazy enough to believe me.

She still looks doubtful. "I don't buy it."

I rack my brain for an appropriate excuse. "I, um, read an article that says trying on wedding dresses helps you get over ex-boyfriends."

"That doesn't sound healthy."

"No, it is. Very therapeutic. They say finding a dress is like finding the perfect man. You know as soon as you try it on. The article was written for women who doubt their judgment in men and recommends that you try on dresses so that you know what discovering the real thing feels like." And if you buy this, I have a piece of oceanfront property to sell you—in Arizona. "It's a new psychotherapy called The One. Very popular in California." She's not going believe it. There's no way. It makes no sense. "I'm surprised you've never heard of it," I add for effect.

"Oh, I have," she says in a rush. "Of course I have. Actually, I was going to suggest it to you, but I heard it's traumatic. I'm not sure if you can take it."

Hook, line and sinker. "So you'll join me?"

"Yes. If you're sure you can handle it, make the appointment and I'll come along. But there's one condition."

"What?"

"You come with me to my parents the next day for Christmas Eve dinner."

I'm Jewish and I get to celebrate two Christmases. Normal? "As long as I don't have to stay over."

"You won't. We'll take the train in and then come back that night."

"Your family doesn't mind that you're not spending the whole holiday with them?"

"Who said I'm not? I'm leaving on Tuesday for a week in Bermuda with my parents. But I have to be here on Monday. Want to know why?"

"Why?"

"Because I finally asked Mark out! And he said yes!"

"Who's Mark?"

She shakes her head. "Don't you listen to me when I talk? He's the library guy."

"Wow, good work. Where are you going?"

"Dinner. Fuck, I'm nervous."

I'd be, too, if I were her. She tends to scare men off. "Just relax, and I'm sure it'll be fine."

"I can't relax." She gestures to her bookshelf of self-help books. "I've done a lot of reading on this. And the first date can set the terms for your entire relationship."

"What does that mean?"

"Like, if the girl asks out the guy, you'll always be the one chasing him. Or if you offer to cook him a home meal, then he'll always expect you to cook. You have to be extra careful."

"People evolve, Heather. Relationships evolve." As I'm talking, I think back to my first date with Cam. It was a Thursday night, halfway through my senior year. Lila and I had been practically out the door when he'd called and asked me if I wanted to get a drink.

"I can't," I'd told him. "My roommate and I are going to the movies."

"Go," Lila had mouthed. "Honestly. I'll catch up on my reading." And I had. Had that set the tone?

"I'm just telling you what I read," Heather says, interrupting my trip down role-cast lane. "So are you going to come to dinner?"

I'm still disturbed, but I try to shake it off. "Oh, yeah. Fine. But I have a condition of my own."

"What?"

"I like you, Heather. I think we're getting along. But sometimes you scare me."

"What do you mean?"

"Like the whole Brad episode. I'm sorry he liked me instead of you. Really, I am. But if you didn't want me to go out with him, you shouldn't have thrown him at me. End of story. We're friends. And if we're going to stay friends, you have to be up-front with me. Okay?"

"Okay," she says, with a sheepish smile. "I'm sorry. It's just that I've had such bad experiences with roommates, and now I tend to keep my guard up. But yes. Friends. And as a friend, I should tell you that you just dribbled toothpaste down your shirt."

Shit. Indeed, there is a glob of white paste on my left boob. "Now what am I going to wear with these pants?"

"As your friend, I'm happy to lend you a shirt."

Friendship does have its perks. Especially friendship with a fashion queen.

On Wednesday in Arizona, Cam and I visit the house again, this time to take all kinds of measurements. This time we also bring—you guessed it—Alice.

She, of course, bounces off the walls in excitement. I'd do the same if I were her. Her son is going to be living only a few blocks away. "You kids will be very happy here," she tells us. She pats the walls of one of the empty bedrooms. "What a wonderful nursery!" Then she studies the kitchen. "All state-of-the-art appliances. Gabrielle, you can make some wonderful meals here. Cammy, has she made you my coconut shrimp yet?"

"I haven't had a chance," I mutter.

"Yum, I love that shrimp," Cam says, and then opens the sliding doors to the yard.

Then move back home with your mother, I almost shout. I follow him outside, feeling an overwhelming need to push him into the pool. And not in a fun, let's-play way, but in a jackass-why-don't-you-drown type of way. Wow. This is so no way to think about your soon-to-be husband. What is wrong with me? Of course, I know the answer to that. What is wrong with me is his mother.

I try to block out the uneasiness in my stomach and the agitation in my brain. The agitation is further aggravated by Alice's running commentary. "Lots of wall space to cover!" she's now pointing out. "You'll need to get a strong vacuum for these carpets! And what a terrific washer and drier! Gabrielle, you can do load after load!"

Am I ready for this? For a house? State-of-the-art appliances? A husband whose Siamese twin is his mother?

I buy the shrimp the next day. Now that I have it, I'm not sure what to do with it. I never did get around to practicing in New York. First of all, the shrimp had already gone bad. Secondly, with my lifestyle, who has time to cook?

He wants the shrimp, I'll make him the shrimp. It's not

as if I have anything else to do with my time here in Arizona. Except pack up the apartment and plan a wedding. And buy Christmas presents. This year, I was put in charge of buying his family's gifts.

"I'm really busy with an insurance-company bankruptcy at work, plus I'm getting our financials together for the house," Cam explained. "And you don't have a job. So it would be great if you can take care of them."

"I don't mind. What should I get them?" Why did I tell him I don't mind? Believe me, I mind.

"I'm sure you'll think of something," he said, making me want to flick him on the forehead.

I blamed my violent tendency on his remark about my unemployment. Sure, it's true I'm not working, but did he have to rub it in? I'm a little touchy about the subject. I called up my former boss Bernie this morning asking if he had any freelance projects that I could tackle. "Please," I begged. "Anything. I'm becoming a desperate housewife and I'm not even married yet."

But no. Nothing. Except work on Christmas and New Year's, which I obviously couldn't do without Cam and Alice and the whole family going berserk. We're expected at Alice's for Christmas Eve and Christmas Day, and we're going to a party with Cam's friends for New Year's.

In an effort to feel useful, I went to the grocery store. And bought shrimp. Even though it pained me to do so, after tossing five whole pounds of it into the garbage in New York. Next time I do a FreshDirect order, I'm freezing.

"Dinner in an hour," I now tell Cam via the phone. "I'm cooking. Or trying to." I cradle the cordless between my shoulder and ear. Before I get my hands all shrimpy, where did I put that guacamole? Oh, there it is. Yum. I'm so hungry in this life. Must be from all that not-working-out.

"Very exciting, baby. I'm sure it will be delicious. Did you put together your account statements for me? I need them for the broker."

"Yes, everything's waiting for you. You know, I didn't realize how gross shrimp are. Did you know they were gray?"

"Yes, I did, hon. I've made this dish before."

"Really? So why did your mother give me the recipe? You could have given it to me yourself." Maybe because Cam asked her? Maybe he wants me to cook for him all the time, but doesn't want to tell me himself in fear of sounding chauvinistic?

"I was planning to make it for you myself, but I lost the recipe and you know me. Can't even boil water without a recipe. And nothing I found on the Internet even remotely resembles my mother's shrimp."

Somehow that sounds a little icky. But still. How sweet is Cam? He was planning to make the shrimp by himself. For me.

He was planning to make *his* favorite dish for me.

"Oh, and hon?" he says. "Don't forget to devein the shrimp. That much I remember."

"I don't have to worry about that. I got them deshelled."

"You still have to take out the vein. Look at the back of the shrimp. There's a blue line. You have to take that out before you cook it. Things you should know."

"That's crazy! Why would they go through all the trouble of de-shelling them and then leave in the vein? It's going to take forever. There are at least fifty shrimp!"

"So forget about the shrimp. We'll have something else."

Cooking is so annoying. But I am no quitter. "It's fine," I say. "I have plenty of time. When will you be home?"

"I'm leaving the office now, so I should be home in twenty."

It's amazing how fast twenty minutes go by when you're in the process of deveining. By the time Cam walks into the kitchen, I've only just started to cook them. But shouldn't I hear some kind of sizzling sound? Oops. Helps if I turn the stove on.

"Something smells delicious," Cam says a few minutes later. He's looking quite handsome in his pressed white shirt and brown pants that I picked up the other day from dry cleaner.

"It's either me or my cooking."

"How did the deveining go?"

"Took forever."

He peers at my platter. "That's because you got small shrimp."

"Huh?"

"You should have bought the jumbo guys. More things you should know. No wonder it took you so long."

"The recipe says shrimp," I grumble. "It does not say anything about jumbo shrimp."

"I'm sure it'll be good." He opens the fridge and pulls out a soda. "Did you get me any more Cherry Coke?"

"Was I supposed to?"

"No. I thought maybe you'd notice we were running low."

"Really?"

"Has anyone ever told you that you speak in questions?"

"Excuse me?"

He finishes off the soda and tosses the empty can in the recycling bin. "You answer my questions with questions."

"Do I?"

He laughs. "You just did it."

"So what?"

"You did it again."

I am this close to throwing one of the miniscule shrimp at his head. "If my manner of speaking bothers you, I'll stop asking questions. I will begin by not asking you how your day was." I contemplate rubbing my shrimp-smelling hands on his clean white shirt.

"I'm just trying to tell you, you should be more assertive. Don't kill the messenger."

"I might if you don't stop nagging me."

He looks genuinely surprised. "I'm not nagging you."

"Ha!"

"Do I nag?"

"Yeah, lately you do. A lot." He's not only nagging. Ever since I agreed to marry him, he's gotten so patronizing.

He leans against the counter and grimaces. "I don't mean to."

"Well you do. You're starting to sound more and more like—"

He puts his hand against his chest. "Don't say it!"

"—your mother."

He tilts back his head and howls, "Noooooooooooooooooo!"

I can't help but laugh. "Oh, yes."

He shakes his head. "I'm sorry. I don't mean it. Do you think it's hereditary?"

"I'm hoping it's nurture versus nature. Nurture that can be unlearned. Why don't you try thinking before you talk?'"

"See, you worded that as a question. You should have just said, 'Think before you talk.'"

I roll my eyes.

He gives me a big fat kiss on the lips.

On Friday morning in New York, Curtis sits on the side of my desk, swinging her loafers.

I look up from my programming. It's only 11:00 a.m. and I'm already on my third cup of coffee. Who needs food when there's a Starbucks in the basement? Anyway, I'm pretty sure that the FDA made mocha lattes one of the food groups in their last nourishment pyramid. "What can I do for you?"

"I saw that you volunteered to help out around here on Christmas Day and New Year's Eve," she says, eyeing me with suspicion.

"Yes. I'm not going anywhere and I know that the network is short-staffed. I'm happy to cover both." The truth is, I'm happiest when I'm here. It's miserably wet and cold outside. Heather will be away for New Year's and it's not like I know anyone else. My dad is still in Brisbane, and my mom is spending the holidays with a new guy. What else am I going to do—go back to Arizona? Why pay for the flight when I travel free every night?

"As long as you're sure," Curtis says. "You definitely don't have to."

I can't tell if she thinks I want to steal her job or if she appreciates that I'm putting in the extra effort. "Honestly, it's fine. I don't do Christmas. And I have nothing planned for New Year's Eve. I'm happy to be working. I'm hoping I can cut out a little early tonight, actually. I have an...appointment."

"No problem," she says. "Thanks for working the extra shifts."

The thing is, I love work. I love being here. I love everything about this place. I love the throbbing of my Black-Berry, and I love who I am. Tough. Strong. Capable. The perfect place to bring in the New Year.

That evening in New York, on our way to Le Mariage on Madison Avenue, Heather hands me a sparkling solitaire ring.

"Aw, you're proposing! You're sick of your parents harassing you about being single, so you've decided to introduce me to them as your committed lesbian partner in order to get them off your back."

She smirks. "Very funny. It's a fake engagement ring. In this city, you can't go wedding-dress shopping without one. I got myself one, too. I might as well try this technique while we're here. Air out my ex-boyfriend issues, too. See?" She extends her left hand.

"What ex-boyfriend issues?" I guess I do ask a lot of questions.

She brushes away my question with a wave of her sparkling hand. "You know. The ones who got away."

"You think of everything," I say, lifting my own sparkler to the sunlight. "Where did you get this?" And yet another question. Damn Cam for making me feel self-conscious.

"From a street vendor downtown. You owe me twenty bucks."

It's a big square-shaped rock on a slim silver band. "It's pretty good. I would never be able to tell the difference between this one and a real one." I think I might like it better than my real one. Who knew?

Still, another question, this one rhetorical. Well, so what? I'm in the news business. Asking questions is what news people do. The only thing I have to stop is questioning myself.

"Trust me," Heather says, "if you had a real one, you'd be able to tell."

I don't think I can tell what's real and what's not these days.

When we get to the boutique, the receptionist hands us two clipboards with forms to fill out. What is your e-mail address? When is your wedding date? Where are you getting married?

The stores are far more organized in New York than they are in Phoenix. I catch Heather laughing to herself as she scribbles on the questionnaire.

"I'm getting married at the Pierre," she whispers. "On Valentine's Day."

Once we've been accepted inside, we're both shown changing rooms. We point to the dresses we like, and our salespeople, or "Wedding Specialists" as their name tags say, get to it. I have a pen and paper in my purse and plan on marking down whatever styles Heather believes are right for me.

"How are you doing over there?" Heather calls from the other room.

My specialist zips my dress up. It's similar to the straight one I tried on at Snow White. "Good! I'm ready. Let me see."

We both step out of our rooms.

"You look gorgeous!" I shriek. She's wearing a long sleek dress that shows off her curves perfectly. "Wow. You should totally get that."

"Thanks. I'm sure my fiancé Frank the brain surgeon would love it." She winks at me as she pirouettes.

I place one hand on my hip, the other on my head, and strike my best glamour pose. "What about mine?"

She looks me up and down. "No."

I love this girl. "No?"

"Definitely not. It's not your style. I can see you in something more princessy."

"Yeah?"

"Oh, yeah. It's awful. You look horrific."

"I get the point."

"That dress was just not sewn to be worn by somebody with your lack of breasts."

"Heather, you're scaring me again." I used to have breasts. In Arizona, anyway. Damn weight loss.

"Friends are allowed to be honest. Let me find you something," she says, charging into my changing room. She selects a simple satin strapless dress with an empire waist. "This one."

I try it on. My waist looks so narrow. And I look gorgeous. I think. "What do you think?"

"It's perfect," she says. "It's the one. Can't you tell?"

I look at myself in the mirror. It's nice. Definitely. But how will it look in Arizona? And is it the one? "I don't know."

"Trust me," she says.

I look at the price tag. "Three thousand five hundred." Eek.

"It's your one special day," Heather says. "You need something perfect."

She's right. "I'll take it!"

"Wonderful. You'll be gorgeous," says the smiling Wedding Specialist.

Heather's pinches my arm. "Um...don't you want to think about it?"

"No, I'm sure." It'll be amazing. Cam will never be able to take his eyes off me. "Can I put it on my credit card?"

"I think you should think about it," Heather urges. And then she whispers, "You're not really getting married. This is just therapy, remember?"

Oh. Right. "I should think about it," I tell the specialist.

The specialist winces. One commission down. I imprint the designer's name and the style number in my memory so I can try it on in Arizona.

I hope it comes in a larger size.

12

Two Turtlenecks and a Partridge in an Orange Tree

Christmas Eve in New York passes in an eggnog blur. Heather's family is loud but nice. There's lots of screaming to pass the this or the that, and her younger brothers keep getting yelled at for turning on the TV.

In Arizona, Alice cooks a feast, and insists that Blair and her brood spend the night. She forces us to watch, again, all their Christmas home videos. Cam rolling himself in wrapping paper. Blair throwing a tantrum when she doesn't get a bike. Alice throwing a tantrum, period.

The entire family congregates around the piano to sing Christmas carols, and I kind of join in when I know the words. Alice tries to insist that Cam and I spend the night, too (what fun, sleeping in Cam's old room a wall away from Alice!), but in anticipation of just that, I purposely forgot the gifts back at the apartment so that we'll have to go home and return the next morning.

I spend Christmas Day in New York working. It's slow; the building is quiet since hardly anyone is here (definitely not running into cute Elevator Boy today), and the stories are all Christmas-hokey.

In Arizona, Cam and I return to Alice's to exchange presents. Honestly, until I met Cam, I never realized how much we Jews miss out on regarding gift-giving. At Hanukkah, parents give their kids presents, but that's it. (Most parents, anyway. Mine seem to have forgotten this year.) At Christmas, everyone exchanges gifts with everyone. At least that's how it is in Cam's family.

The gift-giving thing can be awkward. In college, I got all my girlfriends little trinkets, but none of them got me anything because they knew I was Jewish and didn't want to offend me. The first year I was dating Cam, I got him a baseball hat and he got me a diamond necklace. It was only a small diamond chip, but still. Better than a baseball hat. Cam likes to go all out for Christmas. Last year he got me pearl earrings. It's hard to shop for him, but my general rule these days is to get him something he wants but would never buy himself. Last year I got him a digital camera. This year I got him the latest iPod. Latest for the next five minutes anyway, until they come out with a new one.

I have no clue what Cam's getting me this year. It will probably be jewelry again, since he knows I love it, and I'd never buy any for myself. Although, he did just get me a ring barely two months ago, so maybe he'll get me something different. Like a day at a spa? I was hoping to stumble across it or a clue somewhere in the apartment so I could practice my "This is the nicest (blank) ever," but no such luck.

I picked up toys for the kids, a satellite radio for Blair and Matt (I hope it's acceptable to give only one gift to a couple), a new Martha Stewart book for Alice, and a few DVDs for Cam's dad. Cam carries everything to the car. Still don't see a gift for me. Although, if it's earrings or a spa certificate, it would easily fit in his pocket. Hmm, is it possible I don't get a gift because I just got a ring?

I help him carry all the gifts inside (stopping under the mistletoe—love that mistletoe!) and place them under the massive and overdecorated tree.

After brunch, over more eggnog, we all move into the living room and get ready to open the gifts. The kids go first, and then Alice unwraps her presents from us. ("A new book? That's so thoughtful of you, Cammy. You, too, Gabrielle.") Then Cam starts to unwrap the gift his parents got for us. I'm assuming it's a painting, since it's tall and wide, about half of my height.

"We wanted to help fill up the wall space in the new house," Alice says.

Yup. It must be a painting.

And then Cam opens it. It's a painting. Of Jesus. On the cross.

"Wow," I say. "That's quite a present."

Does she not understand that I'm Jewish? I enjoy mistletoe, and I know the words to "Rudolph the Red-nosed Reindeer," but I have to draw the line somewhere. Besides, religion and interior decoration just don't mix. I liked Pilates, which is kind of yoga-like, and I've been intrigued with eastern philosophy since I did a story on Thailand last year, but you won't see a picture of Buddha on my wall, either.

Alice nods. "We thought so. It will look just perfect over the fireplace in the living room."

I finish my second glass of eggnog and decide I might have to scale down my carol-singing and eggnog-drinking since I'm obviously confusing her. I try to catch Cam's eye to see if he also finds the gift inappropriate. Religious artifacts should be discussed and agreed upon by the couple. How would Cam feel if my dad started sending us mezuzahs and insisting we put them up?

"Thanks, Mom," Cam says, not looking at me. He opens the gift from Blair and Matt. It's a new tie. "Nice," he says. Boring, I think.

I'm up next, and I open the gift from Blair and Matt. I tear away the purple tissue paper to reveal a blue turtleneck sweater. "It's beautiful," I say. Actually, it's really quite nice. Except the neck looks a little small. Outrageously small. It occurs to me that the sweater might not fit over my jumbo-sized head. I reach over to put it on a chair.

"It's cashmere," says Blair.

"That means it wasn't cheap," pipes up Alice.

Please don't make me try it on. Pretty please?

Alice eyes it on the chair and says, "Try it on."

"Oh, I would, but—" I rack my brain for an excuse. I remember that I'm wearing a thick sweater already. "It won't fit over what I'm wearing."

Alice narrows her eyes. "So change in the bathroom. We want to see it."

"Mom," Cam says, "she doesn't have to try it on this second."

Blair snorts. "I think I'm entitled to see what it looks like."

I heave myself off the couch. These people are so annoying. "I'll try it on, I'll try it on," I grumble and head to the bathroom, which still has no lock (is it so hard to fix a lock?), peel off my sweater, slide my arms into the sleeves of the turtleneck and then try to insert my head.

I pull.

I yank.

I thrust.

I give up.

Unfortunately, my head is just not going in. Heather is right. I have a jumbo, freak-sized head. I take a second to nibble my nails, oh, God, I have to stop—they're disgusting in Arizona—and try one more time for good luck, then pull out my arms and put on my sweater.

This is not going to be pretty.

The group is chattering and laughing, but as soon as I join them, they clam up. "You're not wearing it," Alice says.

No kidding. "It doesn't fit. I'm sorry."

"Of course it fits," Alice says. "It's a medium. I'm sorry to tell you, but you're not a small. Maybe if you slowed down on the eggnog—"

"The neck is too tight."

"That's ridiculous," Alice says. "Let me see."

"I can't get it on. I tried."

"Try it on here over your sweater," Blair orders.

My head feels hot. My arms. My tongue. "No. It doesn't fit."

"If you don't like it, just say so," Blair says. "It was expensive."

"Blair!" Cam says, finally jumping to my defense. "If Gabby said it doesn't fit, it doesn't fit. Maybe you can exchange it for a larger size."

"Actually," I squeak, "a larger size won't help. I am a medium, but it's the neck that doesn't fit, and if I get a larger turtleneck to accommodate my head, the rest of it will be too big. So can you just exchange it for another style?" At this point I realize that I'm rambling and stop immediately.

"Try it on." Blair repeats.

For heaven's sake. I shove my hands through the armholes and attempt to ram my head through the neck, and what is wrong with them, why are they so horrible, why don't they see that this stupid sweater just *does not fit?* The sweater is blanketing my face and I'm waving my arms and I'm screaming, "See? See?"

By the time I give up again, I'm sweaty and hot and exhausted. The room is deadly quiet. I fling the sweater onto the coffee table and collapse into my spot on the couch. Cam puts his arm around me in a feeble attempt to appease me.

Blair snatches the turtleneck. "You don't have to be such a drama queen. I'll buy you another one, since I can't exchange it."

Translation: she bought it at a clearance sale.

"Blair, honey, don't upset yourself, it's not good for the baby," Alice coos. "Why don't you open one of your presents?"

Blair picks up the one that we got her and rips open the paper. "A satellite radio! Thanks, Cammy!" she says, clearly ignoring the card that came from Cam *and* me.

"You're welcome," Cam says. "I'm glad you like it."

Matt reaches across the coffee table and shakes Cam's hand. "Thanks, man. Thanks, Gabby."

At least someone in that marriage has manners. Which is perfectly understandable. He's not blood related. "You're welcome."

"Gabrielle, it's your turn to open Cam's," Alice announces. "If you're feeling up to it."

I ignore her. She is not going to ruin the one good part of the day: me opening the present from the man I love. "Which one is it?" I ask, searching under the tree for a small package.

"The red one," Cam says, playing with his fingers. Aw, he's nervous. How cute!

I don't see a small red package. I do see a monster three-foot red box. "That one?" I ask, confused.

Still doing that thing with his fingers, he nods.

I pull it out from under the tree and, sure enough, spot my name on the card. I open and read: *Gabrielle! Merry Christmas! Love, Cam!*

Since when does he call me *Gabrielle?* And this isn't his handwriting. This is Alice's handwriting. Cam hates exclamation marks. Please tell me my fiancé didn't ask his mother to write my card. Please tell me that my fiancé didn't—

I rip away the tissue.

—buy me a vacuum cleaner.

"It's a vacuum cleaner," I say, my voice flat.

"It's a Dyson," Alice says, beaming. "State of the art."

Maybe I can plug it in right now and suck myself away.

I don't speak to Cam all the way home. I don't even look at him. I'm exploding with resentment.

He pops open the trunk and says, "I'm sorry. I should never have given you a vacuum cleaner for Christmas."

I ignore him and concentrate instead on heaving my Dyson toward the apartment door.

"Gabby, talk to me."

I lean the vacuum cleaner against the door while I search through my purse for the keys. Where are my stupid keys?

"I'm sorry," Cam says, unlocking the door. He piles our gifts under the window. "I'm sorry. I should have given you something more fun. But I thought that since I got you a ring, I could get away with something more practical."

Get away with? Is giving me a gift some kind of crime? "No, I don't like it. A household appliance? You couldn't have been more clichéd if you got me a toaster. And does this mean I'm supposed to do the all the vacuuming in the new house? Are you not planning to pitch in with the housework?" I shake my head. "But it's not just that. The entire day was a disaster."

"Was it that bad?"

"Yes, it was. What's up with that painting your mother gave us? Don't they get that I'm Jewish?"

He sits down on his couch and pats the spot next to him. "It's just a picture."

I opt to angrily stride up and down the room instead. "Nothing is just a picture. Is that why she's so horrible to me? Is it because I'm a different religion?"

"She's not *that* horrible to you."

"Are you on crack? Of course she is. And your sister is no better. Is it my fault I have a big head? She didn't have to be so rude about it."

"You don't have a big head. You have a beautiful head. And a beautiful smile. Will you smile? Please? I'll talk to them."

I'm in no mood for smiling. "But why do they treat me like garbage? Do they just not think I'm good enough for you?"

When he doesn't answer, I know I've hit the nail smack

on its tiny, ugly head. "That's it, isn't? They don't think I'm good enough."

"It's normal. No mother thinks any girl is good enough for her only son. It's the same with fathers and daughters. I'm sure your dad doesn't think I'm good enough."

"Yes, he does," I say. Although, in truth, he hardly knows Cam. In truth, he hardly knows me. But one thing I'm sure of. My father would never treat Cam the way Alice treats me. And do you know why? Because I wouldn't stand for it. But there's a bigger problem. The truth is, lately, I don't *feel* good enough. I feel so damn insecure. I have no career. No money. No desire to clean a house. "Look, forget about your family. Let's go back to the gift for a second. How could you think a vacuum cleaner is an appropriate gift for your fiancée?"

"I'm sure we can return it."

"We don't have to return it," I say, kneeling in front of him. "That's not the point. We do *need* a vacuum. It's just that we just got engaged…and I guess I was hoping you'd be feeling more romantic. You normally get me jewelry." Am I sounding like a spoiled brat? "I think that may have sounded awful and I don't mean to sound like a spoiled princess, but I think you know what I mean—"

"I'm sorry. Really. I was going to get you something different. Like earrings or a day at the spa, but then my mom bought it and she said that you really needed one, and I didn't want to disappoint her…." His voice trails off.

"First of all, you should be more worried about disappointing me than disappointing her."

"You're right. I'm sorry." He rubs the back of my neck with his palms.

I'm feeling appeased until I remember the card. "And what was up with the card? Did your mother write it?"

He blushes and pulls me onto his lap. "Sorry about that, too. She said she saw it at the store and bought it and I've been so busy with work and the paperwork for the new house so—"

That's it. I push myself off him and move to the other end of the couch. "Do you know how pathetic that sounds?"

"I didn't ask her to do it," he says. "She just did it."

"You should have said no, Cam. Don't you get it? We have to make our life about us. Not about your mother."

He looks pained. "I'm sorry. Again. You know how she is. I tell her no, but she just keeps at me, until I'm too tired to argue."

I can taste the bitterness in my mouth. "I understand, but it's no good. She's going to push us around our whole life." And I'm going to be miserable, I think but don't say. I'm going to be miserable my whole life.

"I know, I know. You're right. I'll do my best."

"Whatever." I lie facedown on the couch, feeling empty. "It's okay."

But it's not okay. I want to go back to New York. I don't know how it happened, but I like myself better in New York. A lot better. I'm not a wimp there. Or a whiner. And I'm liked. I'm strong and cheerful…and assertive.

"—five, four, three, two—"

I'm in the office in N.Y., watching the ball drop live onscreen at the station. I've always loved New Year's. It feels so hopeful. So fresh. The year ahead is like a blank page. Or in my case, two blank pages.

"—one!"

A cameraman slaps me on the back. "Happy New Year!" he says.

"You, too." We clink our glasses of champagne and get back to work. You'd think I'd be bored, or annoyed that I'm in the office, but I'm not. I love it here. There is nowhere I'd rather be.

I finish my glass and wish the others well, and then get back to work.

"Gabby, can you help with a story?" asks one of the associate producers.

"Sure, I'd be happy to," I answer, and follow her down the hall.

Happy New Year to me.

"—five, four, three, two—"

We're at the Starlight Bar in Tempe with a bunch of Cam's friends, but I have to admit, the countdown is less exciting the second time around.

"—one!"

"Happy New Year, baby," Cam says, and presses his lips against mine.

"Happy New Year," I murmur.

He pulls me into him, brushes away my hair and whispers. "This is our year."

Some say that the first thing you feel in the New Year will stay with you for the next twelve months. The first thing I feel is guilt. There's a part of me that Cam doesn't know. A part of me he'll never know.

"Am I being overly critical?" I ask Lila. "After all, Cam's her baby."

It's the third week of January, and because we've just

finished ordering my wedding dress, I'm treating Lila to a glass of wine. She wanted to get back to work, but I guilted her by saying that as my Number One maid of honor, it was her job to listen to me kvetch. She had taken the news of her shared honor relatively well. We're sitting in a booth at the back of a bar called Grapes, enjoying our chardonnay and sharing our usual cheese plate. Sometimes I try to shake things up by trying to order the chicken wings, but she won't do it. Cheese plate—always.

"No. I think you're not being critical enough. You have to set limits. The same thing happened with my mother and my brother. My mom was horrible to his wife. She treated her like an imposter who was out to steal her baby. Alice can tell that you have no spine and pushes accordingly. You have to lay down the law now before it's too late."

"I can't find my spine," I complain. "It's buried somewhere under all this weight I've gained. Which is something else I'm depressed about."

Lila tilts her head back and takes a long sip. "I want to talk to you about that."

"About my weight or my depression?"

"About *my* depression."

I cover her hand with mine. "You're depressed? Why?"

"I'm lonely in the apartment all by myself. Your move screwed up my whole equilibrium. The place feels so empty. Before, I at least had you to come home to, but now I have no one."

"You need to meet someone."

Lila nods. "Exactly. It's time for me to find myself a boyfriend."

Lila has definitely had her share of flings, but in all the years that I've known her, I've never seen her in a relationship. I've never even heard her say that she wants a boyfriend. She claimed they took up too much space, physically and emotionally. "Wow. That's a big step for you."

"All I'm saying is that I'm going to start dating. I'm open and willing."

"I'll keep my eye out for eligible bachelors."

"Thanks."

She stuffs a slice of Gruyère in her mouth, savors it, then asks, "Maybe Cam has a friend?"

"You'll meet them all at the wedding."

"Speaking of the wedding, don't I need to order a dress?"

"Yes. That's next up. Alice would like you in rust."

"I'm not wearing orange. Alice should mind her own business. How about black?"

"I'll see what I can do."

"Remember your spine."

One week later, we're back in Alice's kitchen, binders open, iced tea poured.

"Next major priority is finding a band," Tricia tells us, pushing a list across the glass table. On it is written: Smokin' Tokin', Starlight, Party Town, Champagne. "I've used these bands before. They're all available on your date."

"What kind of name is Smokin' Tokin'?" Alice asks. "This is your wedding, Gabrielle. You need a band that represents sound family values."

What does she expect? The Partridge Family? "Great," I say to Tricia. "Do they have CDs we could listen to?"

Tricia nods. "Yup. But I think it's best if you go hear them in person. Starlight and Party Town are playing at weddings this Saturday night. It's always best to pop in and see the bands in action."

Fun. Cam and I can go dancing. "And the hosts don't mind?"

"Nah, it always happens. I'm sure you'll have a few crashers at your wedding, too."

"You see?" Alice says, wagging her finger at me. "That wouldn't happen if you got married at home. A hotel is so impersonal. Any stranger can wander in off the street. If they're disruptive, I'm having them tossed out by their ears. And what about terrorists?"

"They're not disruptive," Tricia says. "They're just like you. Couples who want to hear bands."

Alice shakes her head in apparent disgust. "If we must, we must. I'll make dinner for you and Cam, and then the four of us will go."

Spine, I need a spine. "That's very considerate of you, Alice, but Cam and I are happy to go on our own. We'll make a night out of it."

Alice purses her lips and grumbles something incomprehensible.

"Perfect," Tricia says, clapping her hands. "Gabby and Cam will choose the band. Now let's move on to flowers. Gabby, do you have any ideas for bouquets or centerpieces?"

"I—"

"I do," interrupts Alice. Surprise, surprise. "Turn to the flower section of your binders. One thing is certain, we have to have orange blossoms."

First my back tenses and then my spine shrivels. Why not forget the hotel and get married in an orchard? Fine. She can have the flowers. It's not like I care about a bunch of plants. Hey, I'm choosing the band. I'll just have to make sure to regrow my spine in time to argue about the bridesmaid dresses.

13

Live from New York

As Arizona Me works on Alice, New York Me works on, well, work.

I'm in the control room and the show's about to start taping when my BlackBerry buzzes to tell me that a fire broke out at an oil refinery outside of Houston.

"Wait, no one move," I say into my headphone. "Curtis, did you see it?"

"Yeah. Hold on."

"This could be big. Maybe we should hold off taping now and go live at eight," I say. This is a more important story than that snowstorm that's attacking the Northeast. Since refineries are major targets, I'm thinking terrorists. I flip through my BlackBerry trying to find out more, but there's no news yet.

"We hardly ever go live," Curtis says through the headset. "It's too risky."

Ron's face is now featured prominently on the screen in front of me, waiting to begin taping.

"Okay," I say, but then I get another buzz. "A hundred people still inside refinery."

And that's when I get thirsty. Very thirsty. My tongue feels like sandpaper and my eyes start to itch. I know the sign, and it's never let me down before. Something big is going down.

Spine! I need my spine! I sit up straighter and clear my throat. "Curtis? I know it's risky, but I think we should go for it." My BlackBerry buzzes again. "The fire is spreading. I think we should hold off taping. We need to wait for more news. I did it all the time Arizona."

"This isn't Arizona."

No, this is a major network in New York. Hello?

I sit up tall. I'm not backing down. I know this is the right move, and I'm going for it. "This story will be huge. We have to go for it."

"Forget it," says Curtis. "We're taping."

I feel myself sink back into my seat. She's making a mistake. We have to do it. "Let's ask Ron," I say. "He should have the option, Curtis. It's his name out there."

"Go ask him. He won't want to."

I push back my seat and hurry past security into the studio. "Ron, sorry to bother you so close to taping."

He waves me over. "What's up, Arizona?"

"A fire just broke out at an oil refinery outside Houston. I have a feeling it's going to be a big story. The news is still slow to come in, but I think it's worth going live at eight."

He seems to be processing what I've said. "Terrorism?"

"Could be."

"Victims?"

"Possibly."

"What does Curtis think?"

"She wants to continue as planned with the taping."

He stares into my eyes. "And what makes you so sure you're right?"

"I just know."

"Reporter's nose?"

More like tongue. "Sort of."

Ron leans in close and I can see he's wearing foundation and a little too much eyeliner. He looks me over, and I can tell he's deciding. Should he risk his show on a hunch? "All right," he says slowly. "Let's go live. Hope you're right, Arizona."

Curtis calls me over when I return to the control room. "You'd better be right about this fire."

I run to the cooler for water. I need to douse the fire in my throat.

Six o'clock comes and goes, and I'm still thirsty. We are not taping. We are preparing for a live show. My hands are shaking. Not that I wish anyone harm, but if the fire dwindles to a flicker, I'm screwed. I keep checking my BlackBerry. Is it wrong that I'm praying that the fire doesn't stop? A doctor doesn't wish for a person to get sick, but face it, without sick people, doctors would be unemployed. Maybe everyone will be saved and we'll get a few hero stories. Hero stories are upbeat, are they not?

It's 7:58. The fire is still roaring. It's out of control. One of our affiliate producers is there right now, getting us some horrific and overwhelming images. People are trapped inside.

"And we're live."

"Good evening," says Ron, looking directly into the camera. "We have some very disturbing images coming out of Texas tonight. You are looking at an oil refinery outside of Houston, and we believe several people might be trapped inside the smoldering refinery. At three fifty-seven central standard time this afternoon, a gas-tank explosion ignited a fire at a major oil refinery just outside of Houston. Several fire companies are on the scene, responding to the blaze."

We have graphics, we have live images. We have it all. Meanwhile, I'm waving at the assistants, who have been trying to make phone contact with someone inside the building.

"We got one," an assistant whispers to me, ten minutes into the newscast. "His name is Alex Manasin. He's an engineer and he's in the back of the building. Let me connect him."

Holy shit. "Are you sure talking to us doesn't put him in any danger?"

"He's trapped in one of the control rooms. He can't go anywhere."

I adjust the script and tell Ron about the caller through his earpiece. His eyes light up. This is huge.

"We have an engineer, Alex Man…a…ton from the refinery on the phone live with us"

"Manasin!" I scream at the screen. "Not Manaton!"

"Alex, can you hear me?" Ron says in his best voice-of-God.

I hear a man's voice, and it's not Ron's. "Hello?"

"Alex, are you okay?"

"I've been better," says the voice. "It's damn hot in here."

"Stay with us, Alex. They're coming to get you. Can you tell us what's going on in there?"

"It just kinda came out of nowhere. It was a very normal day and then just before four a loud explosion came from the south side of the facility."

"What's on the south side?"

"The south side is the G-sector where refined oil is taken from the facility for distribution."

"How far were you from the explosion?"

"It was just down the hall...maybe five hundred feet."

"Is anyone with you?"

"There's about twelve of us in this control room and another five next door. We're all stuck...there are flames right through the hallways."

"How many employees work at the facility?"

"Could be as high as twelve hundred, depending on the work shifts."

"Mr. Manaton, do you have any idea how this could have started?"

"Tough to say...hold on.... Ted, tell Joan to stay low..."

The phone muffles. Ron, clearly not at his best when live, stares blankly at the monitor for some guidance. This dead air is killing me. I'm about to insert a new graphic when thankfully Mr. Manaton, as he's now been ordained, comes back on the line.

"Sorry about that," he says.

"We certainly understand. Your safety and the safety of those around you is most important here. Now tell us, do you have any idea how this could have started?"

The engineer coughs loudly into the phone. "Tough to say. I don't think it was an accident."

Yes, yes, that's it, say the T-word.

"We've had union issues these past few months."

Ron visually slumps with disappointment.

"But who knows? Some of us here in the control room think it was terrorists."

Bull's-eye!

"What does it look like in there?" Ron asks. "Is there smoke?"

More coughs. "Yeah, hold on again."

We wait a few seconds. Any more dead air and I'm going to get fired.

"Get me someone else! Can we get the mayor on the line?"

"We got him," a bushy-eyed intern yells my way.

I patch the mayor through to Ron, who immediately bursts into, "Houston we have a problem." Oh God, tell me he didn't just say that. "Mr. Mayor," he continues, "what can you tell us?"

For the next twelve minutes, our live coverage of the Houston refinery fire is, well, no need to be modest here, outstanding. I cut to images from the choppers overhead. I insert graphics with factoids about the refinery. I point out how a refinery fire could force gas prices higher.

I cut to commercial.

I glance up at the monitors of the other networks and notice that, except for CNN, they aren't showing the story. Instead they're airing their prerecorded stories about the snowstorm—boring. It's January, people. Snow happens. CNN is just beginning their coverage, but we've already made contact. We beat CNN!

I snap back to the screen with the realization that in one minute and fifteen seconds we're coming back live. "I need an expert on the phone," I scream at no one in particular.

"Someone who can talk about oil, gas, refineries, anything like that. Ron, open with a recap. Two minutes, then we'll get you back on the phone."

Ron's ad-lib skills are practically nonexistent. He changes the location of the fire twice in two minutes—first on the north side, then the eastern section of the refinery. But he does a good job hitting the key points, and the graphics team helps him along.

After the recap, we check back with Alex Manaton/Manasin, then with the fire chief, then move on to an economics expert. Halfway through the hour, all the other major news networks have abandoned their taped segments and are picking up our feed. And I'm feeling damn good about my decision to go live.

The rest of the hour flies by, with other major stories to even it out. Eventually, our time is up and we wind down our efforts. The enthusiasm in the room is palpable. One of our only live outings, produced by yours truly, has been a massive success. We had drama, we had excitement, we had heroes. And adding to the celebration, not only were there no fatalities, no one was injured.

Tomorrow we cover the union dispute. Perhaps, live.

I'm closing down my computer when I notice that Ron is leaning against my desk, a huge grin across his face. "Where do you think you're going, Arizona? I'm taking you to dinner."

"Really?"

"Absolutely. You were a superstar tonight. What's your favorite place?"

Sushi on Third is pretty much the only place I've ever eaten at in this city, except for the Italian place Heather took me to once. "You choose. I trust you. You are one of the most trusted newsmen in the nation."

"Cute, Arizona. Let's go to Gramercy Tavern. I have to get this makeup taken off and then make a few stops, so I'll meet you there at ten."

I do a quick search on the Internet and discover that Gramercy Tavern is one of the best and priciest restaurants in the city. Then I run to the restroom and try to fix myself up. I look down at my running shoes. Shit. I can't go to one of New York's best restaurants in these! Maybe I can just run across the street and—

I glance at my watch. It's already nine-thirty. All the stores will be closed. I'm going to have to make do with what I have on. Which are baggy black pants, a purple blouse and these damn black running shoes. Okay, what can I fix? I unbutton the top button of my shirt. And the hair. I can definitely fix the hair. I remove the elastic from my ponytail, flip my head, add water, shake it out and flip back up. That's better. Unfortunately, I don't carry much makeup with me, except for a lipstick. But that could work. It's rosy. I rub the color onto my eyelids, my cheekbones and finally my lips. And then I smile.

"We'll have a second bottle of the Château Lafite Rothschild Pauillac," Ron tells the waitress.

What will forever be known as the best day ever is getting better by the second. I saw the price list. And that wine cost over three hundred dollars. There is no feeling in the world like getting drunk on a three-hundred-dollar bottle of wine. Although, if I'm going to be honest, Ron has done more than his share of the drinking.

So far, the food is delicious. No, *delicious* isn't a strong enough word. I have mini orgasms every time I lift my fork to my mouth. And there's still so much more to go. I'm only on course three out of seven!

When I realized that just the two of us would be having dinner—Ron said he couldn't find Curtis—I was worried we'd have nothing to talk about. But the conversation is as smooth as the wine. I'm pretty well prepped, since I've read his biography in my other life, and therefore know everything about him. Born in Boston in 1949. Father died when he was ten from a heart attack. Mother remarried twice thereafter. Moved to Connecticut where stepfather worked. Graduated with a B.A. from Yale. Married Janet McKinsey, whom he met in a communications class. Got a master's in journalism from Columbia. Fathered one boy, then twin girls. All three kids are in their twenties. Lives with wife in Greenwich, Connecticut.

Besides, I end up doing most of the talking, since he asks me a million questions. What was it like moving from Arizona to New York? How do I like my job? How do I like working with Curtis? Do I have a roommate?

"Where did you grow up?"

"Just outside of Los Angeles," I answer, savoring my tuna tartar.

"Ah, La-la Land. You didn't want to be an actress?"

"God, no. That world is so fake."

"I know just what you mean," he says, holding my gaze as if I had said something meaningful.

"Half the girls in my class had breast implants by their sixteenth birthday," I add, then wonder if I should slow down on the wine.

Luckily, he laughs, and then asks me about my parents.

I haven't gotten this much attention in years.

Sure, this would be way more fun if he wasn't married. Not that he's my type exactly, being over fifty. But there's something about him that's sexy. The maître d' giving us the best table even though we didn't have a reservation probably has something to do with it. Or maybe it's because everyone in this entire country trusts him. Or because he's powerful and brilliant. Or maybe it's the wine goggles I'm sporting.

"Gabby, tell me, how come you went into producing and not reporting?"

"Not my thing. I prefer being behind the camera."

"You would have been a terrific reporter. That smile would have looked great on camera. But I'm happy to have you as my producer. You're doing a phenomenal job. For the work you did tonight, we could be talking Emmy."

"Thank you," I say, my heart swooning.

I take another bite of my foie gras as the waitress refills my glass with, oh, I'd say seventy-dollars worth of Château Lafite Rothschild Pauillac.

Since we are in the midst of a snowstorm, Ron gives the hostess the TRSN account number and asks her to call for two private cars.

My own car. My very own car. I've taken subways in this city. I've taken cabs. But a black, tinted-windowed car? "You don't have to," I say. "I'm fine grabbing a cab."

The coat guy helps Ron into his black cashmere coat. "It's my responsibility to make sure you get home safely and comfortably. We'll need one car to SoHo, and one to Murray Hill."

"I thought you lived in Connecticut," I say, as the coat guy now helps me with my very-not-cashmere coat.

"I do, but on nights like these I stay at the Soho Grand. Easier that way."

"Got it. Well, thank you so much, Ron. For the car, for dinner, for the job." I feel myself getting teary with emotion, because really, I am overwhelmed with admiration and happiness. This was indeed the best day ever.

"You deserve it." A car pulls up in front of the restaurant. "Go ahead, Arizona. You first."

A burst of winter air blows in as I push open the door. "Thanks again. You were great today," Ron calls behind me.

What would normally be a ten-minute drive ends up taking thirty because of the slippery roads. But I enjoy every second of it. In the back seat of the limo, I feel toasty and happy and brimming with pride.

I've made it.

Back at the apartment, I'm about to drift off into a blissful well-deserved sleep when the phone rings. Perhaps it's Ron calling to tell me what a valued employee I am. "Hello?"

"Hi, Gabby."

I sit up in bed, surprised. "Cam. Hey. How are you?"

"Fine. Good, actually. How are you?"

"You know. The usual. Working hard. How's work with you?"

"Good."

Fortunately, I already know about the insurance-bankruptcy case he's working on. "How's your family?" Still annoying? Of course, I don't say this.

"They're fine. So how was your date?"

Was tonight a date? Wait a minute. Cam wouldn't know

about tonight. And then I remember. Brad. Wow, I haven't spoken to Cam in a while. "Shitty," I say, and then laugh to myself. I feel ew-y all over again.

"Tell me about it."

"You don't want to know."

"Come on," he says. "Tell me. It will make my day."

"It's too awful."

"Please?"

"I'd really rather not. No more dates for me. You were right. Maybe I'm not ready. It's too soon, you know?" Silence on the other end. "Cam?" Continued silence. "Hello? Anyone there?"

"There's something I have to tell you, Gabs."

No one ever likes a statement that starts with *there's something I have to tell you*. "Yes?" I ask with trepidation.

"After you told me about your date—"

"Yes?"

"I was upset."

"Yes?"

And more silence.

Oh God, he slept with someone. I feel the steam flowing from my ears and I reel it back in. I can't get mad. I just can't. I'm the one who broke the engagement. I went out on a date. If he hooked up with someone, I have to deal. I have to handle it. I have to—

"And I called Lila," he says.

Huh?

"To pick up my bookshelf."

Stop. Just stop.

"And we started to hang out. As friends."

No, no, no.

"And then a few weeks ago, she told me she was starting

to think of me as more than her ex-roommate's ex-boy-friend and we...hooked up."

My heart stops. Literally stops. "You did not!"

"I'm sorry, Gabby. I know you're not going to like this. But Lila and I are dating."

The room swirls. He's dating my maid of honor. My fiancé is dating my maid of honor. I try to stay calm, and say simply, "No."

"Excuse me?" he says.

"No. You can't. It's against the rules."

"There are no rules, Gabby. You broke our engagement. I can do whatever I want. You can't tell me who to date."

"But she's so...organized."

"You say that like it's a bad thing."

"You know what I mean. She's like the opposite of me."

"You say that like it's a bad thing." He laughs.

"Go to hell."

"Come on," he says softly. "That's not fair."

I sigh. Damn, damn, damn. Why is he ruining my best day ever? "I know. But she's supposed to be my friend. How could she do this to me?"

"She wanted to call you to tell you, but I thought it should come from me."

"Still, a best friend shouldn't do it."

"Come on. Have you even spoken to her since you've moved to New York? You've moved on, Gabby. And so have we."

A large pit has begun to sprout in my stomach. We've e-mailed a few times in this life. I guess this proves she isn't much of a sister. Best friend by routine maybe.

God, I can't believe I asked her to be my maid of honor. Alice was right. You can't trust friends. Sure, they help you pick out a dress, but they're secretly plotting ways to steal your fiancé. "I'm tired. I'm going to sleep."

"Please don't be like this."

"Just tell me this—when we were together, did you have a thing for her? Tell me the truth."

"I swear, I never once thought of her as anything more than your roommate. If you were here, I wouldn't be going out with her. You know that. It wasn't like I meant for this to happen. I was just so miserable and she—"

"Bye." I slam down the phone and kick my heels into my mattress. Now what am I supposed to do? I am exhausted, yes, but I don't want to go to sleep and return to Arizona. I don't want to see Cam. Traitor.

I cannot believe this. I'm not sure who to be more pissed at. Cam or Lila. They're both assholes. She probably wanted him the entire time that I was with him. Skank.

I need to talk to a friend. Someone who knows Cam. I turn on my light, find my old Arizona Palm and dial Melanie Diamond's number.

"Hello?" she answers in her breathy voice.

"It's Gabby. Did I wake you?" Then I remember it's only eleven o'clock out there.

"Hey, stranger! How are you?"

I realize that this is the first time I've spoken to her in this life, too. I take a moment to update her on the happenings of the last few months.

"I'm so coming to visit. When do you want me?"

"Come in the summer. You have no idea how cold it gets here." I pull my covers tighter to my chest as if to prove my point.

"Maybe I'll move to New York. Guess what? I chopped off all my hair. I got a pixie cut!"

"Adorable. Please move here. You're not going to believe what I'm about to tell you. Lila is dating Cam."

"Your Cam?"

"My Cam."

"How can she do that?"

"I don't know."

"You know, I didn't really like her," she says.

"You didn't? Why?"

"She was too organized. When I came over, she aligned my shoes. Who does that?"

I laugh, and suddenly I feel lighter. Melanie and I trade stories until I'm feeling marginally better. If only I could be more like Melanie. More free spirited.

After we get off the phone, I'm too filled with weirdness to fall asleep. I had the highlight of my professional life tonight. It was perfect, and yet losing Cam to Lila has taken out some of the air.

I put on sweatpants and plan on getting myself a glass of water. As soon as I open my door, Heather pops out of her bedroom. "Good, you're up. I can't sleep." Her face is still tanned from her vacation, and she looks out of place in the coldness of this city. I think she might be prolonging the look with self-tanner.

"Wanna watch TV?" I ask.

"As long as it's not the news."

I pour us both glasses of water, and then we make ourselves comfy on the couch. I tell her all about Cam's treachery.

"Guys are such asses," she says. "Well, not Mark, he's a sweetheart. But your guy—what a jerk."

"How are things going with Mark?" Their first date

was a success and they've gone out twice since. But I still haven't seen him.

"Terrific." She smiles dreamily at the ceiling. "I met him for coffee earlier. What did you do tonight?"

I describe my great day, and my dinner with Ron. "Wasn't that sweet of him?"

"Don't be naive, missy. He's angling to get in your pants."

I almost choke on my water. "Ron? No way."

She wags her finger at me. "Way. I hope you made it clear that it wasn't going to happen. You know—set the right precedent. Otherwise you're heading straight for disaster."

My head hurts enough from the Cam Disaster—I don't have it in me to worry about a Ron Disaster. Surely one disaster in this New York life is enough.

Green light. Headache. I roll over in bed and punch Cam in the arm.

"Ouch! Why'd you hit me?"

"Sorry," I lie. "Bad dream."

Jerk.

That night in Arizona, I'm sitting on the couch waiting for Cam, attempting to enjoy guacamole and chips and a bottle of wine.

But I can't enjoy anything because I'm too pissed off.

How could Cam and Lila do that to me? And what am I supposed to do about it in Arizona? I can't get mad at Cam over here for something he didn't do. Nor can I get mad at Lila for something *she* didn't do. Although, technically, Lila probably always harbored a secret crush on Cam. And I can get mad at her for that, can't I?

Although how would I know that? She never told me.

And she never told Cam. Can I blame her for liking him in secret? It's not like she ever made a move on him when we were together. When we *are* together.

I have no idea what to say to them. How to act. How to feel.

To deal with the people in my lives, I'm going have to treat them as they act in that life only. I can be angry at Cam in New York, but not at him in Arizona. Ditto Lila. It's only fair.

Sighing, I flip through the channels hoping for distraction, and click onto *Ron's Report*. Which is featuring Ron's taped snowstorm instead of the best news hour he ever had. Ha!

It suddenly occurs to me how dumb I am for not calling Bernie, my old boss, to pitch him the refinery fire story. Dumb, dumb, dumb. I knew the fire was going to happen because, well, it happened. I could have gotten myself a camera! I could have flown over to Houston this morning! I could have done some pre-fire interviews that would have been worth a fortune!

Or, I could have stopped the fire.

I am an awful human being. I watch all these news reports about murders, fires and kidnappings, and not once do I think to stop them from happening the next/same day.

Think of the lives I can save.

I have to keep my eyes open for ways to help people. Yes. I have been to the dark side. Now I must use my powers for good.

Although I would only be saving people in one of my alternative universes. One of how many? The number of possibilities is infinite. What difference does just one make?

Who knows—maybe there's another world out there

where Cam and I never even met. Maybe there's a world where I told Cam I couldn't go for a drink with him, I had movie plans with Lila, and he called someone else and fell in love.

If everything is possible, does nothing mean anything?

In New York the next morning, I'm still feeling depressed on the subway to work. There are no seats left so I'm clinging to the pole, trying not to step in the puddles of slush.

The faces of my fellow passengers are all blank and bored. I can't help but wonder if one of these strangers is my soul mate in another life. I can't help but wonder if our paths have crossed somewhere else. If I'm missing out now. If there's a life I'm living where I get everything right.

When I get to my cubicle, there's a memo on my computer. "Come see me. Curtis."

I leave my coat on my chair and head over to her cube.

She finishes typing her sentence and then looks up. "Good call last night."

Right. Last night. I'd almost forgotten. "Thanks."

She takes out her ponytail and then ties it back up. "Number-one show."

I smile. "No!"

"Yes. Best ratings we've had in years. My phone has been ringing off the hook. It took a lot of guts to go against what I wanted. I wasn't sure you had it in you, but I have to tell you, I'm impressed."

I wasn't sure I had it in me, either. And I can't help wondering if this could be it…the world where I'm doing everything right.

14

That's the Way the Cookie Crumbles

"I'm coming! Have you seen my purse?" I ask. Bet Lila never loses her purse. No, I said I'd keep New York Lila in New York, and I meant it. Right now I must stay focused on my Arizona life. And my purse. Where is my purse? Am I forgetting something else? I feel as if I'm forgetting something else.

"You don't need your purse," Cam says. "I'm driving your car and I already took the keys. And I have money. Come on, we're going to be late."

I cannot believe how excited he is to hear this band. I'm pretty excited to spend the night dancing. I even got dressed up. Not ball-gown dressed up, but my pale blue strapless dress is elegant enough that I'll blend in with the guests. I dab on a bit of lip gloss and grab a shawl (it is still the end of January) and run out the door. He locks it behind me.

The clock in my car says 7:08. "Why were you rushing me? We're so early."

He turns on the ignition. "We're picking up my mom on the way."

"What? Why?"

"Because she wants to hear the band."

That conniving little wench. "But I told her we could do it on our own."

He looks at me sideways in surprise. "That's weird. She called me today to tell me to pick her up."

That woman is insufferable. I tried to subtly not invite her, and she invites herself anyway. "Whatever." I should have realized something was up when Cam said he was taking my car instead of his two-seater truck.

"I can tell her not to come if you really don't want her there. Better yet, you call her."

I'm about to pull out my cell, but then I stop. Maybe Alice is a better judge of people than I am, I rationalize. Maybe she should come with us. I am obviously the worst judge of character of all time. I think someone's my best friend, but as soon as I move across the country, she swoops in and steals my fiancé. (Okay, my vow to put it out of my mind is easier said than done.) I cannot be trusted to pick a best friend, never mind a band.

I hope my theory doesn't extend to husbands.

"I don't want to insult her," I say. "I just thought this could be a fun thing we could do together. Just the two of us."

"I know, but she wants to come. We'll see the next one alone. Just the two of us."

"Fine."

When we pull up in front of the house, Alice is dressed in her Sunday best, and staring at her watch.

"Should I move to the back?" I ask.

"No, of course not," Cam says.

Right! I'm Cam's future wife. A wife sits with her husband. Unfortunately, Alice is going to hate sitting in the back. Whenever she comes along with Tricia and me, she always sits in the front. This is the first time she's driving with me and Cam, and I have to set a precedent.

Alice, who has been waiting outside for us, hurries over to the car. She knocks on my window and I roll it down. "The door's not locked," I say. Am I supposed to get out of the car and open the door for her?

"My back is killing me. I don't think I can climb into the backseat."

"This isn't a two-door sedan, Alice," I say. "You don't have to do any climbing." Not exactly assertive, but I think she'll take the hint. I hope.

She sits behind me. "It's a bit tight back here."

I should offer. She should say no, but I should offer. It's the polite thing to do. "Alice, do you want to sit in the front?"

"No, I'm fine. But I'd appreciate if you could lower the music. It's ridiculously loud. I can barely hear myself think back here."

Every word she says grates on my nerves like nails on a chalkboard. No, like teeth on a chalkboard. I turn off the music. Next time I'm around her, I should consider bringing along earplugs. Or better yet, my iPod. That way I can listen to music *and* drown her out.

"Gabrielle, I don't see your binder."

Damn. I knew I was forgetting something. I start picking at my nails again. "I'll remember and write everything down later."

"It's all right, dear. I have mine. I don't mind sitting in the back here, but can you lower the air? It's blowing in my face. Can you hear me up there? I feel so far away."

I want to ignore her. I want to tell her to suck it up. New York Me would have less of a problem saying it. The words are burning my lips, begging to get out.

But Arizona Me can't say them. Won't say them.

"Stop the car," I say to Cam. I unsnap my seat belt, open my door and walk around to hers. "Alice, why don't you get in the front."

"Gabrielle, I'm fine here."

"Please. Really. It'll be more comfortable for you in the front."

"Well, if you insist. That's very sweet of you." She scurries out of the back, hijacking my good mood along with my seat.

Life is happier in New York. I've finally proven myself with the oil-fire story, and now Curtis listens to all of my story suggestions. I'm given a lot more control over segments. I've been keeping my eyes and ears open for ways to help the Arizona world, but so far nothing doable has presented itself.

These days Ron seems to be paying me a lot more attention. Not that he ever ignored me, but since the oil fire he's been stopping by my cube more often for my opinions. It's mind-boggling that this icon, this charismatic mix of brawn and brains, one of the nation's most trusted, considers me, little Gabby Wolf from Arizona, a valued member of his team.

I'm beginning to wonder if maybe Heather was right. Not that he wants to get into my pants, but that he might have developed a small crush on me.

I come out of the ladies' room, there he is.

I'm at the watercooler, so is he.

I run to the elevator, he's one step behind.

It's kind of flattering, actually.

"I still think he's hitting on you," Heather tells me over brunch at Penelope's, pigtails bobbing happily. She's wearing them to match with her navy tunic, leg warmers and Mary Janes, which only she could pull off.

"I don't."

"I do. This week it's 'hello, special friend,' next week it's 'say *hello* to my *special friend.*'"

"Get your mind out of the gutter," I say and stuff another forkful of scrambled egg into my mouth. "Speaking of special friends, I still haven't met Mark. How do I know that he's not an—" I insert air quotes "—imaginary boyfriend?"

Heather claims she has gone out with Mark a few times since Christmas, but I have yet to see him in the flesh.

"He's real, I promise." She motions to the waiter. "Can we get more coffee please?"

"Then why have I never met him?"

"Because I've never invited him over to the apartment."

"But why? You've been dating for a while now."

"Because—" She pauses as the waiter returns and refills our mugs. "Because, I can't sleep with him for another fourteen dates."

"What?"

"I'm training him," she explains, wrapping one of her long pigtails around her thumb. "To put me on a pedestal."

I stare at her blankly. "I don't get it."

"I am a prize. A prize is worth working for. See? If I give in now, he'll never take me seriously. If I make him pay his dues, he'll spend the rest of our lives treating me like a queen."

I think about it for a second and then say, "You're crazy."

"Trust me, it's going to work. All the books say so."

I reach over to her plate and steal a strip of her bacon. "Maybe. But aren't you dying to end your sex drought?"

She shrugs. "Good things come to those who wait. They better. I need to set the pattern now. Otherwise it'll be too late. People don't change."

After we've paid the check, we wrap on our scarves, button up our coats, and head to midtown for some shopping.

"I think I want a new pair of boots," I say stopping to peer at the Saks window display. As I'm checking out the black leather KORS boots on the model's feet, someone ploughs right into me and then keeps walking. What nerve.

"Hey," I shout after him. "Watch where you're going!"

Heather laughs in surprise. "Maybe people can change," she says.

February in Arizona is far less cold. By the middle of the month, I've received my usual two Valentine's Day cards from Cam (as well as a dozen red roses). Plus, we have our band. Alice came with us to hear all of them, and insisted on Champagne. I agreed, mostly because I no longer felt like arguing. And I no longer felt like sitting on the side-lines watching her dance with Cam. We've also chosen the florist (Alice's choice, naturally), and the bridesmaids dresses (also Alice's choice, since she'd already bought the material). "I couldn't resist—it was on sale!" she explained, showing me a nonreturnable, orange bolt of satin. At the moment, we are sitting in Eva's living room. Eva is an invitationer, if that's even a real word. All I know is that she has about a hundred books crammed with every type of invitation inside her house. According to Alice, Eva not only has impeccable taste, but her stuff is half the price of a retail store.

Possibly, but does a store smell like mothballs?

Alice is swooning over one of the samples. "This is just gorgeous. Really beautiful. Let's take it."

After looking though seven books, all the invitations start to blend into one big cursive blur. A black cat is sitting on the nearby windowsill hissing at me. Bet stores don't have those, either.

Alice wants imprinted flowers. Cam told me to get whatever I want, just make sure the writing isn't too swirly. I just want to go home.

I take a look at the one that Alice claims is so gorgeous. It's white, flowered, old-fashioned and boring. It might be the same one my grandmother had for her wedding.

"Do you have anything a little…different?" I ask Eva.

Hiss.

"Well, we do have this one book from New York."

I perk up instantly. "Can I see?"

She heaves a metallic silver tome from her bookshelf and drops it onto my lap.

I open up the book and see green! And blue! And red! I'm like Dorothy who just landed in Oz and my world is suddenly filled with color. "They're gorgeous," I gush.

Alice peers over my shoulder and makes a face. "Too loud."

And orange isn't? "Really? I think the colors are pretty. Really different."

"Definitely different, but color isn't classy, Gabrielle. White is for weddings. This isn't a shower. Speaking of which, we're thinking of having your shower on April twenty-second. Does that work for you?"

"Actually Alice, I've been thinking about it, and I don't want a shower." The last thing I want to do is ask Lila to do anything for me, and that's typically the maid of honor's job. My mother asked me about it just yesterday; I told her to forget about it.

She sighs. "It's really the best day."

"Like I said, I don't want a shower," I snap. My voice sounds a lot more bitchy than I intended, and I refuse to feel bad. "It's too much. I don't want everyone to have to spend more time and money." They're so lame anyway. I don't want to get a bunch of kitchen stuff I don't need.

"You can't skip your shower! That's ridiculous."

"I don't want to talk about it now," I say. "Let's get back to the invitations."

"So we're agreed. The white one from the Crane catalog."

I want to shake her. The word *no* is expanding in my throat, bubbling over. But when I open my mouth, nothing comes out. What the hell? Why can I shout at people in New York but not here? What is wrong with me?

I take a deep breath. Maybe this isn't the right argument to fight. After all, most of the invitations will go to her friends and family. Of the two hundred people invited, a hundred are hers. Thirty are my mother's, thirty are my dad's, and forty are Cam and mine's. And anyway, the invitation isn't that bad. "What do you think, Tricia?"

Tricia is filing her nails. "Definitely. It's gorgeous. People are going to just gasp when they see it."

There is nothing more pitiful than a beaten wedding planner.

"Fine, we'll take it," I say. "But can we pick a different font? Cam doesn't want anything too swirly."

"Of course," Eva says. She shows us a list of fonts that all look a lot alike. "This one is modern-looking," Eva says, pointing to the last one on the list.

Alice nods. "I'm sure Cam will love it."

"Perfect," Tricia says, still filing.

"We'll take a hundred and fifty," Alice says.

"That's enough for three hundred people!" I say.

"I know dear, but the hotel holds three hundred, and I realized I have more people to invite than I originally planned. And of course, we need a few extra in case we make a mistake when addressing them. Eva, did you get that? We need a hundred and fifty, plus the matching thank-you notes. And matching smaller invitations for the rehearsal dinner, which my husband has graciously agreed to pay for."

Ah. I forgot about the thank-you notes. What are the chances I'll be able to get Cam to write the ones for his side? Then again, he'll probably get his mother to do it.

Eva starts filling out forms. "Delivery will take about three weeks. But I need to know your text."

Alice opens her binder, clears her throat and starts reading: "Mr. and Mrs. Richard Winston request the honor of your presence at the marriage of Miss Gabriel Wolf to their son Mr. Cameron Winston—"

"What are you doing? What about my mother and father?" Is she kidding me?

Alice shifts uncomfortably. "It's customary to put the host at the top."

"Perhaps, but you're not the host. My parents are paying."

Tricia finally perks up. "Sherri absolutely has to be on the invite. And she has to be listed before the groom's mother." After all, my mother is the one paying her.

Alice lets out a big sigh. "All right, if you insist. 'Mr. and Mrs. David Wolf and Mr. and Mrs. Richard Winston request the honor.'"

Tricia nods. "That sounds fine."

"No, it doesn't!" I shriek, the bubble bursting. "My mother will go berserk. She hasn't gone by Wolf in years. She tried to get *me* to drop Wolf. It needs to say 'Ms. Sherri Dorowitz—'" Alice visibly grimaces. Not sure if it's the *Ms.* or the *Dorowitz*— "'and Mr. David Wolf and Mr. and Mrs. Richard Winston request the honor.'"

"It doesn't sound right," Alice protests.

"That's the way it has to be," I insist.

"Fine," Alice huffs and turns to Eva. "The thank-you notes should have 'Gabrielle and Cameron,' printed on the front flap, but the envelopes should show 'Gabrielle and Cameron Winston' just above their new address."

Apparently I'm changing my name. "Can you hold off on printing those? I haven't decided if I'm taking Cam's name."

Alice starts fanning herself with her hands. "What?"

"I might want to keep my name."

"You want to have a different name from my grand-children?"

The truth is, I haven't thought it through yet. All I know is that I don't want to make the decision this second. "Let's just wait on them."

Alice juts out her chin. "We need to print the thank-you notes."

"Why don't we just have the address on the back? We don't need to decide on my last name just yet."

I don't know what I want. Hmm, I'd better be careful or I might split again over this decision. Though it would suck either way. Ms. Gabby Wolf or Mrs. Cameron Winston, I get the same mother-in-law.

When I get home, there's a message on my machine from my former boss, Bernie. "Are you up for a freelance gig today? There's a chain of robberies in Phoenix. I'll give you twenty minutes to call me back, otherwise I'll have to call someone else. I tried your cell, but there was no answer."

Shit, shit, shit. I turned off my cell at Eva's and forgot to turn it back on. It's now two. I dial him back immediately. "I'm on it."

"Too late, Gabs, I gave it to Miranda."

"Oh, no. But I'm here!"

"I know, but you just missed it. Next time."

Damn. I flop onto the couch and bang my head repeatedly against the cushion. After a bit of moping and a bit of TV, I realize that's it's already five and that I have to start thinking about dinner. I take out a chicken from the freezer and pop it into the microwave to defrost. Look at me, I'm such a housewife.

Oh God, I'm Cam's house-fiancée. True, relationships involve give and take, but my relationship seems based on give up and get. I give up a career (and maybe my name) and he gets a cook.

A few weeks later in New York, I'm waiting for the afternoon meeting to start when Ron sits beside me and gives me a big smile. "Hey, Arizona."

"Hi, Ron." I say, sharing his smile.

And that's when I feel something under the conference table. Is that his knee? (God, I hope it's his knee.) Why is his knee touching mine under the table? There is no reason for his knee to be touching mine. It presses harder. Maybe he thinks my leg is part of the table. Yes, that's it. He thinks my leg is a pole. It's an accident. He wouldn't be purposefully touching my knee under the table. I'm his producer. He wouldn't hit on his producer. And anyway, he respects me.

Curtis storms into the room. "Guess what? The Cookie Cutter was found in some border town in Mexico."

"No way," I say and reach for my BlackBerry. The knee, thankfully, is gone. "What town?"

"Nogales."

"That's just a few hours from where I used to live!" I say.

"Apparently one of his victims hired a bounty hunter, who busted the Cutter in a diner called Rico."

"Did anyone get a visual?" I ask, in the midst of another knee assault. I look over at Ron, but he's staring straight ahead. I assume he must be knocking into me by accident. He must be.

Curtis shakes her head. "No visual, but he'll be back in the U.S. tonight. We'll do something for tomorrow's show. Any ideas?"

No visual…Nogales…a short drive from Phoenix…

Oh, I have plenty of ideas. But first I have to fall asleep.

"Why are you up so early?" Cam asks, poking his head into the shower. As soon as the alarm went off for the first time (Cam generally hits the snooze button at least twice), I bolted for the shower. "You're never up this early."

I can sleep in any day. But not today. "Got a news tip," I say. "I'm going back to work."

"Can I come in with you?" he asks, pushing back our grungy gray shower curtain.

"Okay, sure. But I'm really in a rush. So no hanky—"

His hands are already on my breasts.

"Cam, I'm serious," I say as he presses his body against mine. "I have to get to the station."

"You can't tease me with the possibility of shower sex, and then not go through with it. You know I love shower sex."

"I haven't even brushed my teeth yet!"

He kisses me and the hot water drips into my mouth. "I don't care," he says. "Let me wash your hair."

Sigh.

Forty-five minutes later, I'm finally on way.

"Bernie! I have a story for you."

"Hi there, Gabs." He pushes off his/my old chair and greets me at the door. "Nice to see you."

"You, too, Bernie. But there's no time for catching up. I got a tip and I want to follow the story," I say somewhat breathlessly.

"What story?"

"The Cookie Cutter story."

He leans against his desk. "I haven't heard any breaking news about it."

"I know. But my tip says that he's going to get busted today in Nogales."

Bernie cracks his knuckles, something he always does whenever he hears something that could be interesting. "Who's your tip from?"

"I can't reveal my source. But I want to get the story. It'll be an exclusive, I promise. All I need is a cameraman. Maybe Jordan? Nogales is only a hundred and seventy miles south of Phoenix. We can drive down in my car. The bust is supposed to take place at two forty-five. Wait. That's New York time. I mean twelve forty-five."

He looks at me warily. "Your source is in New York?"

"Just listen, Bernie. It'll take us three hours to get down there, which means we need to leave now."

Bernie laughs. "Gabby, how do I know this is real?"

"You know me. It's real." And now for my bluff. I say *bluff* because I really, really need a good cameraman. My Kodak throwaways just won't do the job. "If you don't agree, I'm going on my own and selling it to someone else."

"You got the dry mouth?" After working with me for so long, he knows the crazy way my instincts work.

"Drier than the Sonora," I lie. Truth is, I'm not all that thirsty. But who needs dry mouth when you have instant replay?

He considers, then says, "You've been out of it for a while. Maybe I should send someone else."

"Except I'm the only one who knows where in Nogales he's going to get busted."

He grins. "Same old Gabs. All righty, you got it. Take Jordan and good luck. Bring me back something good. And for Chrissake, don't turn off your phone."

When we pass through Nogales, Arizona, Jordan recommends we park the car in a lot and then cross the border on foot to get to the sister town in Mexico. This way we'll avoid having to get Mexican car insurance.

"How do you know that?" I ask him, grateful that he was

at work today. Jordan was always my favorite cameraman. He's been at the job for over twenty years, so he knows exactly what he's doing. He's only about five foot six, but he's built like an elephant, so he can practically pick up all of the equipment with one hand.

"My wife and I come down here to get our prescription drugs. Cheaper."

Ah.

We walk through the border checkpoint, cross the train tracks and look for a spot for lunch on Calle Elias. Somewhere other than Rico, obviously. I don't want the Cookie Cutter to see us. That would tip him off. I can't be responsible for him running off again.

At twelve-thirty, I tell Jordan it's time to get ready. Except I don't see anyone who looks like a bounty hunter. (What does a bounty hunter look like? I envision seven feet of muscle and tattoos, black leather everything and a hoop in the nose.) We head over to the convenience store across the street from Rico and wait for it to go down.

And wait.

I try on a sombrero.

"Not a good look for you," Jordan tells me.

At twelve forty-three, I am peeking out the window.

At twelve forty-five, I'm ready to jump.

At one o'clock, I still don't see any movement.

The woman behind the counter keeps asking us if she can help us ("You want to buy tequila? I have cheap,") but I keep waving her away.

"Maybe I got the time wrong," I say to Jordan. "Wait. Is Nogales in the same time zone as Phoenix? Arizona never changes the clock. You know spring forward, fall behind? Would that make a difference this time of year?"

"What are you talking about? Gabby, do you feel all right? Did you drink the water?"

"Just a bit longer, okay?"

A little bit longer becomes two o'clock. Then three.

I can tell he's getting restless. "I think it was a dead lead," he says.

My cell phone rings at four. From the call display I can see that it's Bernie. "We're still waiting," I tell him. "It's gonna happen, I promise."

"Sorry, kiddo. It already did. You were right about the Cookie Cutter being nabbed today. But he was nabbed in Boston."

Suddenly I'm thirsty. But it has nothing to do with inspiration. That tequila is looking mighty good.

15

Hello, Elevator Boy

I hate March weather in New York. I especially hate freezing rain. Naturally, today, when said freezing rain is hailing on me, I don't have an umbrella. Should I sprint to the subway or flag a cab? I'll try the cab route. Unfortunately, there are none.

"Haven't gotten the hang of it yet?" booms a voice behind me.

I turn around to see Nate, aka Elevator Boy. Funny how I've been hoping to see him for months, and I when I finally run into him, I'm soaking wet.

"Not yet," I answer. Maybe he won't notice my mascara issues and ask me out anyway.

He steps into the middle of the street and tries to wave

down a cab. "Sales exec to the rescue." Within one minute, success. "Here you go."

"Thanks." I'm reluctant to get inside because I might not see him again for another few months. Or at least until the next rainfall. I should just go for it. Ask him out. There's no reason not to. If he says no, what have I lost? I'm strong. I can do it. I can ask out a man! "Hey, you want to get a drink?" There, I said it. Way to go, me!

He hesitates. His glasses have fogged up, just as they did the first time we had a taxi encounter. But then he says, "Sure. That would be cool."

I climb into the cab and face the street, not wanting him to see the huge smile on my face.

Fifteen minutes later, we're in a tiny bar only a few blocks from my apartment, sitting in a booth at the back. The place is dark, the music jazzy. The bar is crowded but quiet, couples talking softly, enjoying their drinks, listening to the music. A candle on the table is flickering between us, making his skin glow. I'm hoping it's doing the same to mine.

At first the conversation is awkward, stilted— "Where are you from?" "What about you?"—and I'm worried that this was a mistake, that I should have just gotten into the cab and gone straight home, but by the middle of my first Cosmo and his first Scotch, we start to loosen up.

"I called you the Mystery Rain Girl to my friends," he says, and takes a slow, sexy sip of his drink.

"You're the Elevator Boy," I admit.

He takes off his glasses, folds them and leaves them on the side of the table. "I don't remember meeting you in an elevator."

I feel my cheeks redden. "It was my first day of work. It was just for a second. Now I feel stupid."

He puts his hand on mine. "Don't. I think it's sweet."

By the time we get through our second round of drinks, we've talked about our jobs, our bosses, our apartments, my recent move. He's from Philly, but he's been living in Manhattan for five years. He has a journalism degree from Penn.

"Then why did you go into advertising?" I ask.

"I shouldn't have. But that's where the jobs were. I should have stuck with it like you. You picked up and moved across the country to do what you wanted to do. Very commendable."

"Thanks. But it wasn't easy."

"Did you have to leave somebody back home?" His eyes are now looking right into mine. They're a deep beautiful brown, surrounded by thick lashes. I like his face. I like this guy.

"I did," I say slowly. "Isn't it against the rules to talk about exes on a first date?"

He grins and gives my hand a squeeze. "I won't tell if you won't tell."

"He wouldn't leave Arizona."

"Stupid," Nate says. "Funny. My last girlfriend and I broke up for the exact opposite reason. She didn't have a life of her own, and it drove me nuts. I'm a busy guy, and she hated that I couldn't entertain her twenty-four seven. It was tough."

I didn't think it was possible. But I think Nate gets it. Gets me.

When the rain finally stops, Nate walks me home. Part of me wants to ask him up, but something stops me.

"Can we do something again this weekend?" he asks.

"Definitely."

"How's Saturday night?"

"Perfect."

He kisses me lightly on the cheek and I watch him leave in a cab. While I'm looking forward to the second date, excited about the second date, I can't help but wonder if it's considered cheating when you live in two different universes simultaneously. This isn't something I can ask Dr. Phil.

Ever since the Cookie Cutter discovery, I've been weirded-out by my two existences.

Specifically, how is it possible that Jon Adams, aka the Cookie Cutter, was discovered in Mexico in one world and in Boston in the other? The only difference in my two worlds is that I moved to New York in one and got engaged to Cam in the other. What possible effect can that have on Jon Adams?

I wave to the doorman and then press Up on the elevator. Here's the thing: If the multiple worlds theory is real, then something that I did in one of the worlds must have changed the chain of events. I've thought long and hard about it and have come up with a million possibilities. It could have been a result of the news coverage on the Cookie Cutter I worked on for TRSN way back in November. Maybe my interview or questions triggered something in his mind and made him decide to go to Mexico, even though he'd been planning to go to his brother in Boston. Or maybe he'd been planning to go to Mexico, but in my Arizona life I somehow did something to get in his way. Maybe I was too long at the taco drive-through, which made the guy in back of me angry, who in turn got a case of road rage and later plowed into the guy who was supposed to meet Jon Adams to give him his fake passport, which made our fugitive decide to go to Boston instead.

As the elevator opens onto my floor, I realize I'll never know. But I don't want to worry about it. I have a date with Nate. That should be enough to keep me happy. In this existence, that is.

"Hello," I call into the apartment. No answer, but the light is on. "Heather?" I walk into my room to find her in my closet.

Her eyes are red, and her hair looks teased and tousled as if it hasn't been washed in weeks. "Where are my black capris?" she screams.

"Are you okay?"

"I'd be fine if I could find my fucking capris. Where are they?"

I back into the hallway. "I don't have your capris."

"Then where are they?" she says, following me. "Huh? Did they walk out of the apartment on their own two legs?" She makes walking motions with her fingers.

"Heather, you have to calm down."

"No, I don't! Go to hell!" she screams, then storms out of the apartment.

Time to hide the steak knives. The psycho roommate is back.

I don't find out until the next day (or two days later, whatever) that Mark, aka Library Lad, dumped Heather. Or, more accurately, she went to surprise him in the library and found him in the stacks, somewhere between F. Scott Fitzgerald and Stephen King, getting it on with another girl.

When I return from work, Heather is lying facedown on the couch, sobbing and kicking her feet. When I try to comfort her, she screams at me for the first ten minutes, then finally tells me what happened. "It was horrific," she wails.

"She didn't even have her shirt on. She was in her bra in the middle of the stacks. What a whore. Oh, and I saw a mouse run out of the kitchen and into your bedroom."

"What? When?" Ew. That's so gross. We never had mice in Arizona. Snakes, yes, mice, no.

"That's not really important right now. What is important is that Mark was cheating on me. I'm so stupid. I should have slept with him."

"If he couldn't wait for you, then he wasn't worth it. You'll meet someone else."

"Oh, what do you know, you moron?" she yells, then storms out of the apartment again.

"Can you pick up some mousetraps while you're out?" I ask, but the door has already slammed shut.

You know, I like Heather a lot more when she has a boyfriend.

I'm almost out the door in Arizona, when the phone rings.

"Hey, it's Lila. Where have you been? I left you like a million messages."

I have to physically stop myself from hanging up on her. "I've been busy," I say flatly. I've managed to avoid talking to her the last few weeks. I don't know what I'm supposed to say to her. I wish I could tell her that I don't want her to be my maid of honor but then I would have to tell her why, that in another world she's sleeping with my fiancé, and she'd probably have me committed.

"Are we still on for next week?" she asks.

My second dress fitting is next week and Lila is supposed to come with me. My mom came with me to my first one—I had to change the appointment three times to work with her schedule, but I really wanted her to see the dress. She played the role right—she oohed and aahed, and yelled at the seamstress that she had to make sure to get all the creases out of the material. She also told me that under no circumstances was I to get a veil.

"Why?" I asked, which led to a lecture about how the veil originated as a symbol of a wife's submission to her husband.

"I thought it was something about making sure the man loves you for who you are on the inside, not on the outside."

"You thought wrong. No veil."

Anyway, my mom wasn't so interested in returning to Snow White's for a second round, so I had asked Lila, and I know I vowed not to hold New York Lila's actions against Arizona Lila but, unfortunately, I don't think I can be in the same room with her without throwing up. Throwing up on my dress would be a huge, expensive problem. "Actually, you're off the hook. My mom is in town and wants to come with me again," I lie.

"All right. You're still coming with me for my fitting, aren't you?"

Alice gave the bolt of orange to a dressmaker she knows in Mesa. They're going to make the bridesmaids' dresses and the ushers' ties. I promised Lila I would accompany her this weekend. "I don't know if I can make it. I promised Alice I would, um, look at party favors. Sorry."

"Oh, come on. I have to make sure it looks good. How else am I going to pick up all of Cam's—"

"All of Cam's what?" I almost scream.

"Friends," she finishes. "Gabby, are you all right? You sound tense."

I take a bite out of my thumbnail. "I'm fine. Gotta go." I hang up without saying goodbye.

* * *

"You're not wearing that in public, are you?" Heather asks me as I'm about to leave the house. She's sitting cross-legged on the couch in the same flannel pajamas she's been wearing all week. Except for going to class, she hasn't left that spot. Her butt imprint is permanently indented in the couch. For some reason, she keeps watching the *Die Hard* DVD. Over and over. "It was our movie," she said when pressed, which I didn't fully understand, and which scared me a little. I offered to Netflix her something more along the lines of *Pretty Woman* but, in response, she just threw the DVD case at my head.

I look down at my jeans and the off-the-shoulder sweater that I thought looked pretty good.

"You look like Cyndi Lauper on acid," my oh-so-pleasant roommate tells me. "You'd better change."

"Heather, I don't care what you think. I like what I'm wearing. Enjoy the movie. Again," I add, and then lock the door behind me.

If she doesn't find a new guy soon, I might need to move. I might need to move anyway. I found a dead mouse in my closet this morning.

I meet Nate at Kittichai downtown. We sit in the corner and drink lychee martinis. "You look gorgeous," he tells me over dumplings.

I beam. I found a winner. He is passionate. He is sensitive. Over pad thai, I discover that he's an Aries.

"We're a perfect match," I tell him.

"That explains it then," he says, eyes not leaving mine.

After dessert, we have a drink at the bar upstairs. We sit on a couch and talk, talk, talk, about our parents' divorces, about how it shaped our views on love and on life. "I would never get divorced," I say. "I know how hard it is on the kids."

"Me neither," he says, and we talk some more until it's 2:00 a.m. and my head feels light, and the cushions feel soft, and his hand is on my knee, and the bar is flashing their lights and asking us, and then telling us, to leave.

We leave the bar, holding hands, and he's sweet and cute and I like him, and on the corner of the street, he pulls me into him.

His mouth is warm and salty. The kiss feels good. Different, but good. When I open my eyes, he's smiling. He hails a cab.

"One stop?" he asks, eyes hopeful.

"Two stops," I say. "This time."

It's 9:00 p.m. Monday and the office is practically empty, but Ron asked me to do some research on a story for tomorrow's show, insisting he needed it tonight. I turn off my computer, pick up my bag and stop by his massive office. He has a gorgeous oak desk, a buttery black leather couch and a view of the city.

"Arizona, come in."

"Hi, Ron. Here you go."

"Thanks, this is great. Close the door and have a seat."

Warning bells are ringing loud and clear in my head, but he is the talent, so I give him the benefit of the doubt, close the door and sit.

He gets up from his desk, rolls up his sleeves and sits next to me so that our thighs are touching. "How are you?"

"Good, thank you." I scoot over so there's some breathing room.

"I hardly get a chance to talk to you anymore."

"I'm always around." The truth is, I've been making myself scarce whenever I spot him in the distance. Trying to, anyway. The way he looks at me, as if I'm a seventy-dollar glass of wine that he'd like to take a sip of, has been making me queasy. "Busy, but around."

"You're not in a hurry tonight, are you?"

"Actually, I am. I have a date." I have a date with myself to wash my hair. Nate and I are not going out again until Saturday, but Ron doesn't have to know that.

He makes these horrendously unflattering puppy-dog eyes. "Cancel. I'll take you for a drink."

I'm not sure what the right thing to do is here. Obviously, it's not to sleep with the talent. I didn't get to where I am by sleeping with anyone, and I don't intend to start now. On the other hand, if I'm rude to him, he can easily have me fired. "I appreciate the offer, but I can't. Honest, I'm already running late." While I talk, I stare at the yellow gold wedding band on his left hand, hoping he'll get the message.

He smiles at me now, bemused. "I like you, Arizona."

"Thanks, Ron. I like you, too."

"No, I mean, *I like you*."

He was never very good at ad-libbing.

"You're married," I say, with a half laugh, trying to keep all this light.

"So?" he says, eyes roaming over my body. "You're very attractive. You should have been a reporter, you know. Come on, one drink."

I stand up. And give him a smile. "Thanks, Ron, but I can't." I take my jacket and bolt through the door.

Fuck, fuck, fuck, I think as I dart through the hallway. How dare he? I'm a professional here, yet he's treating me like some sort of producer-whore.

★ ★ ★

"Do you think Lila is pretty?" I ask. I'm lying on Cam on the couch. He's watching the his all-time favorite movie, *Caddyshack*, and I'm trying to stop thinking. About the Cookie Cutter. About Ron. About Alice. About Nate. About Lila. I'm exhausted. Mentally exhausted. Two lives means two exhausting sets of problems. When did I sign up for that?

"She's all right."

"If you had a thing for her, would you tell me?"

He looks at me funny. "I don't have a thing for her."

"How do I know that?"

"Because we're getting married."

"Are you saying that you'd go out with her if we weren't engaged?" You know, I think all my cooking is making Cam gain weight. He seems softer. Not quite his best.

"Gabby, this is crazy. We *are* engaged."

"But how do I know that I'm the right one for you?" I think about Nate. How do I know Cam is the right man for me?

He pauses the DVD and kisses my neck. "I just know. I promise. Have I ever lied to you?"

"No," I sigh. Unfortunately I can't say the same.

He kisses me again. "And I never will."

It's Saturday evening and I'm alone in the New York apartment. Heather is visiting her parents for the weekend, which is a nice break. She's become the roommate from hell. Without this date to look forward to, I don't know how I would have made it through the week. With Heather yelling and moping at home, and Ron practically leaping on me at work, it's been a disaster.

Ron's glances have become more lecherous. Now that the cat is out of the bag, he sees no reason to hide his feelings, or more likely, his hard-on. I try to come late to meetings, but he saves me a seat. During the meetings he likes to see how long he can leave his hand on my thigh before I push it away. His record is ten seconds, and that's because my hands were above the table showing Curtis something on my BlackBerry.

Every night, he's asked me to do extra research so that we're both there late, and every night he's tried to get me alone in his office. Every night, I tell him I have to leave to meet Nate. I am not going to let him ruin everything I've worked for. No goddamn way.

But I don't want to think about him tonight. Because tonight I have plans. Tonight is the night I plan on sleeping with Nate.

Heather's dating rules notwithstanding, I think going home with a guy on the third date is acceptable. But the truth is, I don't care. I need to move on physically in my New York life. Cam's moved on with Lila; why shouldn't I move on with Nate?

The other advantage to Heather being out of town is that I have offered to make Nate dinner. I will use some of my newly expert housewifery skills to impress the new man in my life. I ordered the colossal shrimp from FreshDirect, deshelled *and* deveined. I privately enjoyed the irony that I'm using Alice's recipe to seduce a new man.

By the time the doorman calls up at eight that Nate is here, my room has been cleaned, sheets changed, apartment swept, candles lit, nails painted, bikini line waxed, hair straightened, wine chilled, Barry Manilow CD on deck, cleavage perfumed, legs and underarms shaved and moisturized.

Oh, baby, I'm ready.

"Hi," I say in my sexy Manhattan demure voice, handing him a wineglass. "Hope you like white."

He's looking extra adorable in a pale blue shirt and black pants. When I kiss him hello, slowly, deliciously, I can smell spicy cologne on his neck, gel in his hair.

"You look beautiful, as usual," he says and hands me a bottle of red. "For the next course then."

The conversation and the wine flow. We're sitting at the kitchen table, which I have set to perfection. I even bought flowers for the centerpiece. The non-orange centerpiece.

"These are amazing," he says after he swallows another bite of the coconut shrimp. "You're a terrific cook."

I've made this for Cam at least six times. And he never once told me I was a terrific cook.

I think my fiancé has been taking me for granted. It wasn't always like that. Not before we were engaged. But ever since I said yes…ever since I gave up New York…

"You still with me?" Nate asks, interrupting my thoughts about Cam.

I shake my head in apology, slightly flushed. I should not be thinking about Cam tonight. I should be thinking about Nate. The hot, sensitive Aries who is sitting in my apartment. "Sorry. I'm here. Spaced out there for a second."

"You look cute when you space out."

Cam doesn't tell me I look cute when I space out. He tells me I have to be more assertive. Which I'm not. Not in Arizona, anyway. Not these days. But in New York, I'm superwoman. I asked Nate out! I think I even ask fewer questions here. I'm the same person; it doesn't make sense that I'd act differently in both. Although, maybe everyone acts differently in different situations. With Melanie, I'm the listener, the comforter. With Lila I'm the talker, the patient. With Curtis, I'm capable. With Nate, I'm confident. Aggressive. With Cam, I'm...weak. When did that happen?

I push my thoughts aside and serve dessert, a chocolate cake made from scratch. After desert, there's more wine, and we move to the couch, where his glasses come off and there's more kissing. And more kissing. Nate is a great kisser. Different from Cam but—

Must stop thinking about Cam. He's certainly not thinking about me. He's probably in bed with Lila right this second. I try to push the ugly image out of my head. "How about we move to the bedroom?" I ask. Yes, it's a question, but it's completely rhetorical. I can guess his answer.

He jumps off the couch, smiling and nodding. I guess that's a yes.

I lead him toward the bedroom, shedding my clothes as I go. Top—on the hallway floor. Bra—in the air, landing over the door handle. When I get to my room, I shimmy out of my jeans and leave them in a heap by my bed. I climb under the covers.

He rips off his clothes in ten seconds flat and slides in next to me. He runs his fingers through my hair.

In the next few seconds, his hands are all over me, and mine all over him. I'm going to do this. I'm really going to have sex with another guy. I really want to have sex with another guy. I get more turned on by the second, and then he whispers, "I can't wait to make love to you."

I freeze.

That's what Cam said to me. The first time. Who is this strange guy I'm in bed with who is using Cam's words? I barely know him.

"Let me get something," he says and reaches onto the

floor. I'm guessing he's searching for a condom in his jeans' pocket, and the thought makes my hands shake.

I can't do this. "Stop," I say, breathlessly.

"Huh?"

"Nate, I can't. Not yet."

"You need more stimulation?" he pants.

"No, that's not it." I pull back from him. There's something else. "I just…well, I thought three dates would be enough for me, but it's not. I need to know you better. I'm sorry."

"Okay," he says, still winded. "We can take it slower." He starts kissing me again, and I kiss him back, and he plays with my hair until we both fall asleep.

Headache. Green light.

"Nate?" I say, his hands in my hair.

"Who's Nate?"

I open my eyes and find myself back in Arizona. Shit. I close my eyes again.

"Who's Nate?" Cam asks again, slightly more seriously.

"I said knot," I mumble.

"Not what?"

"Knot. My hair is knotted."

He wraps his arms around me and pulls me into him. "It sounded like Nate."

"I don't even know a Nate," I say, turning around so he can't look into my eyes. "Not in this life," I add so that I'm not lying. But he'll be able to tell that something's not kosher. How can he not? I was naked in bed with another man. Naked. In bed. I can't look at Cam. I just can't.

He laughs. "I know, I know. In another life when we're

both cats." Cam loves that movie, *Vanilla Sky*. He made me see it twice in the theater and rent it three times.

My stomach hurts. Badly. I feel queasy. What did I do? How could I have almost slept with another guy when I'm getting married in six weeks? What am I doing? I can't do this. I can't. I don't care if it's a separate world. For me, it still feels wrong. I can't hook up with guys when I'm getting married. And what am I going to do when I *am* married? Never see a man in New York? Marriage is supposed to be forever. Marriage means no one else. I can't date other guys and wake up next to Cam. I won't.

I can't deal. I'm never going to get over Cam if I keep seeing him every morning. And I'm never going to feel like I'm being true to Cam, to the idea of marriage, if I keep seeing other guys. Or if I keep living a life that he doesn't know about. He told me he'd never lie to me. I want to— have to—be able to say the same thing.

"Be right back," Cam says and hurries off to bathroom.

Lying in bed, alone, I realize that I can't keep doing both. It's making me an emotional wreck. It's not worth it. I'm never going to be able to give a hundred percent to either life if I'm doing them both. I must get rid of the safety net.

I'm right back where I started, back in November, back in the desert.

I have to choose.

16

Phoneless in Seattle

The only questions now are which life to choose, how to choose and can I choose? I've got to get out of this weird existence warp. If there's a way in, there must be a way out. The whole situation races through my mind as soon as I wake up on Sunday in New York, with not only the usual mammoth headache, but with Nate beside me. I knew he was going to be here, of course I did, but it still weirds me out.

"Morning, beautiful," he says, kissing my forehead.

"Hi." I let him wrap his arms around me.

"How'd you sleep?"

Interesting question. Ever since the switcheroos started, I don't think I do sleep. Not much, anyway. Maybe that's why I'm so tired all the time. "All right."

We have breakfast and, after a quick kiss on the lips, he takes off. He has to get home to pack for a weeklong business trip to Seattle. "I'll call you when I get there," he says, and kisses me again, this time on the nose.

As soon as he's out the door, I search on the Internet for information on how to make wishes come true. I check back on the multiple-worlds sites but find nothing helpful. Getting desperate, I start randomly searching how to undo a wish. *Christmas wish, wishbones, wishing wells, wish upon a star, Make a Wish Foundation.* It would probably be wrong to ask the Make a Wish Foundation for help. If only it was my birthday and I could blow out the candles.

I wonder if killing myself in one life would work. But what if one of them is just a dream (a really weird, lifelike dream, mind you) and I end up killing the real me? Or what if both are connected in some way like Siamese twins? Kill one and we both die. Anyway, how would I do it? Shoot myself? I don't have a clue where to buy a gun in New York. Although, in Arizona you can practically buy them at the local convenience store. But do I want to kill off the Arizona me, or do I want to kill off the New York me?

It's also possible that I'm totally off the mark about this whole multiple-world theory. There's still a chance that I've just gone crazy. And in that case, killing myself won't help.

Moral, practical and theoretical issues aside, the bottom line is that I'm just plain chicken.

I wonder what would happen if I stayed awake all night in the life that I like. Would that close out the porthole to my other life?

Or maybe it has to be a wish. I can try out various techniques to see if they work. If wishing is what got me into this predicament in the first place (I think), why can't it get me out? Of course, first I have to decide which life I want. I start by making lists:

Pro Arizona
1. fiancé I love
2. house with Jacuzzi

3. great winter
4. cool gifts arriving
   from registry
5. can drive a car
   (and park it, too)
6. less expensive to live

Con Arizona
1. psycho mother-in-law
2. house near psycho
   mother-in-law
3. hotter than hell in summer
4. backstabbing best friend

5. disgusting bitten nails,
   fatter body
6. no job

Pro New York
1. job I love
2. adorable Elevator Boy
3. restaurants & nightlife
4. FreshDirect
5. nice nails, slim body
6. more confidence

Con New York
1. talent who molests me
2. psycho roommate
3. more expensive
4. damn cold winters
5. miss Cam
6. miss Cam

Sigh. I wish I could have all of the pros and none of the cons. Oops. Better be careful what I wish for…

Monday: New York

Surely Nate will call me tonight. We'll talk, we'll laugh, we'll make plans for the weekend.

Monday: Arizona

Why didn't Nate call me? He said he would call. He'll call tomorrow. Won't he? If he doesn't, I'll choose Arizona.

Tuesday: New York

I'm sure he's just really busy in Seattle. That's why he hasn't called. And if not, I'll move on. I'm not wasting my time on some guy.

Tuesday: Arizona

But why hasn't he called? I almost slept with him, for heaven's sake. Actually, I did sleep with him, but not sleep-sleep with him. Is that why he's not calling? Because I didn't do it? What, is he sixteen?

Wednesday: New York

I change the channel to the news. Partly for work, partly to see if there's been an accident in Seattle that would explain his lack of calling.

"He's probably met someone else," Heather says. "Maybe he hooked up with a coworker. Late nights, business travel, a few too many cocktails… It happens. When a guy likes you, he calls you every day." She grabs the remote from me and changes the channel to some reality makeover show.

True, when Cam and I first hooked up, he called me daily, but that was in college. I'm sure grown-up daters don't call each other every day. And anyway, Heather is the last person I'd take advice from.

I'm not going to let some random guy turn me into an insecure mess. I clench my hand into a fist. No way. I didn't come this far in this world to slip back to where I was. My nails are digging into my palm, so I unclench my hand and admire them. My beautiful strong nails.

No, I'm not going to let some guy, even if he is an Aries, make me doubt myself.

On Wednesday in Arizona, Alice comes with me to my next dress fitting.

And it's all Cam's fault. I told him I was going, and he said his mother kept bugging him about why I didn't invite her to come and that she wanted to come, and could she come, and then he asked me to please invite her along. If Cam knew I was in the process of choosing between a life in Arizona and New York, he probably would have kept his mouth shut. Not that I even know if I *can* choose. But still. There's no way a full day alone with Alice is going to help his cause.

But anyway, here she is. "What do you think?" I ask nervously, stepping out of the changing room. I don't think I can handle her telling me it's all wrong. I just can't.

But her eyes actually tear up. "You look like a princess," she says, then gingerly pats my satin skirt.

"Thank you." Holy shit. We are having a moment. Is it possible?

"Put on the veil so I can get the full picture," she says.

"I'm not wearing a veil."

"Of course you are, dear."

"No, really, I'm not. They symbolize…I forget, but it's not good."

"You can't *not* wear a veil. Excuse me, Aurora? Can we see some veils, please?"

"Absolutely," says Aurora. She scurries off.

So much for a moment. "I told you, I don't want one," I say, and then I wonder if that's even true. My mother didn't want me to wear one, so I didn't order one. But I'm not even sure if I want one or don't want one, or if they're sexist or sexy or what.

"It won't kill you to try it on," Alice says when Aurora returns, practically invisible behind a handful of veils.

"Personally, I think this one is the nicest," Alice says, grabbing the one at the top of the heap. Its train is at least six miles. She fixes the veil to my head and stands back to scrutinize.

"I think it might be a little much," I say. "I prefer one that comes down just past my shoulders."

She shakes her head. "That's a mistake."

Of course it is. After all, I suggested it. I want to tell her to get off my case. To go nag someone else. I want to, but I can't. I just don't have the energy. How can I be so different in New York than I am here? It makes no sense. Shouldn't my personality from my other life spill over? I want to stand my ground here. I'm itching to tell her where to get off, but I can't. I just can't. I'm frozen in a role I can't stand. "Fine," I hear myself say. "The long one. Whatever."

"So beautiful," Aurora says, nodding her approval. Of course, she approves—the long one is two hundred dollars more. "Your wedding is your day. You should go all out. Soon enough, it'll be all over, the honeymoon, too. Before you know it, you'll be chasing after two or three kids."

"It does happen fast," Alice says.

"Not that fast," I add quickly. I don't want her to think there are grandkids on the horizon. At least not in the next few years. If I choose Arizona, I absolutely have to get my career on track before I even think about having kids.

Alice waves a finger in my veiled face. "You can't wait too long. You never know what could happen."

"I'll be right back," Aurora says. "I'm going to find you some different combs to go with the veil."

Might as well take this opportunity to set Alice straight. "You should know, I'm not even trying to get pregnant until I'm at least thirty."

"And what if you have problems?"

"Why would I have problems?"

"You never know, dear," she says as she fluffs out the top of my veil. "I wanted to have four children, each two years apart."

"But Cam is five years younger than Blair."

She pulls the bottom of my veil so that it perfectly covers the train of my dress. "I had three miscarriages in between," she says matter-of-factly.

I am unable to hide my surprise. "You did?"

"Yes. It was horrible. Absolutely gut-wrenching."

For the first time I notice how tired her eyes look. "I'm sorry," I say. "Cam never told me."

She pats my bare shoulder through the gauze. "That's because I asked him not to tell anyone. It was so hard for me," she says quietly. "The worst time in my life. I pray every day that neither of my kids ever feels that type of pain."

For a moment I'm speechless. And then I sense she wants to tell me more, but that she won't talk unless pressed. "When did you have the miscarriages?" I ask gently.

She stares at the ceiling when she talks. "I miscarried the first time when Blair was a year old. The second time a year later. The third time, about a year and a half after that."

"How far along were you?"

"The first time, seven months. Three months the second time, five months the third. The first and third were boys. The one in the middle, I don't know."

"That must have been terrible." Which might explain why she is so overprotective of Cam and Blair. Especially of Cam, after losing two boys.

"It was. But you move on."

Aurora returns with a handful of sparkling combs. "I have a few options for you."

"That one is beautiful," Alice says, smiling and admiring a jeweled comb. "We'll take it." Her shift in mood is so swift that I wonder whether our conversation took place or if I imagined it.

The closer the wedding approaches, the more I obsess about Nate.

The weekend comes and goes. Nate doesn't call. They must have asked him to stay longer in Seattle. That must be it. He's working his ass off and he's too busy to call. We've only gone out a few times anyway; it's not like we were ever on a daily phone schedule. I'm sure he'll call me when he gets back, no matter what Heather says. She claims that the hardest part of dating in New York is that everyone's always traveling somewhere and that it totally kills the relationship's momentum.

When my phone rings at 1:00 a.m. the following Thursday, I'm certain it's Nate. Finally! It's been almost two weeks since I've seen him, and I was about to (unhappily) write him off. I reach out of bed and pick up the phone. "Hello?"

"Did I wake you?"

It's not Nate. It's Ron. Since I have to listen to that voice all day, I'd recognize it anywhere. I have no idea why he's calling me at home. He's never called me here. "No, I'm still up." What would have happened if I had fallen asleep? Would I have awakened in New York? Or would he only get me after a day in Arizona? Where the hell am I in the middle of the night? "How can I help you?" I ask tepidly. This had better be work-related. And, at this hour, it had better be important.

"I can think of plenty of ways, Arizona. I'm at the Soho Grand and I'm feeling lonely. You can start with coming over here." His words are slurring together. I can practically smell the booze through the phone.

"Ron, you know I'm not coming over."

"You're upsetting me, Arizona. You don't want to upset me."

Is this a threat? I've managed to avoid his stupid come-ons so far, but I'm not sure what I can do if he puts my job on the line. I'm obviously not the first woman this has ever happened to, but it doesn't mean I know how to handle it. "I don't want to upset you," I say, "but I can't come over."

"Is your boyfriend there?"

"No." Mistake. "Yes."

"Tell me what you're wearing," he says, ignoring my answer.

"Give me a break."

"Don't be a baby, just tell me. Do you sleep naked?"

I cannot deal with how highly improper this is. But I can't hang up on him. I can't make him angry. "Come on, Ron. You need to go to sleep. We'll talk in the morning."

"What's the big deal? I sleep in the nude all the time. There's nothing to be embarrassed about."

"Ron, I don't want to be having this conversation."

"You're right. It's ina-inap—"

"Inappropriate," I finish for him. Ad-libbing sober is hard enough for him, never mind drunk.

"But admit it, you're in-in-treeked. We should be having this conversation over drinks."

"I'm already in bed."

"Fine, let's have it at your place."

Patience, I remind myself. Think of your job. "Definitely not. I have a roommate."

"The more the merrier."

And then I laugh. I can't help it. His audacity amazes me. "I don't think that's her thing."

"I've been known to change a girl's mind. What's your address?"

"You are so not coming over."

"All right, Arizona. I give up for tonight. Tonight only. I'll see you in the morning. Wear that silky pink top of yours. The one where I can see down your shirt. Sweet dreams. I know you'll be in mine."

I knew I shouldn't wear that pink shirt to work. From now on I'm only wearing turtlenecks in front of Ron. "Good night, Ron." I end the call and stare at the dead phone.

Fuck. What the hell am I supposed to do? Maybe I should tell Curtis. She can tell me what to do. Although her first warning to me was that Ron was married and that I should keep my hands off. I doubt telling Curtis that I'm having personal issues with her bread-and-butter is going to help me. If she has to take sides, she's going to take his. And if it gets messy, I'm the one who'll be shown the door.

Perhaps I should go to HR. Maybe they can help. Or maybe not. I don't have any proof. Ron = ratings. Gabby = gone. I toss and turn and toss and turn.

Hire a lawyer? Go to the press?

Heather throws open the door.

Wonderful. Just who I feel like talking to now. "Yes, Heather?"

"Please ask your friends to not call in the middle of the night. Some of us are trying to sleep."

I so don't feel like dealing with her right now. "I thought you're an insomniac."

"That's hardly the point. New rule. No calls past eleven."

"Heather, as long as I'm paying half the rent, I'm going to get calls whenever I want."

"Then maybe you should find yourself a new apartment." She slams my bedroom door.

Excellent. A perfectly shitty end to a perfectly shitty night.

A thought occurs to me. If I leave this reality, will it cease to exist altogether? Or will Heather soon be advertising for another roommate? Will there be an investigation regarding my sudden demise?

Will Cam be too busy bopping Lila to give a rat's ass?

Three weeks to the wedding! All the reply cards have been received. (Sent to Alice's of course. "But dear, it makes more sense this way. You'll probably lose them.") The orange flowers, the party favors (silver picture frames), the menu (salad, dumplings, orange chicken or teriyaki salmon), the five-tier white wedding cake—everything has been arranged. Alice has taken care of it all. Except for the part about me in the white dress, I am practically a guest at this wedding.

I am sitting in the living room listlessly watching TV and packing Cam's stuff while he works on his insurance case, so we'll be ready to move into the new place right after the wedding. I wanted to move in earlier and take a honeymoon right after the wedding, but I was told that that was a bad idea.

"It's better that you go after Blair's baby is born," Alice said. "You don't want to have to come home for it."

Of course there's the issue of where to go. I want to go somewhere exotic. Like Kenya or Fiji. Alice disagrees.

"You should go to Hawaii. Richard and I loved it there. And you can get super specials in the summer."

Ever since I found out about the miscarriages, it's been hard for me to put my foot down. Not that I was great at it before, but at least I was trying. These days I'm pathetic. I finally relate to Viagra commercials—I feel seriously impotent. I would have thought that the strength I've been gaining in New York would spill over. But instead, it's inversely related. The stronger I feel there, the weaker I am here.

I think this box can fit one more book, tops. There we go. I close the folds, then tape it all the way around so it stays closed. "Hey," I say to Cam, realizing that he's joined me.

He shakes his head. "That's not the best way to do it."

"To do what?"

"To tape a box. You should tape it up first and then pack it. If you tape it after it's packed, it's going to rip. Let me show you." He sits next to me on the floor, sets up a box, then tapes it. Of course, it looks perfect. "See, that makes more sense."

"Things you should know," I say warily.

"It'll make packing easier. Trust me."

"Do you know everything?"

"Yes," he says and winks. He must see the weary expression on my face because he asks, "What's wrong?"

Sigh. "Nothing."

"Something's wrong Gabby. I can tell something's bothering you." He sits down beside me. "You seem kind of unhappy lately. What can I do?"

"I'm fine." I say and bite my thumbnail.

"How come you started biting again?"

I take my hand out of my mouth. "Just nervous. Wedding stuff."

"Don't be nervous," he says soothingly. "Everything is going to be fine."

I take a deep breath. "It's just that, well, sometimes I feel kind of useless."

"What are you talking about?"

"Like I can't do anything right."

"That's ridiculous," he says, sounding like Alice. "You shouldn't be so insecure."

You shouldn't be so patronizing, I think but don't say. It occurs to me that he's gotten more patronizing as I've gotten more insecure.

"Anyway, you do a lot of things right."

"Like what?"

He pushes aside the box and kisses me on the mouth. "You kiss pretty good."

I smile through my sadness. "That doesn't count."

"It definitely does. You're a terrific kisser. And you're smart and sexy. You're brimming with usefulness. Overflowing."

If I'm brimming, why do I feel so empty? Sometimes I feel like a ghost. As if no one can see or hear me.

As if I'm not really here at all.

17

Don't Forget to Smile

"Surprise!"

Not again. Not another surprise party. Only this one isn't an engagement party. I have just stepped into my surprise bridal shower, and all the guests are female. At least fifty women are gathered in Alice's house, a few I recognize, most I don't.

Orange streamers are draped on the walls; platters of square sandwiches and potato salad line the countertops; piles of gifts are stacked by the fireplace. I was told to come over for an emergency seating-plan crisis, but I realize too late that the pleading phone call was just a ruse.

"You have to see the look on your face!" shrieks Jessica. "You had no idea, did you?"

I scan the room to see just who exactly is here and am

relieved to spot my mother, in the corner, with a none-too-pleased expression on her face, eating a dry celery stick, and then Melanie, on the couch and deep in conversation with Lila.

Oh no, Lila. I've pretty much come up with every excuse in the book so I won't have to see her. But here she is, in all her fiancé-stealing glory.

I say hello to strange faces as I make my way toward my mother. "Surprise," she says, with more than a touch of bitterness.

"I can't believe you didn't warn me," I whisper.

"What, and ruin all the fun?"

"I said I didn't want a shower."

"I know. So you can imagine my surprise when I got the invitation in the mail. It was so nice of her to consider consulting me on the date."

I sigh. "I've learned to just shrug it off."

"Now you're going to have spend your whole life shrugging things off. You should have confronted her at the beginning and nipped this mother-in-law problem in the bud months ago." She stabs her celery stick in the air to make a point. "You're in for years and years of aggravation."

Have I ever confronted anyone? "That's a wonderful thing to say to your daughter the week before her wedding."

"They don't pay me to sugarcoat."

"What does that even mean?" I grab onto her arms. "I need to say hello to my two friends. Come with me?" I'm afraid to leave her alone in case she attacks someone.

"Go ahead. I want to check out the house. I was thinking of sneaking into Alice's sock drawer and mixing them all up so none of them match. I bet that would drive her nuts. Then maybe I'll just hide in her closet until this is over."

"Try to control yourself. I'll be back soon." I reluctantly let go of her arm and head over to my friends. Along the way, I notice that Alice's friends and family (which is ninety-nine percent of this party) are staring at Melanie, the Monica Lewinsky of Arizona.

"Thank you so much for coming," I say, hugging her, feeling awful that she has to endure all this unpleasant attention today. Next to Alice's yapping friends, the tabloids seem tame.

Melanie squeezes me tightly. "Wouldn't miss it for the world."

I guess now I have to hug Lila. "Hey."

"I can't believe it's your shower!" she sings. "You're almost a married woman."

"I know."

"You sure you're ready for this? You'll never have sex with another man."

"That's usually what marriage means."

Melanie puts her arm around me. "You guys are meant to be. I just know it."

Lila winks. "It'll be a sad day for the singles of Arizona when you two are officially off the market."

I know she's kidding and that her comment was entirely appropriate (within the context of this conversation), but it still sends willies down my spine. You don't just wake up one morning and find your roommate's ex-boyfriend sexy. You harbor a crush on him, waiting for your chance, waiting to pounce. Waiting for his girlfriend to move to New York. No, I'm convinced that even in this world, Lila has a thing for Cam.

There's a sourness in my mouth, a sourness I can't swallow away. I look for the platter of celery to clean my palate, but don't see it. "Has either of you seen the veggie plate?"

Melanie shakes her head. "I don't think there is one."

So where did that celery stick come from? Oh, God. My mom brought her own carb-free snacks from home. I start biting my fingers again. How insanely embarrassing. How insane, period. I should never have let her go off on her own. When my mother is in one of her insane phases, she's a serious danger—I'd better find her before she does any serious damage to Alice's sock drawer, I decide. "I'll be right—"

"Excuse me! Excuse me!" shrieks Alice. "It's the time we've all been looking forward to. The time to play How Well Does the Bride Know the Groom?"

I wonder if I can join my mother in that closet.

"Gabrielle, you have to sit here," says Alice, pointing to a chair that has been decorated with—shock of all shocks—orange streamers. "I've asked Cam twenty questions about himself, which he answered. Now I'm going to ask you the same questions. Every time you get an answer wrong, you have to take another piece of gum." She points to the bowl on the coffee table, which is overflowing with Bazooka bubble gum.

I cannot believe I am going to have to participate in such a lame game. I cannot believe how embarrassed I'm going to be when I get all these answers wrong. This is the most miserable game I have ever heard of, obviously invented by a group of sadistic mothers-in-law hoping to humiliate their future daughters-in-law. I fake a smile and sit.

My mother takes this opportunity to rejoin the party. She leans against the wall and waves. She unzips her purse and removes a plastic bag filled with celery sticks.

"Here we go!" chirps Alice. She takes out a stack of white index cards and begins reading aloud. "What is Cam's favorite color?" She leers at me, waiting for me to get the answer wrong.

The pressure, the pressure! The crowd of strangers is staring at me, waiting for me to say the wrong answer. But wait! I know that one! It's... "Purple!" I say triumphantly.

"Yes," says Alice, checking the back of the card.

The crowd claps politely.

"What was his first pet?"

"Ruffles the cockatoo is the only pet he ever had."

"Right again," Alice says and the crowd claps.

I look up at my mom and she gives me a thumbs-up.

"What is Cam's favorite movie?"

Hmm. That's a tough one. "His true favorite movie is *Caddyshack*. But there's no way he'd admit that, so I'm going to go with *Vanilla Sky*."

"Right again," she says, sounding more than a little surprised. "Plus you got the next question right, too—what's his favorite movie that he's too embarrassed to admit?"

More clapping. I'm on a roll! Except my audience is starting to fidget. I think they're getting bored.

"What is Cam's favorite meal?" Since Alice's eyes are twinkling for this one, it's not too hard to figure out.

"Coconut shrimp."

She smiles, but then the questions start coming fast and furious.

Alice: "How old is his oldest pair of underwear?"

Me: "Eleven years." I have to admit it makes me uncomfortable that Alice has any information regarding Cam's underwear.

Alice: "What is my son's favorite sports team?"

Me: "The Cardinals." And this is supposed to be hard?

She fans the index cards. "You know, this game is getting a bit tedious. Let's play something else."

Hey, I was just starting to have fun! Sure, they were all excited about the game when they thought my mouth would be stuffed with gum. "No, let's continue," I say. This is my chance to show Alice that her son confides in me. That I'm important to him. That I'm the next queen of his court.

"How about bridal bingo?" the very pregnant Blair asks.

"I think we should finish this game," says my mom from the back of the room.

Alice rolls her eyes. "But it's boring."

"My daughter wants to continue, so let's continue." There is an edge to my mother's voice. One I recognize.

"I don't want to," Alice says, eyes slit.

My mom reaches into her purse, then into a plastic bag, and slowly, purposefully, removes a celery stick, lifts it high above her head…

Oh, God. She's going to do it. She's going to throw the stick at Alice.

…tilts her hand into tossing position…

Don't do it! Mom, no!

"I think Gabby should finish the game," Melanie pipes up.

After an audible gasp in the room at the sound of the quasi-celebrity's voice, Alice mutters a quick, "Fine, we'll finish the ridiculous game. What does Cam like on his pizza?"

The celery stick pauses in midair. Then, instead of soaring across the room, it finds its way to my mother's mouth.

Chomp.

Whew. "Pineapple and pepperoni," I answer.

My mom winks at me, and I wink back.

When I get home, Cam is waving a bottle of champagne. "What's this for?" I ask.

He's smiling. "We closed the house today."

"Really? Wow. Congrats."

"Congrats to us." He pops the cork and it flies into the ceiling, making a smacking sound and a slight dent in the paint. "Whoops."

"At least we don't own this place."

He pours the champagne into two glasses—two glasses we registered for. "In the new place, we'll be opening all bottles outside."

Tuesday, the week before I get married, I step out of the elevator and there he is.

There *they* are.

Nate and Mystery Woman. They're standing outside the building, on the other side of the glass doors, talking. But not regular how-are-you talking. Not that I can hear them. Not that I need to. You know how in TV shows, the characters are always standing absurdly close together so the cameraman can get the right shot? And you hope that the actors carry around breath mints or spray because their faces are barely a millimeter apart? That's how close Nate and Mystery Woman are. His hand is in fact touching her upper arm. I peer. At least, I think it's her upper arm.

My feet are stapled to the lobby floor. Heather was right. Nate has hooked up with someone else. A coworker, perhaps? Jerk. Ass-wipe. He sleeps with me (yes, yes, not sleep-sleep, but still) and says he'll call, but doesn't even have the courtesy to tell me he's seeing someone else. Or the courtesy to tell me that I should no longer be waiting for his call! It's been many weeks and I haven't been staring at the phone, praying for it to ring, but I have occasionally glanced at it while cursing its silence.

He steps into the street and hails a cab. He and Mystery Woman get inside. And I thought that hailing was something he did just for me.

I feel like crying.

But the crappy part is, the absolute worst part, is that it's not because of Nate's rejection. No, I feel like crying because I feel empty. Like a shell. Because I realize that I don't really care that Nate rejected me. Because as much as I wanted to find someone new to be in love with, Nate didn't really matter to me at all.

And that's what makes me want to scream, to kick, to cry.

The fact that I may never love anyone the way I love Cam.

"Follow me, everyone," instructs Tricia, physically placing us in order. It's Thursday evening and we're in the middle of the wedding rehearsal at the hotel. So far the evening is going relatively smoothly, except for a few small concerns: one, my mother has been eyeing Alice like a lion eyes a gazelle; two, Blair looks so pregnant that I'm afraid she might give birth at the ceremony; and three, I'm concerned that I'm going to feel like a guest at my own wedding, since I barely know any of the people on the guest list. And I only like one of my bridesmaids. Furthermore, I didn't choose the menu. Or the flowers. Or the tablecloths. Or the band. Safe to say, it's nothing like that beach ceremony I used to dream about.

And the groom? Is *he* the man of my dreams?

"Now you have to walk slowly," Tricia is saying. "One foot in front of the other, and don't forget to smile."

First the grandparents, then the bridesmaids and ushers, then Blair and Matt, Alice and Richard, Cam, Lila, my mom and then my dad (yes, they each walk on their own).

As I wait my turn, I feel like a fraud. And it's not because I'm wearing a blue sundress, although that isn't helping. It's because I promised myself that I would have to decide ASAP which life I want, and ASAP has already passed. I still don't know. I don't want to be married in one life and remain fancy-free in another. It's just wrong. I'm getting married in four my-time days (two Arizona days) and I'm still torn. One second I think I should get married, the next second I think it's a mistake. I have to choose one life over the other, once and for all. But I can't make up my stupid mind. And the worst part is, even if I do finally make a decision, what then? Will I even be able to actually choose? Deep down I believe that the act of choosing a life will block the other one out, but what if I'm wrong? What if I'm destined to spend my whole life divided?

"Your turn, honey!" my mom calls from down the aisle. "Keep your shoulders down!"

"Yes, Gabs," says my dad. "You don't want to look like a quarterback."

Hey, look at this! My parents are getting along.

"No!" both Alice and Tricia shriek simultaneously. I stop in my tracks.

"The bride absolutely cannot be part of the rehearsal," Tricia says.

Alice runs up the aisle. "It's bad luck," she says, at my side again and breathless.

It's a wedding miracle. My parents are agreeing. Alice and Tricia are agreeing. I better not have entered another parallel universe. I really shouldn't joke.

Tricia says, "The maid of honor is usually the stand-in."

"Blair, get over here!" calls Alice.

"I'm tired," whines Blair, who's plopped her body and unborn child on one of the folding chairs.

"Lila!" I call down the aisle, but she's immersed in a conversation with my groom. Surprise, surprise.

"I'll do it," Alice says.

Tricia tries to block her. "I don't really think that's appro—"

Alice pushes us both out of the way, turns toward the front of the room and begins walking down the aisle, singing the wedding march.

Everyone in the wedding party has their mouths open. Even Richard, my future father-in-law, looks uncomfortable. It's not every day you get to watch your wife marrying your son.

Tricia squeezes my hand and mutters just loud enough so I can hear, "Gabby, I promise I will watch her like a hawk at the wedding. If she tries to pull anything, I will personally take one of her orange flower arrangements and knock her over the head."

Afterward, we all go over to Alice and Richard's for dinner. Richard is wearing an apron that says Kiss the Cook, and Alice is scurrying around making sure everyone's glasses are filled.

Once the main course is over, before dessert is served, Richard takes off his apron and taps his wineglass with his fork. "If you can all be quiet for a second, I'd like to make a toast."

I have to admit, I'm surprised. I don't think I've ever heard Richard speak in public. In fact, I can't remember the last time I heard him speak, period. Cam puts his arm around me and squeezes my shoulder.

Richard clears his throat. "We're here tonight to celebrate the upcoming wedding of my son Cam and his fiancée Gabby."

Everyone cheers. Richard waits for quiet and then continues. "As some of you might know, Alice and I will be celebrating our forty-first wedding anniversary next week. Some people scoff at the idea of love at first sight, but the day Alice walked into my father's store where I was working the register, that was it for me. It wasn't just her big smile and shining eyes, although she was, and still is, the most beautiful woman in the world. It was just a feeling I got. But what a feeling. No denying it, it was the real thing. I knew right then and there I wanted to spend the rest of my life with her. I told her that her purchase had come to eleven ninety-nine, and she shook her head and told me that instead of paying she would redesign my display window, and the rest is history."

The crowd goes "Aw!"

"One day a little over three years ago," he continues, "Cam came into my store and told me he was seeing someone. 'Tell me,' I said. 'What's she like?' 'She's beautiful,' he answered. 'She's smart, she's funny, she's sweet. But it's a lot more than that. I can't explain it,' my son said, 'but I just know it's the real thing.'" He raises his glass. "And now, please join me in a toast. Those of you who are parents all know that we want our kids to have twice as much as we do—to be twice as happy, live twice as long, be twice as successful. So to my son—I wish you two houses, four children and eighty-two years of marriage to your beautiful young bride."

Tears spring to my eyes, and Cam and I both walk over to hug Richard, and then, yes, hug Alice. I can't believe how sweet that was. Married for forty-one years...I can't even imagine. Do I want to imagine?

"You should have seen those window displays before I got my hands on them," Alice says. "They were embarrassing."

After another glass of wine, I find my father in the sea of people.

"I can't believe my favorite kid's all grown up," he says, hugging me and rubbing his chin into the top of my head.

I smile. "I'm your only kid." For a fleeting moment I'm a little girl again and I feel safe in his arms. "Daddy...is this the right choice?"

He pulls away and searches my face. "Honey, if this isn't what you want—"

I laugh nervously. "Don't worry. I'm fine. Just prenuptial jitters. I know what I'm doing."

If only that were true.

It's Friday in New York, one Gabby-day before my wedding, and I'm still stuck. After an exhausting (but exhausting in a good way) day of work, I manage to avoid running into Ron, but see Nate and Mystery Woman in the elevator.

Funny, how in the beginning, months and months went by and he was MIA, and now that I wish he really was MIA, I see him everywhere.

"Hi," I say, looking at the floor.

"Hey. How've you been?"

Now that's awkward for ya. I mumble something even I can't understand and head out to the subway.

I don't get a seat. Great. What else can go wrong today? Somewhere underground around Fortieth Street, it grinds to a halt and goes pitch black.

Wonderful.

That had better be a woman's purse rubbing against my leg. I clutch my own bag tightly to my side. A few minutes later, we start up again and finally I'm at my stop. When I step outside, it starts to rain.

Lovely.

Soaking wet, I rush to the apartment and I go straight to the bathroom to wash away the grime of the city. Then I realize that I'm starving and that I should have picked something up for dinner. I'm about to open the fridge when I spot a note on the freezer door: "G: You drank my apple juice. I did not give you permission to drink my apple juice. You owe me two dollars and fifty cents for my apple juice. H"

I did not drink her apple juice. She is crazy. I take the note off the fridge, crumple it and toss it into the garbage can. The disgusting, smelly garbage can. Everything in this city is smelly and gross. I hate this garbage can. In my new house with the Jacuzzi, I'm going to have a garbage disposal.

I spend the rest of the evening watching TV. Heather storms in around eleven and yells at me for not emptying the garbage.

As I get into bed, I look forward to falling asleep. Look forward to Arizona, where the streets are clean, where disposals rein over cans, where Cam is waiting for me. Just as I'm floating in that fuzzy place between wakefulness and sleep, the phone rings, jarring me. Hoping it's Cam, I feel my heart speed up. "Hi, baby," I murmur.

"It's me," says Melanie.

And then I remember where I am. Or more precisely, where I am not. Which not for the first time causes me to wonder, what would have happened if I had been asleep? Would someone else have answered the phone while I was nestled in Cam's arms, back in Arizona? Someone with my body? (Or my clone's body?) Where the hell am I when I'm asleep?

"Yoo-hoo," says Melanie. "Anyone there?"

"I'm here," I say. Though at this point in my life, I'm not entirely sure.

"You're not going to believe who I just saw." There's a lot of static and I can hear loud noises in the background.

"Who?"

"Cam and Lila. On a date."

Surprise, surprise. "Where were they?"

"You mean, where *are* they. I'm at China Grill in Tempe. I'm on a blind date and I just passed them on the way to the bathroom. I'm in a stall right now. She was feeding him with her chopsticks."

I feel sick. They've gone public.

"It was so nauseating," she continues. "But I had to tell you. I mean, I'd want you to tell me, if I were in your place."

"Did they see you?" I hope they did. I hope they did and felt horrible and guilty and had a big fight.

"I don't think so. But they will. I'm going right over to yell at them. I'm going to tell them—"

A siren goes off outside and I don't hear the end of Melanie's sentence. "I missed what you said. Sorry. It's loud here."

"I said I'm going to tell them that they suck."

Right. That'll crush them. "No, don't say anything to them. Please. There's nothing either you or I can do."

We chat for a few more seconds, and then I hang up and stare at the ceiling. Another siren goes off and then the phone rings again, but I just let it ring. It's probably Melanie calling me back to tell me he's kissing Lila now, they're making out right in the middle of the restaurant, or even worse, he's on his knees proposing. I can just picture it: the whole restaurant applauds when she throws her arms around his neck and yells, in *When Harry Met Sally* style, "Yes! Yes!" But when I check the caller ID, I see it's Soho Grand. I groan. Just what I need, Ron wondering what I'm wearing, or hopefully, what I'm not wearing. I want him to stop calling me. I want him to go away. I put the pillow over my head to stop the ringing.

"I'm going to kill you!" Heather screams, pounding on my wall.

I hate that he calls me at home at night. I hate that Nate never called. I hate that I don't really care that Nate never called. I hate that Brad barfed all over my bathroom. I hate how cold the winters are. I hate that I share a wall with a crazy woman. I hate that somewhere, in another life, right now, Cam could be proposing to Lila.

As the third siren of the night wails in the distance, I toss and turn, and toss and turn, and realize that I'm sick of the subway, sick of the men, sick of the cold. Sick of the garbage.

And then I hear the squeaking in my closet.

You've got to be kidding. On top of everything, the mouse is back. I have to get out of here. What if all this noise keeps me up and I can't fall asleep and then my Arizona porthole closes and I'm stuck in this world forever? I need to go to sleep. Right now. I throw on jeans and a shirt and my sneakers, grab my purse and run like hell.

All the way to the Bolton Hotel in Times Square. No phone. No Heather. No mouse.

"I'd like a room please," I say to the man at the service desk.

"For how long?"

"Let's start with one night."

"Would you like the king-sized featherbed?"

"Sure. Why not? A quiet room please."

"Something high up then. That'll be two hundred dollars."

I hand over my credit card. For two hundred dollars, those feathers had better be goose.

"Do you have any baggage, ma'am?"

Oh yeah, do I ever. "No."

"Then you're all set," he says, his face devoid of expression. I guess he's used to women with no luggage checking in after midnight. "Here's the key card for room 2715."

I wait for the elevator, and when it opens, I'm face-to-face with Brad.

He turns red when he sees me. "Hey, Gabby. How's it going?"

"Good, thanks. You?" He's the last person I feel like dealing with now.

"Okay. Um. Listen I want to apologize for the night we went out. I don't remember most of it, but it couldn't have been good."

"No worries."

"Cool. Take care," he says. "Um, is Heather with you?"

"No. Why?"

"I just thought…oh, never mind."

What an ego. He was probably worried she'd pounce on him. I think about the last time I was here, and how he ignored her. I step into the elevator and press the button for floor twenty-seven. Or maybe he thought there was a party in one of the rooms. The last thing on my mind is partying. I'm so dead, I can hardly keep my eyes open.

I kick off my sneakers, strip off my clothes, close the blinds and pull down the covers. I flop down on my two-hundred-dollar bed and go straight to sleep.

18

Viva Las Vegas

It's Friday morning, the day before our wedding, and Cam's alarm has just gone off. Half-asleep, he snoozes it, then pulls me into his arms.

I love this man, really I do. I want to marry him. And maybe, just maybe, once we go through with it, the deed will be done, on earth as it is on (the other) earth. Once we get married, that's it. For better or for worse. If I prove to the powers or whatever that yes, I want to be Cam's wife and live happily ever after in Arizona, then maybe just maybe the heavens or whatever will smile down on me and end the insanity once and for all. In other words, I'll be proving to the cosmos that I'm no longer torn mentally, so please, will you stitch me back together?

In other words, when I marry Cam, I'll be making a

statement that I choose this life, and maybe the other Gabby will cease to exist. It's possible, isn't it? Please?

My heart starts to race. It suddenly occurs to me that all this craziness started when he proposed. That somehow it's all tied up in the wedding. Hence the solution: cancel the wedding. (*This* wedding, that is. Not the marriage, obviously.) I never wanted it in the first place. I don't want to marry him at the Sunset Hotel, in front of people I don't know, at a party I didn't plan, in a veil I don't want. A wedding should be a magical event, a meaningful ritual symbolizing the union between two kindred spirits. Besides, if I'm going to make a statement to the cosmos or whatever, it had better be *my* statement, not Alice's.

"Cam, let's elope."

"Hmm?" he says, nuzzling his head in my neck.

"I said I think we should elope."

Cam, now completely awake, tickles my side. "We're getting married tomorrow. We don't need to elope."

"Just hear me out. Getting married is about you and me, not about your mother, or my mother, or flowers, or bands, or bridesmaids, or anything else." The words spill out in a rush, tumbling over each other. "Eloping would be private. Just us. Something meaningful that the two of us can share on our own without all the fuss."

He must sense the urgency in my voice because he pulls away from me and sits up against the headboard. "That's the craziest idea I ever heard."

"I know, I know! It sounds crazy, but let's do it anyway. For once let's be crazy."

"It you wanted a private ceremony, you should have said so before."

Is he kidding? "I did. But you, and your mother, wouldn't

listen." I run my finger down his arm. "But it doesn't matter. That's past. It's the future that counts. Let's start the future right now. Come on, let's do it—screw the rest of it!"

He shakes his head, laughs, then puts his feet on the floor. "I have to get ready for work. Why don't you get some more sleep, then take a bath or something?"

I reach out for him, stopping him from leaving with a touch to his shoulder. "You don't get it. Our wedding is about *us*. It shouldn't be a show. It has to mean something." For more reasons than he can understand.

"It's too late," Cam says.

"It's not! You have to listen to me. It's so easy. We'll drive to Vegas. We'll go tonight. It'll be romantic. "

"Vegas is romantic?"

He's missing the point. "Forget Vegas. We can elope in Sedona. We already have our Arizona marriage license, so that won't be a problem. Or Tucson. Or how about the Grand Canyon? I've never even been there. But I don't care where we go. As long as it's not here."

He laughs again. "We can't call off the wedding, Gabby. It's all paid for. Your parents would kill you if we wasted their money. Everyone's already in town. It's not right."

"I think my parents would rather me be happy. And I'd pay them back. But if that's what you're concerned about, we don't have to cancel the wedding."

"Now you're talking sense." He kisses me on the nose.

"Yes! That's it," I say. "We'll get married our way today, then get married again tomorrow. Why not? We can still go through with the whole shebang. Tomorrow will be *their* party. The real wedding will be today. Say yes! Please, please say yes!"

"No. That's nuts. My mother will never go for it."

"It's not about your mother! It's about us. Cam, I want to marry you more than anything in the world."

"And we *are* getting married. To. Mor. Row."

"No, today. We won't tell your mother. It'll be our secret." It's so romantic, I can't take it!

His eyes are flickering with annoyance. "You want me to lie to my mother?"

"No, not lie. Just not tell her."

He shakes his head. "I won't. And the reason I won't is because it's not happening. Just go back to sleep, Gabby."

I punch the mattress. "Why can't you do this one thing for me?"

"Because it doesn't make any sense."

"It makes sense to *me*." I close my eyes. "Come on, Cam. Think about it. Every year your mother is going to want to do something for our anniversary. We'll never be able to celebrate it in private. This way we'll have the real day to ourselves without denying her a thing. Don't you see? It's perfect."

He sighs. "Come on, Gabby, you know I can't do that. I know you think my mother hates you, but she doesn't. She's trying. She really is. I think you're the one who hates her."

"I don't hate her," I say. And it's true. Sort of. She's annoying as hell (I'm being polite here), and I feel sorry for her. "Our wedding isn't about your mother. Why can't you see that?"

"Forget it. It's not going to happen. I just can't condone it."

Condone it? He can't condone it? It's then I realize that the problem isn't the wedding. The problem isn't even Alice. The problem is Cam. My throat feels like it's closing up, I'm so upset. "It can't always be about what's good for you. Sometimes you have to do what's good for me."

He slaps his forehead. "Oh. God. Is this about New York? Is that what you're talking about? Can't you give it up already?"

"That's so not the issue," I say shaking my head and feeling myself explode. "But now that you've brought it up, tell me something. Why did you make me think that I could have my dream *and* you? The moment my dream came true, you proposed. But it wasn't just a proposal. It was an ultimatum."

"What are you saying? I never—"

I can taste the bitterness. "Oh, not in so many words. But you made it clear that I couldn't have both." I think back to that morning I was getting ready to go to Mexico and bust the Cookie Cutter story wide open. When Cam joined me in the shower, and I thought he was being loving. But he was just being controlling. Possessive. Macho. "My career is a threat to you, and always has been."

"You're talking crazy."

"Am I? You wouldn't even try long distance. It's always been your way or no way at all. That's not how marriage works. I needed you to do one thing for me. Elope. Today. And you wouldn't." With a shock, I realize that I'm talking about us in the past tense.

He moves to get up, and this time I don't try to stop him.

My eyes fill with tears and I'm having trouble breathing. I place my hands facedown on the bed and try to steady myself. "It's no good. It's not going to work."

"Of course it is. You'll take a bath, I'll go to work. By the time I get home, you'll have calmed down. The wedding tomorrow will be perfect. The flowers, the tables, the ceremony. It's all taken care of."

Precisely the problem. Everything has been done by someone else. I've had no say whatsoever. "No, Cam. I meant, we're not working."

He stops at the door. "Excuse me?"

Tears are now spilling down my cheeks. "It's you, Cam. You and me. It's these roles that we've created for each other. For ourselves. We have to stop before it's too late. I'll never be happy like this."

He rolls his eyes. "You're happy."

"I'm not happy! Don't tell me I'm happy! I'm whiny and I ask too many questions and I have no confidence! I'm miserable!"

"You're hysterical. All brides get hysterical before the wedding."

Breathe in, breathe out. Then with all the calmness I can muster, I say, "It's over. *We're* over." I get out of bed and join him at the door. I put my hand on his arm and look into his eyes. Eyes I have to say goodbye to.

Eyes that are now steely. Cold. Angry. "You can't cancel the wedding."

Prove me wrong, I silently beg. Make all this hurt go away. "Then let's elope. Please, Cam. Please." *Make this one gesture, just for me.*

"You're being ridiculous. We're getting married tomorrow or we're not getting married at all."

Another ultimatum. Except this one is not disguised. As his words cut through me, I know what I have to do. "How's this for ridiculous?" I walk into the closet and take out my red suitcase. "I'm going to New York."

I'm in a window seat on a plane to New York.

I needed to make a decision, for my own sanity. And, in

spite of the winters, a crazy roommate and the lack of garbage disposals, in spite of the Brads and the Rons and the Nates, I chose New York.

Cam, of course, thought I was bluffing. "I'm getting into the shower," he said. "When I get out, that suitcase is going to be back in the closet, you're going to be back in bed, and we're never going to discuss this again." Then he slammed the bathroom door, leaving no doubt in my mind that I was making the right decision.

"Can I have some more water?" I ask the flight attendant.

"Sure thing," she says, handing me a plastic cup, a water bottle and a small bag of peanuts.

The truth is I don't know what's going to happen. All I know is that I can't marry Cam at the Sunset tomorrow. And here's what I'm thinking: if my two bodies are in one place, and my head is in one place, maybe the split will end and I'll become whole. I don't know if it's going to work. But it's all I got.

So I drove to the airport, left my car in the long-term lot and bought a ticket on the three o'clock flight. Hopefully, once I land, one of my two lives will disappear. I'm rooting for the survival of New York Gabby. In that life, I have my dream job. I can handle Ron, and even Heather. I've got the tools to do it. I've got confidence. But if New York Gabby disappears, I'm prepared. I'll have confidence, either way. And if neither disappear? If I'm still leading two lives? Then at least I'll be home in both of them. And home for me is New York.

I stare at my bitten fingers. My bitten fingers that are so nice and long in New York. My bitten left hand that's still sporting my engagement ring. Oops. I remove the ring and hide it in my purse. I'll have to give that back one day. Though if Arizona Gabby disappears, I don't see how that's possible.

As I race through the time zones, I watch the sky fade from blue to orange to red to navy. Throughout the entire flight, I watch the night take over, and I think about how one step leads to the next, and how people change, and mature, like the hues of the sky.

When the sky is black, I realize it's almost Saturday. My wedding day. As the plane lands, I feel a pang of regret. And then I prepare to disembark.

I roll my suitcase to a taxi line and wait. When it's finally my turn, the cabbie lifts my belongings into the trunk. "Where to?" he asks.

"The Bolton Hotel, please."

Since it's late Friday night, traffic is light, and we arrive at the Bolton in just twenty minutes. "Thanks," I say and pay the driver. "Can you pop the trunk?" I ask as I'm climbing out. He pops it and heads to the back to take out my bag.

I push open the door to the hotel and spot the bar I visited in my other life. I head over to the service desk and wait behind an elderly couple until it's finally my turn. "I'd like a room, please."

"For how long?"

"No idea. Let's start with one night."

"Would you like the king-sized featherbed?"

"Yes, I would."

"Terrific. That'll be two hundred dollars."

"Thanks." I hand over my credit card.

"Do you have any baggage, ma'am?"

"Just one bag. But I can wheel it myself."

"As you wish," he says. "Here's the key for room 1817."

"Actually, can I have room 2715?" Same city, same hotel, same bed. The exact same space I occupied at the exact same time in my other life. Maybe this is what I need to do to make one life disappear. "Let me check. Yes, it's available. Here you go."

Key card in hand, I head to the elevator.

I push the key card into the door. I kick off my sandals, close the blinds and pull down the covers. I shove my suitcase into a corner and flop down on my two-hundred-dollar bed. Almost instantly, I fall asleep and, for the first time in six months, I dream.

I open my eyes to a new day.

For the first time in six months, there is no intense headache. No forks bashing into my forehead or temples. All I see is the white hotel wall. No swirling green hot light burning behind my eyelids.

I didn't change universes. It worked. It worked!

There is just one me.

But which one?

Since I was Arizona Gabby last night, and I didn't change universes, I should still be Arizona Gabby today.

I made my decision. I chose New York. And here I am. I am Arizona Gabby, but I am no longer Gabby in Arizona.

Which means I have to start looking for a job. And an apartment. King-sized featherbeds are great, but at two hundred dollars a night, they're a bit out of my price range.

I turn the TV on to the news, intending to listen while I scrounge through a suitcase. After a shower, I'll need a change of clothes.

I want to look fresh and smart, like a true New Yorker, when I go looking for an apartment. I have one small problem. My suitcase is gone.

What the hell? I know I wheeled it into the corner. Fine, I was out of it last night. Maybe I didn't. Maybe I stashed it in the armoire. I open the armoire. Empty.

I call the hotel desk. Nope. No suitcase downstairs.

And that's when I hear it. The anchorman on the news is talking about my Cookie Cutter. How his appeal has been denied. How authorities are talking about beefing up the security at the Nogales border.

Nogales? What happened to Boston?

I look at my nails. My unjagged, long nails.

I'm not just Gabby in New York; I'm New York Gabby.

But what does that mean? Am I New York Gabby for good? Or am I going to wake up here in the morning?

Crestfallen, I dress, grab my purse and return to the lobby to return my key card. As the doorman hails me a cab, I feel despair expand inside of me. It's never going to end. I'm never going to be able to live one, normal life.

"Thirty-fourth and Third," I tell the driver flatly. As he drives, I keep blinking, and blinking, and blinking again attempting to hold the tears back.

He brakes in front of the apartment. "Six-fifty," he says.

I reach inside my purse for my wallet. And that's when I feel it. The smooth, cold band. The hard diamond. My engagement ring. I lift it out of my handbag and let it sparkle in my palm.

I don't know how it got here, or why. It's as if it leaked out from my other life. My heart pounds faster, as if I'm running or having a first kiss. What does this mean? Have my lives merged?

I quickly pay the cabbie and then rush up to my quiet apartment (Heather must still be sleeping), all the while marveling at my ring. My key works, so I know I still live here. My room is exactly how I left it. The mouse is probably still in the closet.

Everything about me is New York Gabby. Everything. Except the ring. I'm *only* New York Gabby.

Yes!

I sit on the corner of my bed and let the tears flow, but they're tears of relief. How about that. It worked. Except for the ring, it worked. Arizona Gabby is now defunct. I look back at the sparkling diamond. Well, no one ever said the universe was perfect. I slip the ring onto my finger, but it's loose. It looks much better with these nails, I have to admit. I reach into my jewelry box, find a silver chain and slip it around my neck.

So I'll never forget.

19

You, Again

I head over to the deli to pick up breakfast, and another mousetrap. Then I return to the apartment. By now Heather is awake and wanting to know where I've been. "Finding myself," I answer. I'm not quite sure what else to tell her.

I think I know what happened. I'm not certain, mind you; it's just speculation. See, one of my days was really two days: Part One in New York, Part Two in Arizona. The split had to mend at the end of a day. A full day. So on Saturday I started fresh. I didn't change into Gabby New York; I simply stopped becoming Gabby Arizona. I stopped becoming someone I wasn't meant to be.

Of course, there's always the other explanation: by making a decision, I became who I needed to be.

"Guess who called me!" Heather says, as I hand her the mousetrap.

"Who?"

"Brad!"

"No!"

"Yes! He asked me out." Pause. "But I won't go if you don't want me to."

"Go, please, I want you to." Just don't give him too much to drink.

On Sunday night, I fall asleep in my own bed in New York. And wake up in my own bed in New York. I was right. No more switching, no more headaches.

No more Cam.

On Monday, while I'm in the shower, I wonder if the past six months were just a dream. Maybe I imagined it all until I could feel certain I had made the right choice. And then I feel the ring and remember.

It's now Monday evening, and I'm standing outside Ron's door. I'm determined to make my life work here in New York, and I'm going to start with my job. Which means I have to talk to Ron. No, not talk to him—confront him. Lay down the law. Now all I have to do is knock. I hesitate before lifting my hand, and then bang on the door.

"Come in!"

"Hi, Ron," I say. I step inside and shut the door behind me.

He winks suggestively. "What can I do for you?"

I walk up to his desk and face him. "Here's what you can do for me. Stop making me feel like I'm here for the wrong reasons. Stop making me feel uncomfortable."

"Sorry?"

"Ron, you're a jerk. You put me in a bad situation. The way you've been treating me is wrong. You devalued my job. You devalued *me.* You made me want to go to HR. You made me want to quit. You made me want to tell your wife. You made me want to sell you out to the tabloids. You made me want to sue both you and TRSN."

"Arizona—"

I put up my hand. "Let me finish. Here's the thing. I love my job. I'm good at my job. So this is what I've decided to do. Stare you in the face—" I look up at him and into his beady eyes "—and tell you that if you ever do that to me, or anyone, ever again I will pull out all the stops. Do you understand? I will not shut up until everyone in this town knows what a creep you are." I pause for effect and watch his expression harden. "Sure, you can fire me, but I'm not afraid of that. Of you. Nothing about you scares me. You need me. This station needs me."

I cross my arms in front of my chest. I feel tall. Strong.

Ron, on the other hand looks shrunken. "Have it your way, Arizona," he says. His voice is weak.

"Don't call me Arizona. My name is Gabby." I turn on my heel and slam the door.

Ha. I did it! The truth is I don't know what will happen now. Maybe he'll fire me, anyway. It's possible. Anything is possible. But I'm taking control. Learning how to, at least. I'm not going to let anyone push me around again. Sometimes you have to take a chance and go for it. Without a backup plan.

In the elevator downstairs, I realize that my hands are shaking. I think I need a drink. I hail a cab.

"Where to?"

"Gramercy Tavern," I answer before I can think too hard.

I deserve my own three-hundred-dollar bottle of wine. Okay, not three hundred. That's just crazy. A hundred. Tops. Though what good is an expensive bottle of wine without someone to share it with?

I take out my cell and dial. She answers on the first ring. "Heather?" I say. "Wanna meet for a drink?" Okay, so she's a little psycho. Big deal. When it comes to love gone awry, who isn't?

The week passes by. Work is tough but manageable. *Flash floods. Kidnappers. Political scandals. Is another starlet too skinny?* But I don't get fired. And Ron keeps his hands to himself at the morning and afternoon meetings.

By the time I get home on Friday, I'm wiped out but happy. I skip into my lobby, smiling, my briefcase swinging by my side.

And I see Cam, sitting on the visitor's couch. My heart stops. What the hell?

"Hi," he says, with a sad smile and a wave.

My feet are frozen to the ground. "What are you doing here?"

He looks different. Thinner. Tired. Unshaven. His jeans and T-shirt look slept-in and rumpled. "I have to talk to you."

I try to clear my mind. I haven't seen *this* Cam since November. *This* Cam is dating Lila. I don't know what *this* Cam is doing here. "There are phones."

"I know, but I needed to see you. You look amazing, by the way."

Yes, I do. "Thanks. Well, you might as well come up."

After a silent elevator ride, I unlock my door and he follows me inside. "Heather?" I call. No answer. I'm not surprised. She's probably out with Brad. She's been seeing him all week, which means she's been in non-psychotic mode, which also means I haven't had to hide the steak knives. "Have a seat," I say to Cam, pointing to the couch. "Can I get you some water?"

"I'm fine, thanks."

I sit on the other end. "How was dinner at China Grill?"

He doesn't answer right away and for a fleeting, crazy moment, I wonder which Cam he is. "How did you know I was there?" he finally asks, bringing me back to my senses.

"I have my sources."

He half smiles. "Always the news person." His smile fades. "It's over."

"Really. Why's that?"

"Because she's not you."

I reach to bite my nail, but stop myself. "I'm not sure what that means." Although, maybe I do. I tried—and failed—to find a replacement for Cam.

"Your leaving me was the worst thing that ever happened to me. I was miserable. Broken. The world just bottomed out and Lila…" He shakes his head. "I shouldn't make excuses. But being with Lila, being with someone else, made me realize how much I'd lost when I'd lost you."

I take a deep breath. "I don't know what to say."

He leans over to me. "Say you'll give me another chance."

"I have a life here. My job is important to me. I know it was shitty of me to take off on you, but you weren't even willing to consider long distance, let alone moving with me. It was your way or no way at all." Though an echo from another life, the words are still true.

"I know. And that was idiotic. That's why I'm here now. To show you how important you are to me. I'll do anything. Anything it takes to keep you by my side."

"I'm not the same person I was in Arizona." Literally.

"Neither am I," he says. "People learn. People change. *I* changed. It can be different this time. Please."

My head, my lungs, my heart are all overflowing. This is too much. Maybe I've become the type of woman who's right for Cam. Someone strong. "You're willing to try a long-distance relationship?" I ask. Of course people learn. And people can change. But after everything that happened, I realize that so much of who we are, who we become, is dependent on circumstance, on where we live and the people we interact with. Bottom line, how long would it take before his mother wore him down?

"I'm talking about moving. *My* moving. I'll move to New York. I'll take the bar here." He gives me a lopsided grin. "I might have to still root for the Cardinals though. But the Giants aren't bad. Hey, what are you wearing around your neck?"

I touch the ring. "It's a long story."

His fingers look so soft. So warm. I take his hand.

And then his cell rings. And rings. I pull his phone out of his pocket and glance at the caller ID. Alice's number is flashing across the screen.

"It's your mother." I toss the cell in his lap. "Just answer it."

He takes the phone, presses Talk and then immediately presses End. He places it back on the coffee table and scoots closer to me on the couch.

"She'll get over it," he says.

I'm not sure if he's talking about the phone call, or the move, or me. But I laugh and reclaim his hand.

"It's time for her to let go," he says.

And suddenly I'm thirsty. Very, very thirsty.

AFTER

We're lying on the terrace in our bure in the Yasawa Islands of Fiji. Cam's forehead nuzzles into my neck as the stars above scribble across the sky like ink from a silver marker. I raise my hand into the air, my wedding band shiny in the moonlight, the wedding band I acquired earlier this afternoon on the beach. Then I follow one of the stars, the brightest star, with my index finger as it shoots diagonally across the blackness. And I make a wish.

I wish that Cam and I will be together forever. A wish people in love make every day. The starlight burns out and I close my eyes. And then I drift off to sleep, in my husband's arms.

Who says wishes can't come true?

From *USA TODAY* bestselling author

Carole Matthews

With or Without You

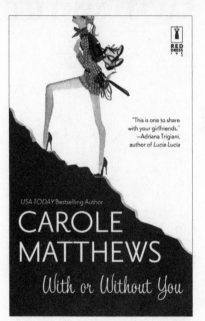

When Lyssa Allen decides she needs a little
adventure in her life, she sets out for Nepal, and
embarks on a journey that changes her life forever.

On sale wherever
trade paperbacks
are sold.

**RED
DRESS
I N K**
™

www.RedDressInk.com

RDI593TR

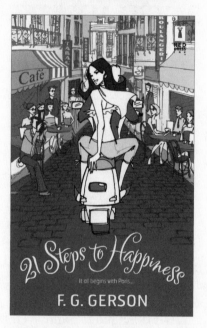

More great reads from international
bestselling author Sarah Mlynowski

As Seen on TV

Sunny Langstein has done what every modern-day
twenty-four-year-old shouldn't do. She's left her life
in Florida to move in with her boyfriend in
Manhattan. But don't judge Sunny yet, because
like any smart woman she has an ulterior motive—
to star on *Party Girls,* the latest reality-television
show. Here's the catch—*Party Girls* have to be
single. Free designer clothes and stardom versus
life with her boyfriend. What's a girl to do?

RED
DRESS
INK
™

It's time to tell your own story!

From bestselling
Red Dress Ink® author Sarah Mlynowski
and veteran chick lit editor Farrin Jacobs
comes the essential guide to writing chick lit.

Me vs. me /
FIC MLYNO   **3105701007694**

Mlynowski, Sarah.
WEST GA REGIONAL LIBRARY SYS   12/2006

Write
A Girl's Guide to Writing
Chick Lit

BY BESTSELLING AUTHOR SARAH MLYNOWSKI
AND FARRIN JACOBS

Featuring tips and advice on every stage
of developing, writing, and selling your novel.

SEE JANE WRITE:
A Girl's Guide to Writing Chick Lit
$14.95
ISBN-10: 1-59474-115-8
ISBN-13: 978-1-59474-115-9
In stores now

QUIRK
BOOKS

www.quirkbooks.com